WIREWALKER

WIREWALKER

MARY LOU HALL

VIKING

VIKING
An imprint of Penguin Random House LLC
375 Hudson Street
New York, New York 10014

First published in the United States of America by Viking,
an imprint of Penguin Random House LLC, 2016

LIBRARY OF CONGRESS CATALOGING-IN-PUBLICATION DATA
Names: Hall, Mary Lou, date– author.
Title: Wirewalker / Mary Hall.
Description: New York : Viking, [2016] | Summary: "Fourteen-year-old
Clarence Feather tries to survive in his impoverished neighborhood in
the aftermath of his mother's murder"—Provided by publisher.
Identifiers: LCCN 2015042376 | ISBN 9780670016464 (hardback)
Subjects: | CYAC: Conduct of life—Fiction. | Poverty—Fiction. | Single-parent families—
Fiction. | Fathers and sons—Fiction. | Drug dealers—Fiction. | BISAC: JUVENILE FICTION/
Social Issues / Physical & Emotional Abuse (see also Social Issues / Sexual Abuse). |
JUVENILE FICTION / Social Issues / Violence. | JUVENILE FICTION / Boys & Men.
Classification: LCC PZ7.1.H284 Wir 2016 | DDC [Fic]—dc23 LC
record available at https://lccn.loc.gov/2015042376

Book design by Nancy Brennan
Printed in U.S.A.

1   3   5   7   9   10   8   6   4   2

FOR RUSSELL, ALWAYS, IN EVERYTHING

CONTENTS

WIREWALKER

BOOK **1**

SUMMER'S END

MONA

....

HE SAW THE DOG every day. The dog was part of the afternoon walk he made each day to the Kwik-Bi-Handi-Mart, where he would buy a snack and a soda and then just head out to wander. If he had money, it was sometimes the money his father left him after a night full of plenty to drink. Once in a while, after long evenings of booze and sports radio, his father dropped sticky coins and vitamins on his bedside table as he slept. On most days, though, the money was what he got from the errands he ran for Johnnyprice, a friend of his father's who had taken him under his wing. Johnnyprice was called Johnnyprice, like it was one name instead of two, and Clarence had never known either name to be spoken without the other. He wasn't a tall man, but his thick freckled body was a wall of meat and muscle. If you touched him, poked him, slid into him, even punched him, nothing moved and nothing gave, and Clarence was glad Johnnyprice was part of his family, even if they didn't share the same blood. Come the end of his weekend errands, Clarence almost always ended up with a couple of twenties in his pocket, and he'd head to the Kwik-Bi and spend a few dollars on Andy Capp's and Mr. Pibb, his all-time favorites.

When he got home, after his dad and Johnnyprice had settled in around the kitchen table with the sports radio squawking, he'd creep into his closet to stash the rest of his cash in his mama's big-buckled purse, hidden way back under his puffy winter coat. His mama's purse still held her baby-powder smell, and he'd lift it to his face and suck her into his lungs, the same way he'd done most every day for almost three years. Next he'd pull out her red leather wallet and open it like a book, gazing down at her driver's license photo to make sure he still remembered her alive face, not just her dead one. Making money made Clarence feel important, like he was holding his own, on his own. Before long, he thought, he'd be one of the men.

The dog lived toward the end of his street, a few blocks away from the Kwik-Bi. In the afternoons its huge white head floated ghostly in the big downstairs window, watching. The dog never barked, never made any noise Clarence could hear. It just kept its eyes on him, from the moment he walked into its sight until the moment he left it. Most days, he would speak to the dog in his mind. *I see you*, were the words he would silently form. *I see you, dog, seeing me.*

One steaming night in mid-July, his father sent him to the Kwik-Bi for frozen pizza and toilet paper. He took his usual walk, past the empty lot growing the wild, twisted tree, past the house with the stacks of rusted metal in the yard, past the house of the old man who asked him was he staying out of trouble like a good boy should? The walk was the same as always until he got close enough to see that things had changed at the house of the white dog. Tonight the dog's head wasn't floating in its window but was attached to the dog itself, which was outside, unfenced, and the size of a small pony. Everything else was the same: the dog was watching him, just like always, but this time, there was nothing between them but air and skin. *I see you,* Clarence said in his mind, though this time, the words felt phony, on account of his terror.

"Oh, she won't hurt you!" A tiny beige woman in a Bar-B-Q Palace uniform waved at Clarence from the open door. "You can come on over and pet her if you want. She's nothing but a big baby." Clarence found himself drifting toward the dog, hypnotized in spite of his fear. Given a saddle, he'd be able to ride that dog. "Her name is Mona," the woman said. "She's a Great Dane." The woman scampered down the stairs in little red sneakers that seemed meant for a child, and her feet didn't seem to want to stay still, not even when she stopped and laid her bitsy left hand on the dog's white globe of a head. She seemed just like an amped-up, Slurpee-sucking kid, except for her eyes. Her face seemed to be caving in right there around her eyes, and it was a look Clarence had seen on certain women who carried on with Johnnyprice: a heaviness under the skin. "She's an albino," the woman said now. "That's why she's all white, with the baby-blue eyes. Come on over and pet her if you want."

To Clarence, it seemed like a long time passed before he reached the dog. It was like something was wrong with his legs, or with time. When he finally got close to her, he stopped and stared into the pale sky of her eyes. He'd never seen an animal with blue eyes, and those eyes made her seem a little bit human, a little bit like him. "Hi, Mona," he said to the dog, and then he held out his hand, like the woman at the bottom of the steps was showing him. A dripping tongue the size of a cold cut escaped from Mona's mouth and danced over his fingers, leaving them wet and shiny in the streetlight. He couldn't help but laugh, partly from fear and partly because it felt so funny, a big tongue like that tickling his fingers until they were sticky with spit.

Truth was, he'd never been that close to a dog before. Truth was, the only dogs he knew about lived in the wild stories told at the kitchen table, now that his mama was dead and gone. What he knew was that these dogs were off in training somewhere, learning how to kill one another. What he feared was that one day, he would have to watch them do it.

"She likes you," the woman giggled, and though he knew it wasn't cool, Clarence found himself smiling. "My name's Gina, by the way." Gina's red-sneakered feet kept moving as she spoke. It seemed that at any moment, she might just lift off of the grass or burst into song. "So . . ." she continued. "This guy I know is putting up a fence for Mona, so she can be outside sometimes. She gets lonely cooped up in the house all by herself, and I'm working a lot of doubles lately. So you should stop by—I mean, if you want to. I think she'd like that. I think she likes you, you know?"

Clarence understood what Gina was saying about Mona, but he had more pressing things on his mind, like how to make his mouth stop smiling. He'd learned, from watching Johnnyprice and the other guys and especially his father, that there was something a man lost when he smiled. So he made his mouth back into a straight line and slid his hands into his pockets. "I've got to go," he mumbled. Mona licked at the space between them, at nothing. "I've got to go to the store for my dad now." He turned away from Gina and her dog and headed out onto the street, and he didn't look back this time, not like he usually did when Mona's head floated ghostly in the window. But even without seeing her, he knew she was watching him, and he carried that knowledge home, right into his room, where the weight of the night fell hard, and he fussed the edges of his sheets while the radio blared in the kitchen. He stared up at the ceiling, remembering her human eyes, reminding himself that those blue eyes still watched him and would watch until he slept.

— — —

The fence went up on the morning of Clarence's first fight. Johnnyprice and his dad had decided he was ready, based on his performance in whatever it was they were judging him on. He felt this judgment deeply but couldn't name it, regardless of whether he was doing well or majorly screwing up. What he knew was that he'd been running on luck when it came to the two of them. There were no rules he'd been able to figure, and if there were, they were keeping them to themselves. What was wrong one day was the right thing the next, and then the next day it might suddenly be wrong again.

So he just shut up and did what he was told, on whatever day it was and no matter how it had been the day before. This was especially true if the two of them had been drinking. He found that if he shut up while they were drinking, they sometimes patted him on the back and told him he was all right, and if people came over, his dad might tell those people he was all right, and at moments like these, everything would stop while the whole room raised their drinks to him, and for a moment he'd forget his mama toppling from her chair at the table where these strangers now sat, lifted drinks in their hands, his name on their lips.

The fight was to be between one of Johnnyprice's older dogs, the one called Nasty, and one of the puppy pits owned by the guy they simply called Y. Y was a boy-man, not a man-man like his dad or Johnnyprice. Clarence imagined they called him Y because he was always shrugging like he was asking a question with his body. *Why?* his body demanded every time he moved, his narrowed eyes daring anyone to answer. *Why, goddammit? Why?*

Clarence didn't know why; he only knew that sometimes when he delivered for Johnnyprice, he'd run into Y coming around some corner, hands disappearing into ass-dragging jeans, that same shrug asking and accusing. "Whatcha got there, Itty?" he'd ask, motioning with his head toward the folder where Clarence carried the little bags for Johnnyprice.

"Nothing," Clarence would answer. This is what Johnnyprice had told him to say, especially if the question was coming from Y. "Schoolwork is all." He'd hug the folder a little more tightly and move slowly past Y, usually looking down at his own feet, though he knew he should keep his head up and make his mouth into a straight line, the way the men did.

"A'ight," Y would say, turning so that his shrug followed Clarence as he passed. "Run along then, boy. Get on home with your schoolwork. And go get a few more inches on you while you're at it. Itty-bitty thing like yourself . . . it's hard to believe you're just a few months away from high school."

Clarence had both Y and the fight on his mind as he walked to the Kwik-Bi to get his dad's noon cup of coffee. On weekends his life was better if the coffee was waiting when his dad rolled off the sofa and stumbled into the kitchen. At 11:30, Clarence would start walking, and by 11:55 he'd be waiting on the back porch while his dad leaned over the sink, spat, then ran himself a cloudy glass of water. When his dad finally turned around, Clarence would step in, hand him the coffee, and then leave as quickly as he came. He'd gotten good at buying time, and at knowing when he needed it. Today was a fight day, and his dad would be extra-ornery or stupidly happy, and stupidly happy didn't last, now that his mama was gone.

As he passed Gina's house, he noticed some young-dude versions of Y standing around in her yard, admiring a fence that seemed to have popped up out of nowhere. They weren't all that much older than Clarence, but they talked like men—running their hands across their dripping faces, bragging about putting the fence up, muttering foul-mouthed smack about who'd done more work and who should get paid the most. A towering dude with tiny braids glanced up at Clarence as he passed, giving him the slow, Y-boy nod. Clarence dropped his eyes and picked up his pace.

He knew Mona was right over there in the living room window as he passed, but he kept his eyes fixed in front of him and refused to look back at her. He couldn't let the Y-boys see that he cared about a dog, especially on the day of a fight. But he still spoke to her in his mind, like he always did when he walked by Gina's house. As best he could tell, no one could get into his mind, at least not yet.

I see you, Mona, he thought, and he realized she could hear him. He didn't know how, any more than he'd known how she watched him as he slept, but he sensed her presence like he sometimes sensed the presence of his mama, as a warmth settling in his blood. As he opened the door at the Kwik-Bi, he found himself wondering if Mona was listening in. Then at home, as he handed his father the coffee and slipped out the kitchen door, he realized he was telling her things he'd never told anyone. *They're testing me,* he said to her silently, taking the back steps two at a time and wandering off down the alley. *I don't know how to be. I don't know how to be. What. They want.*

He rode out the day by keeping his feet moving. He knew

Johnnyprice and his dad were thinking big thoughts about him and the night to come; he just wasn't sure what those big thoughts were. But he knew one thing most definitely. The him he'd been up to this point was not the him he needed to be later. He just hoped the him-he-needed-to-be showed up at the fight.

He walked as the afternoon grew gold, then orange, finally bluing into a deep, hazy dusk. He'd talked to Mona all day long, wandering the same alleys and sidewalks he always did, but today the walking had brought no relief. He passed the Kwik-Bi one more time and then forced himself to turn down Bedford Street. It was time to go home. It was time to face whatever was to come.

By the time he passed back by Gina's house on Bedford, Mona stood alone on the other side of the new fence, and the Y-boys were gone. It was strange, seeing her out in the yard without Gina, just the flimsy, see-through fence between the two of them. He wasn't scared, exactly. That wasn't the feeling. The feeling was a vibration in his backbone, something like the one he'd get when the grown-ups raised their glasses to him, but quieter. Less like someone hollering, more like someone humming.

He took his time walking over to the fence and then laid his hand against the wire. "I see you," he said, and Mona ambled her largeness over, pulled herself up onto her back legs, and settled her front feet on the fence above him. She was taller than he was, much taller if he counted how far up her paws reached above her head. On any other day he would have backed off in fear, but at this moment he had a hum in his body, some desire greater than fear, and so he closed his eyes, kept his hand on the fence, and waited. Seconds that felt like minutes passed with his eyes closed and his hand on the fence. He listened to himself speak to Mona in his mind. *Hey, Mona,* he said, hoping that this might be the day she'd finally answer him.

In front of him, just inches away, he could hear her breathing. He could smell the rot of her warm fishy breath. Then all of a sudden he felt her tongue slap against his hand like the slimy back of a catfish. It was a feeling he both loved and hated at the same time, like when he was little and his dad used to tickle him until he cried. Clarence always came back for more, too, often taunting his father, a man who suffered from what his mama called a "short fuse" but who back in the day knew how to keep that fuse from blowing. When he thought about it now, Clarence could see he'd almost always been a boy who came back to the things that scared him.

He thought about his dad's tickling, thought about Mona, and then he smiled, realizing there was no one around to see it one way or another. The air felt cool on his wet teeth, and he liked it. He was getting tired of keeping his smile locked up behind the hard straight line of his pulled-tight lips, so he smiled again. He kept on smiling. Then he opened his eyes, looking up into the baby blue eyes of the dog. "Hey, you," he said. Mona nuzzled her pink nose into the shape his hand made against the fence, and once again the hum passed through his body like music. "Hey, girl," Clarence said. "I see you, girl. You're a good girl, now aren't you, Mona."

Mona's name had barely left his lips when he heard the voice behind him. Y's voice. "'Sup, boy?" Y asked. Clarence kept his face right next to the fence; he kept looking into the eyes of Mona. "That dog likes you, don't it. That's a real big dog now, ain't it, boy." Clarence could tell from the way Y's voice circled him, dancing, that he and Mona were together in the wrong place at the wrong time. "Well, why don't you bring that dog to the fight tonight, Itty? That is, if you're coming. That is, if you're allowed to come, is what I mean."

"Oh, I'm coming," Clarence spat, and as he looked into the almost human eyes of Mona, he suddenly felt afraid. Not of her, and not even of Y. He could hear Y's feet kicking asphalt, moving in the direction of the Kwik-Bi, away from him. He was afraid of the boy he'd been all day: fourteen years old and talking to a dog in his mind. He was afraid he was starting to like that boy, the very same boy who'd be heading to a dogfight that night. "Don't look at me," he suddenly said to Mona, and he took his hand off the fence and wiped it on the front of his jeans. "Don't look at me like that, dog," he said, and he turned and walked toward home.

When he got home, Johnnyprice and his dad were sitting at the kitchen table, listening to sports radio and drinking beer. "So, how you doing there?" Johnnyprice asked, grabbing Clarence and pulling him in close, then rubbing his knuckles on Clarence's head until his scalp burned. "Just look at your little old self. Gotta toughen you up, Itty. Those dudes don't mess around in high school." When Clarence was younger and his mama was alive, this would have been just a tickle, but since her murder, these two tickled him with sloppy hands. In what used to be her house, a little bit of pain meant all was well. In what used to be his mama's house, his one and only goal was to keep the pain under control.

"I'm fine," he mumbled as he freed himself, then just kind of stopped and stood there in the middle of the kitchen, feeling gangly. Saturdays were when Johnnyprice paid him for the errands he did after school on Fridays, when the three of them had to playact like nothing was happening. They'd been playacting for over two years now, and each of them knew their parts by heart, though Clarence was starting to tire of their little production.

"So, I've got a little something for you, my boy." Here it was. It was time for Johnnyprice's voice to dip low, grow thin and quiet. His green left eye twitched into a clumsy wink while his brown right eye sat still and glassy. Clarence's dad nodded, then shot Johnnyprice a look that was first hateful, then as blank as a board. This was his usual look for Johnnyprice—and for Clarence—these days. The nodding was part of the act, but the dead look: that part was for real. His dad took his time getting up from the table, stretched, and let out a dramatic, make-believe yawn.

"The beer," he said, pointing to his stomach as he headed down the hallway toward the bathroom. "Can't hold the beer for anything these days." It was true that his dad couldn't hold his beer, but that was the only honest thing being said in the kitchen at the moment. Once his dad was gone, Johnnyprice reached into his pocket and pulled out a wad of money, fanning the bills out like a poker hand. Johnnyprice was playing his part too, though Clarence was starting to wonder why either of the men bothered. It wasn't like the truth of the matter would change anything. It wasn't like he could walk away and do anything but what they wanted him do.

"Take something extra this time," Johnnyprice said with a grin that showed plenty of teeth, but no joy. "Big ones, little ones—you choose. You done good, my man. You always do good work for me." Clarence took two twenties and just stood there in the fluorescent light, folding the bills into squares. It was his turn to act, but today he didn't have it in him to pretend to be grateful. "You ready for the fight to-night then?" Johnnyprice changed the subject, leaning back in his chair and yawning. Clarence nodded because he had to, but he didn't look up from his hands. He kept folding the twenties into smaller and smaller squares.

He was trying to forget the part of him that had awak-ened that morning, the part that knew something bad was about to happen. His mama never tolerated talk of dogs in the house, and she would never—no matter what his age—let her own son go to a fight. But his mama, she was gone, and these two men were all that was left. "You know, it's just the big guys get to go to the fight," Johnnyprice assured, and he pulled Clarence in close again, knuckle-rubbing the top of his head more gently this time. "So I guess you're one of the big guys now, huh?" Clarence felt his mouth fall into a hard straight line on its own, no effort necessary.

"Yeah," he said. "I guess I am."

THE FIGHT

•••

THE DRIVE TO THE fight wound through a neighborhood no one seemed to live in. Tired-looking houses with
dark-eyed windows leaned, and broken-down cars littered
the empty streets. It was hot, even now after dark: the wet,
clinging hot of someone breathing down your neck, making
threats. *This heat is angry heat,* his dad would say some evenings, holding dripping cold beer bottles against his red-
rashed neck. This was his way of explaining what might
happen later, what he'd blame on his Irish temper in the
light of the next day.

But Clarence wasn't convinced his father was Irish. Being white didn't make a man Irish, and neither did red hair.
He'd met his so-called Irish grandparents once, and they
didn't seem any different from the other white people who
would look at him, then at his dad, then at his mama, then
quickly look away, like they'd just seen an accident. But with
his mama gone, the white people's eyes lingered. There was
no reason now for them to mind their manners. Their eyes

settled where they pleased, openly searching for the link between the black boy and the red-headed white man, for that missing puzzle piece, the one that was dead.

At times like these his father's lips sat sealed, but even in silence Clarence could hear him screaming. "Keep walking," he'd eventually mutter, laying a hand on his son's shoulder and tightening his grip. And so Clarence walked. He just kept on walking.

It seemed like Johnnyprice drove a long time, deep into the fight neighborhood, until finally the empty houses became tall brick buildings with long broken windows. Then there were fewer buildings, then hardly any buildings at all. In time Johnnyprice pulled up next to a long cinderblock garage that sat back from the road, behind a patch of skinny dead trees. Clarence told himself that the feeling in his stomach came from the heat. *Angry heat*, he thought, and then he thought, *Scared heat*, and then he stopped thinking. He followed his father and Johnnyprice through a patchwork of streetlight scattered out across the dirt, and Johnnyprice knocked on the wood of a high fence that squared off the backyard of the building, a fence that was higher, even, than the fence at Gina's. In a moment, the fence opened wide enough that Clarence could see a mouth full of teeth gleaming there in the half dark. "Park down the street somewhere," the mouth said, and the open crack narrowed.

"Cops," the mouth said, and then the fence slammed shut.

His dad and Johnnyprice stood there for a while, just looking at each other, basically doing nothing. Sometimes it took them a while to come up with a plan. There were sounds coming from the other side of the wooden fence—friendly, happy sounds, like the kind at one of his dad's glass-raising parties. These sounds briefly changed the feeling in Clarence's stomach, made it almost flutter with excitement. "I'll move the car," his father finally said, and then Clarence felt a hand on his shoulder.

"I'll wait here." Johnnyprice nodded at his father, and Clarence moved himself in a little closer so he could feel the man that was made of Johnnyprice's muscles and bones, but not close enough to seem afraid. A few moments passed, and then he heard Johnnyprice's voice above him. "You know, you've always been kind of soft, Itty. Not your fault, I mean, your mama babied you like you were a little girl. But this night? This is a big one, and I'm mighty proud of you." His left hand gave Clarence's shoulder a little squeeze. "It's always been like you were my own son, you know. You must know that by now." Clarence wished Johnnyprice (and everyone else) would stop calling him Itty, and he also wished his mama's name would be kept far away from topics like dogfighting. But he knew Johnnyprice had just paid him a compliment, and lately compliments were hard to come by.

"So . . . where's Nasty?" Clarence knew that Nasty was the dog Johnnyprice intended to fight that night. He felt like this was the time he should say something about the fight, something that would take his mind off the fact that he could feel Mona sniffing around the corners of his mind, trying to get his attention. He tried to imagine what it was like, two dogs fighting, wondered if it was like people fighting, only with teeth and claws and no words, all sounds and pain. He wondered what made men gather around to watch it, raising animals to be killers.

He thought of Mona.

"Nasty's already in there," Johnnyprice said, casting his gaze out over the dirt around the building, then out beyond the ramshackle street, toward whatever lay beyond the orange streetlights sweating in the darkness. It was always this way with Johnnyprice and his gaze. It was like he knew someone was watching him, and he refused to be surprised when they rounded the corner, speaking his name.

"So, you scared?" Johnnyprice asked. Clarence knew this was an important question. He knew by the way Johnnyprice's hand had been on his shoulder one moment but wasn't there anymore, by the space that now lay between them.

"Nah," he lied, and he wondered if Johnnyprice could tell. He could feel Mona listening in. He knew *she* could tell.

"They're just dogs, you know," Johnnyprice said, and

then he pointed to the spot where Clarence's father was now stepping from the shadows, his hair a shimmering sunset in the amber light. "Just keep remembering they're nothing but dogs, Itty. Keep remembering this ain't nothing but a thing." He opened up the gate, walked in, and then turned back to Clarence. "Come on, now," he said, and Clarence followed him.

Inside the big square fence was a smaller, lower fence that formed a kind of pen. People stood around the pen, drinking beer from cans, and music drifted out of the open door of the cinder-block building. A group of hard-haired women in high pointy shoes stood on the building's back steps, swaying. Y stood a few feet away from them, watching them dance. When Clarence walked in, Y glanced over and nodded at him. *Where's the dog, boy?* he silently mouthed, and Clarence felt his face go hot.

"There he is. . . . There's Nasty," Johnnyprice suddenly said, and he pointed to a dark corner of the pen where Clarence could make out the shape of a dog chained to a big metal stake. "I don't know where Y's dog is," Johnnyprice added, spitting into the dirt. "I don't know but that he doesn't have a dog at all."

"True that," Clarence's father agreed, and he walked over to a plastic tub and pulled out two wet cans of beer. He handed one to Johnnyprice. "No sodas here, I don't think," he said, looking around the yard. He opened his beer, took a sip, and then handed it to Clarence.

"Have a taste," he said, and he glanced over at Johnnyprice.

"A big night," said Johnnyprice.

Clarence's father grunted in agreement. Clarence raised the can to his lips. Once the beer hit the inside of his mouth, he realized it tasted like what pee might taste like if you got it real cold and then poured it into a can. Not that he'd ever tasted pee. It was just the first thought that came to mind. What he really wanted was a Mr. Pibb and a bag of Andy Capp's, but he went on drinking: one, two, three gulps on account of the fact that his dad and Johnnyprice stood, nodding there in front of him, and that beyond them, over by the swaying girls, Y slumped against a railing, watching, drinking his own beer, and nodding. Seemed almost everyone was watching him and nodding. Apparently he was doing something right.

"Whoa, now," said Johnnyprice, suddenly grabbing the beer from Clarence and handing it back to his father. "Like father, like son," he kidded, and Clarence watched his dad's body stiffen as he took one step forward toward Johnnyprice.

"That's right. My son. My beer for my son." Clarence looked down at his feet, which was always the best bet when the two of them started in on each other. He'd noticed that, since his mama had died, his father was usually the one doing the starting, and more so with each passing year. Way back in the day the two of them had been all jokes and tall-assed tales, and he remembered that these were what they'd called the "good times." These days, the good times were harder to come by.

"Well, I'm about ready to get this show on the road, don't you think?" Johnnyprice nodded at Clarence's father, and then both men turned so that their eyes, though shadowed, were burning a line in the direction of Y. Y still nodded, watching the women dance. Over in the back corner of the pen, a low rumbling sound came from the throat of Nasty while, at the same moment, the women backed up flat to the fence, and a young dude was all but dragged down the building's steps by a lanky pit on a short, gleaming chain lead. Y grabbed the lead out of the kid's hand and choked it up tight, pulling the dog in close to his body. "This is Black!" he yelled out into the yard, but the white dog's name remained a mystery to Clarence, as there was nothing black on its body but the marks around its eyes.

Y walked the dog through the crowd of people, who backed up and let them pass. As Y chained Black to his own stake in the pen, Clarence thought the dog didn't look so different from Mona, just smaller, and part of him wondered if its breath, too, smelled like rotting fish.

Mona. The Superdog. The dog that could see and hear everything.

Around him, people were moving in closer to the pen, opening fresh beers and lighting cigarettes. Johnnyprice elbowed his way over to the pen, to the corner where Nasty panted. Someone turned off the music inside, and the yard hushed: just the murmur of voices and the growling of dogs. A man with a handheld spotlight elbowed his way up to the pen and fastened the light on to one of the corners that didn't hold a dog. "Welcome to the show!" he yelled out into the yard. "Last bets have been made inside," he added, and then he stepped back and gulped the beer that one of the dancing women had handed him.

In the far right corner, Johnnyprice leaned over the pen and attached his hand to the back of Nasty's collar. In the front left corner, Y did the same with Black. Inside the pen, the dogs' eyes were fixed on each other. Behind them, the men's eyes were fixed on each other's eyes.

The man with the spotlight held a hand up in the air and started raising fingers. "One, two, three," he said, and then he yelled, "Fight!" and before Clarence knew what was happening, the dogs were free and on each other, lips pulled back to show teeth and gums and thick white spit. In a split second they were raised up on their hind legs like humans, wrestling. Then they started moving their mouths, going at each other's necks with wildly grinding jaws. *They are eating,* Clarence thought, his stomach churning with cramps like from that belly sickness when he couldn't leave the bathroom for hours. *They are eating each other's faces.*

Clarence felt his father's hand on his shoulder. The white pit's face was wet and red with blood, but it was hard to know which dog the blood belonged to. But Clarence could see, as Nasty raised his head to get a grip on Black's ear, that the blood was coming from a wide-open wound that had replaced Nasty's throat. Nasty folded onto his back legs, and Black, jaws thrashing, went in for the neck again. *He will eat him whole,* Clarence thought as the crowd began to scream, "Black, Black, Black!" like a chant. *He will eat him and there will be nothing left but blood.* Clarence sank to his knees and tasted blood himself, just before the backyard went black.

When he awakened, he was in the backseat of Johnnyprice's car; he could tell by the smell of pineapple air freshener and dirty ashtray. The inside of his mouth throbbed and tasted like warm salty meat. In the front seat Johnnyprice and his father were discussing the fight and, more specifically, him.

"I don't know what that boy was thinking," Johnnyprice muttered. The car came to a stop, and Clarence listened to the rhythm of the blinker as Johnnyprice waited to turn.

"He wasn't thinking." His father's voice was floor-flat and quiet, like it always was when he was holding in his temper. "Damn," he said. "And everyone looking on like that, like they felt sorry for me or something."

The car pulled into a left-hand turn, and Clarence closed his eyes and prayed for sleep.

"Well, it *was* his first time, Rowley," Johnnyprice said. "And he's a pussy. You know that as well as I do." Silence. The scream of a car horn. Clarence heard his father clear his throat, then roll down the window and spit.

"You better watch your mouth," he growled, and Clarence knew that growl so well, he could picture exactly what his father's face looked like at that moment. His lips would be pulled into his mouth like he was trying to swallow them. His eyes would be narrowed down to creases and lashes. "In case you'd forgotten, that's my son you're talking about, and no one talks shit about my son. Not even you."

For a moment silence swallowed the front seat, but it wasn't true silence; it was a silent scream. Finally Johnnyprice spoke. "Come on now, for the millionth time: *We agreed not to do this*. Nothing good will come from it. Nothing good *ever* comes from it." More silence, this time quieter. Then Johnnyprice's voice again. "And what I'd like to remind you, by the way, is that I've been carrying your ass, in one way or another, ever since Evie died."

Sleep, Clarence thought, closing his eyes so tight, he saw stars. The car squeaked to a stop. *Sleep*, he thought again. His next thought was of the open bleeding neck of Johnnyprice's Nasty. Then he felt Mona licking at his thoughts, and so he let her in. He didn't want to be alone in his head anymore. He didn't want to be alone at all.

"You awake yet, boy?" Johnnyprice asked as he opened the car's back door and stood, blocking the streetlight. Clarence didn't budge, didn't flinch, didn't open his eyes. "I'll get him up," Johnnyprice mumbled, but then his dad came back with, "Oh no, you won't," and then there was just the slamming of the car door and a siren's faint wail. Clarence lay stiff as a stick in the backseat, his eyes closed tight, his mind traveling back to a time, not so long ago, when either of these men would have happily lifted him out of the car, when he would have disappeared into strong arms around him, into the man-smell of security. And while he knew he'd feel shame at still being little enough to be carried, stronger than that shame would be the pleasure of being held, like back before his mama died, when he was still a small thing worthy of love.

Instead, he lay sweating in the back of a stinky-assed car, alone. "Superhero," he whispered, as he often did when he felt lost. Even though he was too old to believe that he could whisper himself into special powers, just saying the word comforted him. Sometimes it even worked as a kind of spell that would bounce him out of his mind and body, dropping him into a world of his own making. He kept his eyes shut tight, and then he said it again. "Superhero." He willed himself away from the car, right into a memory.

In this memory he and his mama were in the Walmart when he came upon some Spider-Man sheets and decided he had to have them. "I just bought you a Batman bedspread, didn't I? I thought you were all about Batman," his mama said. "And you know we're not made of money, Clarence Feather." She stood there, shaking her head, trying to look stern, but she really just looked like she loved him, like she always did.

"Well, I like them both," Clarence answered. "I mean, I like them all. All the superheroes are the same, when you really think about it. They have different powers, but the powers have to come from the same place, don't they? Doesn't that make sense?"

His mama laughed and shook her head some more. "So there's some central power plant where superheroes get their powers or something?" Clarence paused and thought about it.

"Well, there's only one sun for all of us, right? Everything in nature gets its energy from there, but the energy gets used different ways, depending on what's using it." He looked up at the store ceiling as if he might be able to see beyond it, right up into the sky. "And all those lights up there on the ceiling, they're running on the same power, aren't they? So yeah, I guess that's what I mean. Makes sense to me."

His mama walked over and laid her hand on the top of his head. "Sometimes you think too much for your own good," she said quietly, and she picked up the sheets and started walking toward the checkout counter. Just like that, the memory vanished. He said, "Superhero," again, but he couldn't make it last.

There he was, back in Johnnyprice's nasty-smelling car, and the men he couldn't please were now inside the little gray house, right down the hallway from his bedroom, where the Spider-Man sheets from his memory lay beneath his Batman bedspread. He was too old to be still using either of them, he knew, but he didn't want anything new on his bed. He washed his linens in the tub himself and then hung them out himself on the porch railing to dry. He didn't let the men touch them. They were his, all his, bought for him by the mama in his memory. And he needed to get back to them now, to pull their years of softness up over his face and vanish.

He pushed himself up off the sticky vinyl car seat and heard himself sigh. Inside his mouth, his tongue was a torn, aching mess of meat. "Superhero," he mumbled, and then he opened the car door and slowly climbed out onto the street. He looked at the lit-up kitchen window and then turned left, walking toward the dark square of his own bedroom window. He knew he'd left it open from his last nighttime walk, and there was no way he was facing those men again tonight.

Once in his bed, scooched way down under his sheets and invisible, he closed his eyes and focused on listening. He wasn't sure his father was finished with him yet, so he strained to hear the men's conversation down the hall, something about Johnnyprice needing to clean up what was left of Nasty, about finding a place to dump the body. He pictured Nasty, dead inside a dumpster or in one of those little ditches running by the side of the road. Then it was Mona lying by the side of the road, her white neck wet with blood, so he concentrated until his mind finally went blank, until the back door slammed, Johnnyprice's car engine revved up, and his father walked down the hallway toward his room. Until his father's footsteps stopped right there at his bedroom door. Until there was nothing, no sound at all.

"You in there?" his dad shouted in from the hallway.

"Yeah," Clarence mumbled. He wanted to ask for aspirin or something to take the edge off, but he knew he wouldn't. He wouldn't be the first to reach out, not this time. He was grateful when he heard his bedroom door shut and the combination lock on the outside click into place. His dad would unlock it later before he crashed out on the sofa, once his anger lost its fire. Or at least that was how it usually happened. That was the purpose, his father had explained to him more than once. He wasn't punishing him. He was protecting him, or so he said.

It's just that sometimes you're hard to look at. I don't know how else to say it. It's your face. I don't know; it just gets to me sometimes. There's something about your face that can make me . . . His dad had about fifteen ways of saying this one thing, but the message was always the same. Clarence's face was wrong. Clarence tried to figure it out when he looked in the mirror: he saw a meaty little nose like his dad's, his mama's full lips, her hot-chocolate eyes, and her dimples in the soft meat of his cheeks. And then there were his freckles, just like his dad's, and just like Johnnyprice's. His face looked a little bit like each big person in his life, and he used to think this was a good thing.

But it didn't matter what he thought. Since his mama's death, it was usually a relief when his dad locked the door, and sometimes Clarence locked the door from the inside, too, just in case. His dad mostly left him alone, once he'd put him away, out of sight. And so far, his dad's plan was better than what happened if there weren't two locks between them on a night like this.

— — —

The next day Miss Vernetta Wilmer from down the street showed up at the door. He wasn't sure how she'd heard; somebody at the fight must have known somebody else who went and gossiped the news to the biggest mouth in Mayfair Heights. "First thing is: why in the world has this child not been to the doctor?" she screamed at Clarence's dad when he opened the door. "His tongue is about half bit off, is what I heard. Get out of my way." Clarence was lying on the sofa in front of the television, and Vernetta Wilmer shoved her way past his dad and came and stood over him.

"Let me see," she said. Clarence stuck out his tongue, looked away from her, and pretended it didn't hurt. Vernetta was a deaconess at his mama's church, but his mama never liked her, and Clarence hated her wagging finger and voice like a crow. She took up every inch of space when she walked into a room—the inches he could see and those he couldn't, even the ones that lived inside of him, in private. In his mind he called her the Space Snatcher, and he kept his eyes on the top of her cotton-candy hairdo while she inspected the inside of his mouth. People entered one another through their eyes, so when in doubt, he made sure no one had the chance to get in.

Vernetta Wilmer laid her hand on his head like she was checking for fever. "Child," she finally said, and for a moment her voice quieted. "What in the world happened, child?" Clarence's father slunk away from the front door, but he offered no answers. For some reason his dad had never trusted Miss Vernetta, even when Clarence's mama'd been alive. Johnnyprice himself had warned Clarence many times to stay far away from her house. He said that if she didn't like the looks of a thing, whatever it was, she'd call the cops, just to get them digging around in somebody's business. Some said she'd even put her own illegitimate son in jail, and the rumors also mentioned a loaded Glock in the yellow handbag that always dangled from her wrist. Since his mama's death, she'd bang on the door from time to time, pretending to be interested in Clarence's welfare. Clarence wanted nothing to do with her.

"What Evie saw in you, I'll never know," she said now, still looking into the eyes of Clarence. Like so many grown-ups, his dad and Miss Wilmer talked to each other by talking *at* somebody else. "So, you going to tell me what happened then?" Behind Miss Wilmer, Clarence's father looked down at his feet.

"Don't know," he said. "Wasn't there when it happened. And I reckon it's none of your business, one way or another."

Vernetta Wilmer raised her hands from her sides and locked them onto her hips. "Um-hmm," she said, still looking down at Clarence. "Okay, then—you want to tell me what happened, young man?" Her eyes searched his eyes, looking for clues. Clarence quickly glanced away, back at the TV screen.

"I fell down," he said. "Going to the store. It was dark outside. I fell down and hit my chin on the pavement and bit my tongue." There, behind Vernetta Wilmer, Clarence's father smiled.

"Right," Vernetta mumbled, shaking her head. "Going to the store. But just let me tell you this, Rowley Feather. Dog-fighting is one thing, and make no mistake, one day I *will* shut you people down. Rest assured, though: if you ever lay a hand on this child, you'd better know I'll have the police on your porch just as fast as you can say 911."

Oh, he's laid a hand on me, Clarence thought. In front of him, on the television, a skinny woman was excited about a cup of coffee. *He's laid a hand on me, but he doesn't mean it.*

"Now, you come see me anytime, all right, Clarence?" Vernetta Wilmer stretched her palm across his forehead once more, and while he almost liked the way it felt there, he knew he'd never set foot in her house. She didn't care about him. She only cared about the story she'd be able to tell about him. "Oh, you miss your mama, don't you, baby? Stuck up in a house with a ne'er-do-well nobody like him night and day."

Behind Miss Wilmer, Clarence's father rolled his eyes. "Go on and get, Vernetta," he said, and then he turned and walked toward the front door. When he got there, he opened it wide and stood there, waiting. "I mean it, woman. It's time to go now."

"Oh, don't you worry. I'm leaving," Vernetta crowed as she left Clarence on the sofa, waltzed up to the open door, and for the first time during the visit, looked Clarence's father in the eye. "You know, I've never trusted a white man—not one day in my life. I told Evie that myself, back when she started carrying on with you." Vernetta's gold-nailed forefinger almost grazed his father's nose as she shook it. "But Evie was young. She hadn't seen what I've seen."

Clarence's father didn't blink as he watched Vernetta Wilmer stomp out onto the porch and slam the door behind herself. "High-and-mighty nigger bitch," he finally mumbled, but it wasn't as if Clarence couldn't hear him. Just like that, Clarence felt a hot wind kicking up inside him. It blew in out of nowhere, and he recognized it as a new feeling. If Vernetta Wilmer was a nigger, that made his mama a nigger, and if his mama was a nigger, then he was a nigger too. His dad had just called both his mama and him niggers.

The hot wind in Clarence hissed.

His father walked away from the front door, back into the living room. He took his time and then stopped right in front of the TV, blocking the picture. "Thanks," he said. "You're all right, you know." He reached over and placed a hand on Clarence's head. Clarence just lay there, looking past him at the stained white wall. The wa

its own screen, as walls did sometimes sinc

death, and as usual a scene played itself ou

movie. He was watching his father—younger, fatter, straight-shouldered, smiling—chasing a seven- or eight-year-old Clarence around a yard. The sunlight painted everything yellow; even his dad's fiery hair was the color of August grass. Clarence remembered this kind of chasing, the kind that ended in giggles and squeals and fingers skittering under rib bones. Tickling, never hitting. Just an open, laughing mouthful of sun.

In the room where he was, this dingy little living room with this dad, his father now said, "All right, then," but Clarence didn't bother to watch him shuffle past the sofa and down the hallway, toward the kitchen. He just waited for the sound of the opening refrigerator door and the chatter of sports radio, and then he got up from the sofa and left by the front door, walking away from the house, into the heat.

When he walked into the Kwik-Bi, Mr. Khabir sat behind the counter, watching a silent black-and-white TV. From time to time he reached up to scratch a deep-red map-shaped mark on his right cheek. This was the way Clarence usually found him, and these three things—the man, the TV, and the little red map on his face—felt warm and predictable, like the sun coming up in the morning, no matter how dark the night before had been. "Hey," Clarence said quietly as he stopped and looked over Mr. Khabir's shoulder at the TV screen. Mr. K spun around on his stool, faced Clarence, and nodded. "Well, good morning, sir," he said, and then he folded his hands in his lap. "Are you here for your father's coffee then?"

Clarence shook his head and kept his eyes on the screen. He wanted to be here at the counter with Mr. K. He knew that much. He also knew he didn't feel much like talking, and he hoped Mr. K didn't feel much like talking either. He didn't even know if he'd be able to make conversation, given the state of his mangled tongue. Soon the two fell silent, but Clarence could feel Mr. K studying his face.

He didn't really like the feeling of being so closely watched, but when Mr. K was doing the watching, Clarence found he didn't dislike it either. With Mr. K, he knew he was really being seen, but it felt different from the way the men in his house sometimes inspected him, always looking for places that needed repair. Mr. K had a soft way of seeing, like the way his mama used to sit across from him at the dinner table and quietly ask about school. That softness made him want to hide the parts of his life that would cause her worry, like the fact that, as he'd gotten older, most people—including Johnnyprice—had started calling him Itty—short for Itty-Bitty—which was short for *You're going to do what we want you to do, because you can't do anything to stop us.*

Though Mr. K's big tinted glasses mainly hid his eyes, Clarence could feel those eyes trying to see through his skin, straight into his heart, like his mama's eyes used to. Clarence was careful to keep his own eyes glued to the silent screen, biding time until Mr. K's stool spun back around to face the TV. "So, you are liking the golf, Clarence?" Mr. K asked, and while Clarence could see that the sport called golf was on the TV in front of him, he couldn't understand how anyone could honestly claim to like it.

"I guess it's fine," he fibbed. "I haven't seen it much, and guess I don't really get the point." He tried to speak clearly without hurting his tongue, but it wasn't working. He squinted against the pain, but Mr. K didn't seem to notice that anything was wrong. He spun around on his swivel stool and went on talking.

"The point, sir, is to simply execute each swing as if there was no swing before it, and as if there will be no swing after it. Each swing becomes the only swing, and each moment, the only moment." As always, Clarence's eyes were first drawn to the mark on Mr. K's face, then to his eyes, which were just blurred shadows behind his tinted glasses. "The man who is thinking only of the present swing, this is the man who is mastering the game. It is all a practice of the mind, you see."

Clarence nodded, but he felt his mind wandering. On most days, he enjoyed hearing Mr. K's thoughts about, well, most everything. He'd been coming to the Kwik-Bi since he was a little kid, and when he'd turned ten, his mama had started letting him come on his own. Now, without his mama around, there wasn't really a reason to go home, and Clarence would sometimes just stand there in front of the silent black-and-white TV, listening to Mr. K. tell him about the world. Today, though, was different. It wasn't just that his tongue hurt. Everything about him hurt: his insides, his outsides, his mind, the place in his heart where he could still hear his mama's voice. He—the whole entire boy named Clarence Feather—throbbed like the meat of his tongue, and he just couldn't sit around and chitchat with a man who, sooner or later, would see that this was no ordinary Saturday morning.

"I need some dog biscuits," Clarence suddenly blurted out, and Mr. K cocked his head to the left, which meant he was about to ask a question.

"Dog biscuits? You are having a dog now, yes? And when did you get this dog? Or were you having one all along?"

Clarence shook his head. "It's not my dog, Mr. K." He glanced down at the counter for a moment while he thought about how to answer. "It's just this dog I know. A big white dog named Mona." Mr. K nodded, but in the grown-up way that meant he thought he knew something Clarence didn't.

"You stay away from those fighting dogs," he whispered, lowering his head and moving his eyes around the store. "I hear the stories, left and right. The men who fight these dogs, they are bad men. You stay away." Clarence wished Mr. K had said something, anything else. "Dogs are to love," Mr. K suddenly continued with great feeling, and then he raised his head and scratched the dark stain on his cheek. "If dogs are not to love, then what is the point?"

Clarence agreed. What was the point then? Yet there was still the fact of the night before. There was still the blood and the dead dog and the blackout and the part of his tongue he'd nearly taken off with his own teeth when he fell.

There in front of him, Mr. K's mind left his body for a long moment, which it did sometimes. Clarence knew Mr. K was the kind of person who was always thinking, who was always seeing above and under and around and beyond what everybody else saw. Clarence watched as right there behind the cash register, Mr. K traveled to a place where dogs were never loved, where they were hurt and even killed by men like Y and Johnnyprice. Mr. K sat very still, his face dark with sadness, and then all at once, he shook his head and stepped right back into the conversation like he'd never left it. "Pick out any biscuits that you care to, Clarence. There will be no reason to pay today."

Clarence walked to the back of the store and stopped in front of the pet food section. *I'm sorry, Mona,* he thought as he picked out a box of biscuits. A fluffy white dog wearing a cowboy hat was featured on the label, and just the sight of the little dog made him want to cry. *I'm so sorry for last night,* he continued, and he hoped that by the time he got to Gina's house, Mona would have forgiven him for what he'd witnessed in the fighting pen. He picked up the biscuits and walked slowly toward the front of the store, passing behind Mr. K, who was once again facing the golf game. "Thanks, and see ya later," he muttered, tossing a couple of dollars onto the counter for the Andy Capp's he'd grabbed on the way back to the register. He was out the door before Mr. K had a chance to spin around to face him.

DOG DAYS

••

HE MADE HIS WAY across the Kwik-Bi parking lot, letting the sun sink into his skin and hoping it would ease him. He slowed down into his walking, letting his body walk itself until it found a quiet spot on the side of the Kwik-Bi that faced out at Bedford Street. In time he sat down in a dry patch of grass, pressed his back against the building, and carefully sucked at the Andy Capp's so as to keep the salt off the raw spots on his tongue. Across the street sat a tiny brick building with a FOR LEASE sign in the window, but the last *e* had faded, and someone had used a black marker to color in an *F* before the *l* in *lease*. He couldn't help but think it was funny, the way that the empty building was now *For Fleas*, but he was careful not to let the thought show on his face. He just leaned back into the warm brick until there was only his body, the sucking of his mouth, and the vacant brick building there in front of him, waiting for fleas.

Before long, something moved into his vision, over on his left side. He turned his head and saw it was Y. "Whatcha got there, Itty?" Y asked in a way that seemed more of a threat than a question. Clarence held the hot fry still in his mouth. Its spicy red salt burned the wounds on his tongue, but he couldn't seem to get it down, so he just waited until Y stopped right in front of him, then he shifted his eyes to the pavement. He finally swallowed. "Give me one of them fries, why don't you now."

Y pulled at the red underwear poofing up over his sagging jeans. He adjusted the gold frames of his sunglasses, then fingered the thin black hair slicked back against his scalp. A sad little mustache sat just above his top lip, looking like something scribbled, a mistake, and he swayed there in the sunlight until Clarence held out the bag of fries. Slowly Y removed one and inspected it, holding it in the open palm of his hand. "What else you got?" he asked, nodding toward Clarence's pockets. Clarence swallowed, then held up the box of dog biscuits. "So you're still loving up on that big white dog, aren't you now, Itty? A real pretty thing, you and that big white dog."

"How's Black?" Clarence heard himself ask the question before he'd even formed a thought about his next words. His belly was kicking, the same way it had the night of the fight, and it was a feeling he knew well, always coming on strong when he was afraid. Asking stupid questions took his mind off his nerves, but he'd learned that men didn't like stupid questions. Especially not boy-men like Y.

"So, is he okay?" he continued, unable to stop speaking. Y moved in on him close so that his crotch stopped right in front of Clarence's face. He stood there for a moment, then another, and then he squatted. When his eyes reached the level of Clarence's eyes, he smiled.

"Why yes, thank you for asking. Black is good as gold." Y was smiling with too many teeth, and Clarence knew he was in trouble. Men didn't smile that big unless they were drunk, telling dirty jokes, looking at women, or looking to kick someone's ass. "You might be better off asking Johnnyprice about how Nasty's doing, all things considered. Or have you already forgotten how last night went down?" Y ran the tip of his tongue across the surface of his mismatched teeth, and Clarence waited for the worst. Without any notice, though, everything about Y suddenly changed.

"But enough about dogs, Itty." He stood and pulled up his ass-dragging jeans so the belt was almost at his waist. He straightened the collar of his silver jersey and then crossed his hands carefully in front of his sparkling belt buckle. "I'm not here to talk about last night. I'm here to get your opinion on some matters of business." Suddenly Y sounded like a teacher or a preacher, someone who wanted to earn Clarence's trust. "I mean, you're not a kid anymore, and I'd like to ask you if you're happy with your business arrangement with Johnnyprice, if you're getting what you think you deserve."

This question didn't sit well with Clarence, for a couple of reasons. Number one, no one was supposed to know he did errands for Johnnyprice, not even his dad. This was why, when he showed up after a weekend run, his father left the room before Johnnyprice ever busted out the twenties. Number two, his work for Johnnyprice wasn't a business arrangement. Johnnyprice was like family. He'd just always been around for as long as Clarence could remember, and pretty much all the time since his mama had died.

During the winter of bone shivers and no heat in the house, a few months after his mama's murder, Johnnyprice had come on strong with a story about delivering cheap medicine to poor people as a community service. He'd said he had connections and that he could get medicine for next to nothing, and he just needed Clarence's help in getting it out to the sick folks while he minded the business end of things. After that, Clarence had just never stopped running. Even after he learned the truth of what he was doing, it was all he had to offer. When he finished each run, he'd walk back into the kitchen, and for minutes and sometimes hours the men in his house would be happy. His own happiness had all but died with his mama, and he craved these full, bright moments as much as his belly craved food after a long fitful sleep.

He still craved them—even at fourteen—but he'd learned to live without them. With each year that passed since his mama's death, the two men in his house liked him less. He didn't think he'd changed much; he'd barely grown an inch, and he worked hard at staying out of their way. But the air they shared in the box-of-gray had soured little by little. The moments of brightness were pretty much over, and thinking about it now, he could see Y's point. Johnnyprice still paid him like he was eleven, like he was a kid who didn't know what he was risking to run crack. Y was right about the money, but that didn't change what Johnnyprice had told Clarence's dad the night before, on the way home from the fight. Johnnyprice kept a roof over their heads. If Clarence wanted to stay under that roof, he'd have to keep being what Johnnyprice wanted him to be.

Clarence shadowed his eyes with his hands as Y stepped out of the blinding sunlight, and into shadow. Apparently Y wasn't finished with whatever business he thought he was conducting. "So . . . Johnnyprice, then. I just have to ask, you know. I mean, he pays you what you're worth? He pays you what the other runners make?" If Y was just going to beat his ass, Clarence wished he'd get it over with.

"I don't know what you're talking about," Clarence faked, figuring that denial was really the only safe response. He wiped his forehead with the hem of his T-shirt, noticing that the afternoon seemed to be getting hotter with each second and that the heat wasn't just around him, it was in him now. Y squatted down again and gently shook his head, like he felt sad for Clarence, like he could see a wrong there in front of him and just wanted to make it right.

"Itty. No . . . I'm sorry. Clarence." Y smiled a perfectly quiet little smile, a smile so unlike any expression Clarence had ever seen on his face that Clarence had to catch his breath and hold it for a moment. This wasn't a Y-style grin; this was a smile, and the smile seemed real, like a Mr. K smile, like there was something solid behind it, holding it steady. "Maybe it's time to be done with Itty, don't you think? Would you rather I call you Clarence?" And just then, right after the question, Y's voice went lady-soft for a moment, and in that moment Clarence felt himself get lost. He felt himself forget who he was talking to, and he felt himself let it happen.

Soon he found himself nodding because, yes, he would very much like to be called Clarence. He would like very much to be called the name his mama gave him instead of some stupid, made-up name that wasn't even a word. He knew that people still called him Itty because it made him feel small on the inside, like he was on the outside. He also knew it made them feel bigger than they actually were, and he was tired of it.

Y just squatted there and nodded, and the nodding became a rhythm that was comforting to Clarence, like the beating of a heart or the hushed creaking of a rocking chair. Y took off his shades, and his eyes held Clarence's eyes, and Clarence couldn't help but notice that Y's eyes were going soft, just like his voice. He'd never seen Y's eyes when they weren't burning a hole right through him or Johnnyprice or whoever or whatever else he was looking at. "Okay, so listen now, Clarence," he soothed in a bedtime-story voice. "I think you need to do a little something for your own good, my man. I think you need to simply have a little chat with Johnnyprice, you know, ask him what the going rate is for what you do. Ask him does he want to pay that rate, and tell him that if he won't, I will."

Clarence sat, looking at Y's face, but he really couldn't see it anymore. His eyes were open, but at some point during Y's talk, a door had closed behind them, back in the part of his mind that told him what things meant. Y smiled sweetly once more, and for a split second Clarence wished this boy-man would just reach out and hug him. The last real hug he'd gotten was from his mama, just minutes before she'd sat down at the kitchen table on that warm October night. The window had been cracked to air out the kitchen. She'd cooked up his favorite supper—mac and cheese with collards—and from her chair facing the window, she'd reached over to hand the plastic red basket of rolls to Clarence when a *pop-pop-pop-pop* sound had bounced off the kitchen walls, her chair had toppled over, and as she'd twitched there for a moment on the linoleum floor, the front of her shirt filled up with blood.

Clarence could feel Y still watching his face, could feel him nodding like Mr. K did when he understood something but wasn't ready to say it. "You miss her, don't you?" he whispered, like he was inside Clarence's own memory, and Clarence let him stay there, all the while hating himself for enjoying the comfort of the hand that now rested on his arm. For a few more minutes neither of them moved, but neither said anything else. Eventually Clarence just closed his eyes and let the sun swallow him. In time he heard Y's voice above him again: still soft, still sweet, saying he was sorry about Clarence's mama and that he needed to make sure to take good care of himself.

Clarence sat, silent, unable to find a flaw in Y's reasoning. Y was right. He did need to take good care of himself. What Y knew now, for whatever reason, was something he'd been knowing himself for the better part of two years but had never dared put into words.

If he didn't take care of himself, there was just no one left who would do it for him.

— — —

When he got to Mona's yard, he put down his things, then sat down on the sidewalk in front of the fence. He looked around to make sure no one was coming in either direction, that no one was around to see him be soft. Then, "Mona!" he yelled, knowing that on a hot day like this, she'd probably be in the backyard, sleeping in the shade. "Come on, Mona!" It seemed like the words were still leaving his mouth when she galloped into the front yard and flung herself, paws first, against the fence.

Slowly he stood, and the top of his head came up to the top of her shoulders. He had to cock his head way back to even see her face. *Thank God this fence is bigger than you, dog,* he thought, fighting the urge to jump back and wait for his breath to settle. But he stayed, and he stood very still, breathing as best he could, and then he slowly raised his hand and laid it against the fence, like he'd done for the first time just days before.

His hand was greeted by the great dripping wetness of Mona's tongue.

In time, he slid his hand down the fence to his own eye level, and Mona followed his hand with her tongue, letting

her paws drop from the fence to the ground. Clarence squatted and took a minute to enjoy the buzz in his body that
meant something good was happening, and then he remembered the biscuits, so he bent down to get the box while Mona
watched him, her blue eyes blinking. "I've got something for
you," he said, and he looked down the street in both directions. The coast was still clear, except for the old man on his
porch, but he didn't count. The good thing about old folks
was they no longer cared who was cool.

Clarence reached into the box and pulled out a yellow
biscuit that smelled a little like a graham cracker and a little
like his mama's vitamins used to. Slowly he slid it through
the fence while Mona drooled on the other side. Then, when
the biscuit was midway through the chain link, Mona shifted
forward in a flash, and Clarence felt a sudden whoosh against
his hand: the hot wet wind from her open mouth, then that
mouth slobbering right up onto the biscuit, onto the meat of
his own hand. He closed his eyes against the feeling, riding
it out in all its nerve-frazzling glory. Then the moment was
over. And he wanted another one like it.

Because, as it turned out, his fingers were still there, all
five of them glistening in dog spit, and on the other side of
the fence Mona's mouth hung loose and happy, like she was
laughing. This was an animal that could eat anyone's face

anytime she wanted, just like Black had eaten Nasty's the night of the fight. What he didn't understand was why she wouldn't. With so many things that could do him harm, why wasn't this huge beast of a dog one of them?

The afternoon faded while he slowly fed Mona through the fence until the biscuits were gone. Everything was forgotten in the time that passed between the two in silence. With Mona, he felt light and full, like a regular kid in summer. With her, it didn't matter that he was a runner, and he didn't need to try to be a man. With her, his Superdog, he didn't need to try at all.

Around him, the day cooled, its light slanting low toward evening. Gina, Mona's owner, would probably be home soon. Just one minute more was all he needed, but in one second's time, that minute disappeared. Time stopped with the loud sucking of teeth, and the sucking stopped right behind him. "Looking good, y'all are," Y said, and Clarence kept his breathing low and slow. Y was behind him, and he didn't know what that meant. Had he followed him? What more could he possibly want? "Dog's lucky to have you around." Clarence heard another set of footsteps nearing as Y softly singsonged, calling out to whoever was walking toward them. "Hey there, pretty lady. Got a little something special for you today." This time Clarence could hear the falseness beneath the sweet sugar of Y's voice. It was the same sugar he'd laid on Clarence just a few hours back, but now Clarence could smell the stink it hid.

"Hey, Y," answered the woman. The voice clearly belonged to Gina. "That's sweet of you. God knows I'm running on empty, but I've got this house to pay for now. I could really use a little help making it through the night shift." There was a brief silence, and that silence gave Clarence time to fully realize what was going down. He knew what Y would be giving Gina to keep her awake. He *ran* what Y would give her to stay awake.

He also knew, given that she worked the register at the Bar-B-Q Palace, that Y's little pick-me-up wasn't something she could afford. "So, I'll catch up with you later, Y—cool? You got me covered, then?" Clarence's mind traveled back to the prior afternoon, to those Y-boys in Gina's yard yesterday, before the fight, and then he remembered how she'd told him that a guy she knew was putting up a fence for Mona. And now, here was Y himself, sniffing around, spreading on the love. Whether he liked it or not, Clarence could see how the pieces fit together.

"Oh, hey there," he heard Gina say now, like she was talking to someone else. Then there were more footsteps, then a hand on his shoulder. He flinched without even thinking about it. "Whoa now, Clarence," Gina said, and she moved around to his right side and then sat down next to him. "Why so jumpy? It's just me, Gina. I don't bite, baby." Clarence turned his head and wondered if Gina was officially a girl or a woman. She didn't seem much older than Y, but there were those riverbeds around her eyes that said a lot had happened, that a lot of water had run there. "So, how you doing there? You and Mona having a good time?"

Clarence nodded but didn't answer with words.

"Well, why don't you walk around back with me, Clarence. I have something to ask you. Got a minute?" Clarence nodded again, and he pushed himself up onto his feet, taking care to keep his back to Y. Gina led the way to the gate, and he slid in right behind her when she opened it.

"See y'all later," Y singsonged again behind them. Clarence had already guessed that he'd been hanging back in the shadows somewhere, watching him and Mona. "Looks like you have some important business to attend to." Clarence thought about Y, then Gina, and then he let his mind linger on Mona. In front of him, Mona just stood there, grinning, her pink tongue flapping happily. *You'd better stay away from this dog, Y,* said Clarence's mind, and he knew his mind spoke the truth.

Gina dragged her feet as she walked along the side of the house toward the backyard. She was so different from the Gina he'd met that first day with Mona, the one whose red sneakers could barely keep their soles on the ground. Now he knew why. She'd been working doubles, and smoking rock helped her make it through double shifts, and Y was her guy, and she was currently running low. As Clarence followed her along the side of the house, Mona thunked along between them, looking back at him from time to time, like she was checking to make sure he was still there. Mona. Gina. Mona. Y. He couldn't help but wonder how deep Gina was in with Y, or why he was paying so much attention to Mona. Why had Y's boys put up a fence for her? What had Y meant when he said she was lucky to have Clarence? As far as Clarence could tell, Y only saw dogs two ways: killing another dog or dead. He was glad when Gina finally spoke. He needed something else to think about.

"Oh, Clarence . . . I'm just so exhausted," she quietly moaned as she sat down on the back stoop and turned her face toward the dimming sky. Clarence heard her draw a long breath, like she was pulling hard on a cigarette. She blew the air back out loudly and then just sat still and silent, like she'd forgotten what she'd meant to say or do. Mona smelled the back of Gina's left hand, glanced at Clarence, then at Gina, and then she hunkered down at Gina's feet and started licking Gina's ankles. "Hey, girl," Gina muttered, letting her hand drop onto the top of Mona's head. "These hours are killing me, girl. What am I going to do?" Before Clarence really knew what he'd done, he'd walked right up to Gina and laid a hand on her shoulder. He didn't have an answer for her, but sometimes a hand on the shoulder was enough. "I mean, I just got home, and I've got to be back for the night shift in a hour. Not even enough time for a nap." Clarence slid his hands into his pockets. What was there to say?

"Sorry, Gina," he offered. It was all he had.

"Well, you know . . . I've been hoping you might be able to help me out with Miss Mona here." She looked down at her dog and weakly smiled. "I'm working doubles most every day to pay for this house my mom left me. I can't afford the place, but I don't want to let it go. I guess it's complicated." She grew quiet. Her dark eyes drifted. "Maybe you know how that is."

Clarence knew all about what *complicated* was, but he didn't want to talk about it. He quickly brought the conversation back to Mona. "So, you want me to look out after Mona when you're gone?" He tried hard to keep himself in check, to play it cool. He didn't want to get his hopes up.

"If you could. I mean, if that would be all right with your parents and everything. I couldn't pay you, but I'd keep snacks around, and you could—"

"I'll do it." The words flew out of his mouth on their own, and Clarence knew he'd spoken too quickly, too eagerly. He could feel himself smiling, exposing his teeth to the world.

He had to bring the conversation down a notch, find some cool. "I mean ... you know ... that would be all right, I guess. I guess I'll do it if you really need me to." He set his mouth into a straight line, but inside he was laughing at his luck. Gina thought Mona needed his help, and maybe she did—for food and water, all the things that kept her alive. But he needed to stay alive too, and he needed more than food and water to do it. He needed to be loved, and as he watched Mona glance back, giving him a slobbery grin, he knew he already was.

— — —

It was almost midnight in the box-of-gray, and the men were at it again. Clarence sat on his bed, with his back to the wall and his headphones pulled down tight over his ears. In his lap, the opening credits of *The Dark Knight* scrolled on his player's screen. Even with the headphones on, he could hear that his dad and Johnnyprice were having another argument down the hall: maybe about sports, maybe about dogs or crack, maybe about him, maybe about nothing. It could go any which way at any old time between them, and the topics switched back and forth as quickly as the ads on the radio. One moment they'd be cursing each other's mothers, and the next they'd be hugging it out like a couple of church ladies.

Today was Thursday, and they'd been going at it all week long since the dogfight. The hotter it got, the more they drank, and the more they drank, the more they either loved everything more than it deserved to be loved, or were convinced that the whole world had gone to shit. By the time the sun disappeared into the rooftops, most anything was possible, and tonight, the fact that Nasty—Johnnyprice's prized fighter—had been killed by Black only made matters worse. Tonight these men loved nothing. There was nothing to do but wait it out.

Clarence knew it was a Thursday because every morning when he woke, he checked the calendar hanging on his closet door, the one that Mr. K had given all his regular customers for Christmas. He usually didn't think about calendars once school was out, but this summer was different. He wasn't checking the calendar to find out the date or day; summer was just summer until it wasn't anymore. But soon, in just a few weeks, he would walk over to the closet door, look at the calendar, and the day would be August 24, and on that day, he would pull his clothes out, just like always, and he would dress himself, just like always. Everything would be the same, but he would be different. He would be a high school student, and he was scared shitless.

Each and every morning this summer, he'd checked the calendar and realized he wasn't ready, and yet the days kept on coming. It was already August now, and he was no more ready than he'd been back in June, when Stonewall Jackson had let out. Based on the pencil marks on the closet's door-frame, he hadn't gotten any taller, either. And to top it off, he couldn't seem to figure out what would *make* him ready, at least not while he stayed cooped up in the box-of-gray with the loudmouths in the kitchen. For the better part of August they'd just planted themselves in front of the fan in the kitchen window, only leaving to buy beer or smokes, or to check in on what they called "business."

"Business," aka crack and dogs, had lately meant they were going broke, and the broker they got, the more they holed up. He'd hoped that by now they'd need a breather before another weekend got rolling, but by the sounds of things—sportscasters yapping, fridge door slamming, hands and cans banging against the tabletop—they were just get-ting started. Since Nasty's death, Johnnyprice had soured, and where Johnnyprice went, Rowley Feather followed. If Clarence wanted peace, he would have to find it on the street.

He stopped the DVD and took off his headphones. He shook his head, like his mama used to when his dad did something stupid or hardheaded. If his mama was here, she'd put an end to all this constant carrying-on, and if she knew how they made their money, or that they'd tricked her son into running crack? She would probably call the cops herself.

But the men were different men back then; they'd had

what his mama had called *common decency.* His dad had actually worked for a living—he even had his own uniform with a SANITEC patch on the front—and he'd brought a paycheck home every week and handed it over to Clarence's mama during Friday night supper. All three of them were at their best when she was around, because she loved them enough to expect it, and because they loved her back. Even Johnnyprice. Clarence never knew what Johnnyprice did for work, but without Johnnyprice, his dad and mom would have never even met. His mama knew Johnnyprice from *way back in the day,* she'd said, and she kept him in line, always shushing him when he said the wrong thing and even sometimes making him leave if he crossed a line.

"*Mama,*" he whispered now, keeping his voice down, knowing he wasn't allowed to speak of her in the house. "*Mama, Mama, Mama,*" he softly said until he swallowed the word whole, for fear of never being able to stop.

In time he swung himself down from the bed and went over to check the lock on the door. He stood there a moment, just listening to the clatter down the hallway, and then he turned and left through his window, dropping down behind the scraggly line of bushes at the front of the house. When he got to the street, he made a left and started his regular walk. He passed Gina's house, said hello to Mona in his mind, and then soon the Kwik-Bi's lights became a starry smear in the thick August air. They reminded him of his wishing stars, and he knew if such stars were to fall, they would surely fall there, into the life of the nicest person he'd ever met, besides his mama.

He knew it was late, and that Mr. K would probably have already gone upstairs to his apartment, but he walked toward the lights anyway. As he got closer to the store's glass door, he saw that the inside lights were burning bright and that Mr. K sat on his stool behind the counter, his face turned toward the black-and-white. Clarence just stood there, watching. He wanted to knock, but it was late, and Mr. K worked such long days, with so little time to himself. Still, he didn't want to leave, either, so he just stood there, watching Mr. K as he rubbed the little red map on his face, then looked away from the TV and out into the aisles.

Minutes passed, and then Clarence noticed that there was something in Mr. K's hand—maybe a book or a picture frame—and that occasionally Mr. K would raise it up, look at it, and then gaze back into the aisles again. Suddenly Clarence felt uneasy, like he was seeing something he shouldn't be seeing. He was about to walk away when Mr. K turned his head toward the front door, and their eyes locked and stayed locked. Mr. K's actual eyes were just blurs behind his tinted glasses, but Clarence could sense the power of their focus, maybe even more so because they lay hidden.

Before Clarence could move in one direction or another, Mr. K had slid down from his stool, unlocked the door, and opened it wide. "It is you, here in the night's wee hours! Why are you wandering about so very late, Clarence?"

Clarence shrugged. He couldn't tell Mr. K that lately he was out in the night's wee hours more than he was in his own bed. "Couldn't sleep, you know?" he mumbled, looking down at the toes of his sneaks. "Just happens sometimes."

Mr. K stepped out of the way and let Clarence slide by him, into the store. Clarence kept his eyes down until he was seated on a stool, and then he quickly turned his eyes to the black-and-white, hoping that without eye contact, Mr. K would lose interest in questioning him.

"Well, then. I was just about to make a nice hot cup of tea, you know," said Mr. K from behind him. "I take the tea with the last of the paperwork, before I go upstairs for the night. Would you join me in a cup, perhaps?" Clarence nodded and made an *umm-hmm* sound, though he'd never had tea without ice in it, and he couldn't see why anyone would want a hot drink on a summer night that was as slippery as a porch-hanging girl. Mr. K seemed to read his thoughts, which didn't surprise him. "You see, the heat of the tea will make you sweat, and the damp sweat will cool down your body. This is simple science, and in my country, it is an ordinary thing to take the hot drinks in the hottest of weather.

And my country is much hotter than yours is, my friend. Trust me. You will see!"

The heels of Mr. K's loafers *click-click-click*ed back toward the kitchen, and Clarence was left alone at the counter with the silent television. He was glad Mr. K had already turned down the volume. He was glad for the quiet and the soft comforting sound of running water back in the kitchen. No voices. No other noises. He put his elbows on the counter, laid his forehead in the palms of his hands, and finally, for a moment, he let himself rest.

He awoke to the sense of a hand touching his shoulder, and he jerked away. For a moment he didn't know where he was or who had touched him. "It is only me with the tea, Clarence," Mr. K reassured, backing up to give him room. "You are all right. It is only me." Clarence spun around on his stool and faced the man with the tea. Slowly and gently, he took the cup Mr. K handed him but found he didn't know what to do with it. It was tiny and looked like something that fancy women in long gowns might drink punch from as they fanned themselves with their pale hands. He glanced over at the store's glass door, making sure no one would catch him drinking tea out of a lady-cup. "It is all right," Mr. K said. "You are not going to hurt the cup. Just blow a bit on the tea to cool it off, and then you will find it most refreshing, I think."

Mr. K walked around the counter and settled himself on his own stool, on the other side. He gently placed the teacup on the counter in front of him. "Well. We have known one another quite some time now, have we not?" Clarence nodded and studied the row of painted roses along the edge of his cup. He couldn't believe he was drinking from a lady-cup with little roses on it, and he couldn't believe that he liked it. The air conditioner above the register hummed and sputtered, and Clarence sighed. This felt good. Drinking tea with Mr. K in the middle of the night felt good.

"You know, your father and his friend, they come for the beer and the cigarettes, and they have been bringing their business for years, since even before you were born. But they are not the same men they were. This much I know. Now their words—they are ugly and sharp. Now their eyes are like the eyes of the dead." Clarence sat very still. The lady-cup trembled a little in his hand. "Too much has changed for you, Clarence," said Mr. K, and Clarence stared at the row of roses around the cup's edge. Rose after rose after rose after rose in a perfect circle that never ended.

THE STORM

....

AT JUST AFTER TWO the next day, the faded blue sky
went the yellowy-green of a week-old bruise. Johnnyprice
ran around the kitchen closing windows and doors, but
each time the wind kicked, the back door blew back open.
"Damn that door," he growled as he dropped the little plastic bags onto the kitchen table. It was Friday. Delivery day.
Clarence watched him and couldn't help but think about
what Y had said about the other runners and what they
got paid, and this thinking made him belly-sick like certain kinds of thinking always did. This Friday there were
only five bags on the table, but Johnnyprice still saw fit to
give him the speech about doing the neighborhood a favor.
"Thank God I've got these connections," he proclaimed,
but as usual he kept his head down and his eyes away from
Clarence's eyes. "Bloodsucking pharmaceutical racket.
Poor people need their medicine too, goddammit."

Clarence ignored him and stared down at the table, and
there, on the scratched-up wooden tabletop, he saw an image

of himself at eleven, on the afternoon when Johnnyprice had first told him the Story of the Medicine. *You're doing a good thing,* he heard Johnnyprice reassure as he laid his hand on little Clarence's small bony shoulder. Little Clarence—his eleven-year-old self—stood at the same table that fourteen-year-old Clarence stood next to now, and his younger self's gaze quickly moved beyond Johnnyprice to the big kitchen window. Right there, in its center, a single bullet hole was captured in a web of shattered glass. *I don't want to,* he heard little Clarence say. *I don't want to go out there. I'm scared. Please don't make me.*

Johnnyprice pulled little Clarence in close, just like he'd done the night of the dogfight. *I know it's scary out there, but you've got to face it, Itty. It's the only way to beat the fear. Think of Batman. Those bats scared the shit out of him, so he made himself into a bat, right? You've got to get back out there, like Batman did, or you'll never get over this.* Clarence watched little Clarence lean into Johnnyprice, and he watched Johnnyprice slide in closer, returning the lean. He watched Johnnyprice point to the little bags on the table and nod. Johnnyprice had always been like a second dad and sometimes like a better dad than the one he'd actually been born to. Or so it had seemed. He couldn't tell anymore. *Your mama would be proud of you, little man,* he heard Johnnyprice say to little Clarence, and then he watched his younger self glimpse his actual father—his blood—drifting by the kitchen window like a ghost. He watched his father cast a look at little Clarence with wide, sad eyes. He watched him disappear.

Now, in the same kitchen, Johnnyprice was about to send him out in a thunderstorm over five lousy bags of crack. This didn't sit well with him, all things considered. "Hey, it's looking pretty bad out there," he mentioned as Johnnyprice strolled over to the refrigerator and leaned casually against it, like he'd ended up there by accident. "Maybe I can wait until the storm passes?"

Johnnyprice shook his head. A fake pout played at the corners of his lips. "People don't stop being sick just because it's raining, Itty," his mouth said, but the message behind the words was *Don't even* think *about questioning me, boy.* Clarence walked over to the table, lifted the plate, and slid the bags into the pockets of his plastic red folder. Outside the kitchen window, beyond the front porch, the scrawny trees bowed down to the wind. All around the house, the bruise of the sky darkened, and Clarence realized that the weather outside and the weather inside himself were doing the very same thing. He wondered if Johnnyprice could see it or feel it, if he knew that a boy could change as quickly as an August afternoon.

"You're doing a good thing," Johnnyprice mumbled as

he slid into his jacket. He picked up the folder and walked over to the fridge, pinning down Johnnyprice's eyes with his own before Johnnyprice could look away. He wanted Johnnyprice to see his eyes, to watch the hot wind blow across little Itty's face and then to wonder, later, what he had witnessed. He wanted him to know, when the storm finally exploded, that he'd been given a warning.

He walked down the back steps into a fierce, stinging rain. Water seemed to be blowing in all directions, and he pulled himself as deep into the jacket as he could go, glad for once that he was small enough to almost disappear into the hand-me-down slicker that used to belong to his father. He marched through the dirty water that frothed along the curbs, smacking his feet hard on the pavement beneath. Goddam those men. Goddam them for putting him in harm's way when he didn't know any better. Goddam them for taking advantage of a child. The two of them deserved each other. Let them destroy themselves and destroy each other. He was done with them. This much he knew.

As he splashed deeper into Mayfair Heights, in the opposite direction of the Kwik-Bi, he remembered that this walk made him nervous, and on an afternoon that now looked like the edge of night, it seemed especially spooky, first because the landmarks were wrong, but the landmarks were always wrong in this pocket of the neighborhood. No twisted tree.

No rusted metal in the yard of the tattooed artists. No old man who called him boy as he waved at him from his porch. No Superdog named Mona, watching him from her living room window. The landmarks he passed on his way to the apartments felt like shifty-eyed strangers, though he'd seen them dozens of times. So he watched his back as he made his way. He never felt truly alone, though he couldn't imagine why anyone would be out in a storm like this.

He hunkered down into the wind, noting the tiny yellow house with the red towels for curtains, its doghouse nearly eaten by the weedy front yard. He'd never seen a dog there, but he'd never seen a person, either. Not fully, anyway. The porch light was always on, even in the daytime, and he believed he'd seen someone peeping out from around one of the towels once, just before dark. He was sure there'd been a dark profile, the shadowed side of a face. He even thought he'd glimpsed the eggy white of someone's eye. He wanted nothing to do with this house today, and he looked away from it just as a jagged white lightning bolt sliced the sky right in front of him. He stopped, held his breath, and waited for the thunder, and there it was, rising up from the very earth, it seemed, straight into his body. He closed his eyes and waited for it to end, which it did, and he pressed on.

Goddam Johnnyprice, he thought again, and he readied himself for the house with the porch-hangers, girls not much older than he was, who called to him in the voices of women. Loud, cool, slippery, sweet. He always dreaded walking by the girls, but his trips were on Fridays after school, and on Fridays after school, girls hung on stoops or in the parking lot of the Kwik-Bi or in the picnic shelter of the park, where they drank sodas and hiked up their short skirts as they shifted positions on the picnic tables. He hoped that the storm would have driven them inside by now, and he got his wish, except for the big one who carried the height and shoulders of a man, plus the everything else of a woman. This was the one they called Mornay, and she stood, hunched up close to the front door, smoking a cigarette. *'Sup, Itty?* he imagined he heard her holler, though her voice was probably carried away on the wind.

Passing Mornay meant he was almost to the park, and the trip through the park was the worst part of this walk. Everyone knew the park belonged to Y. Clarence hated the park, but he only knew one other way to the apartments, and that was through the woods. The stories he'd heard about the woods were worse than the stories about the park, or even about Y, for that matter. So he made himself face the park every Friday, hoping Y might be elsewhere in the neighborhood, walking his walk, maybe holding court with the boys in the parking lot of the Kwik-Bi. So far, there'd been no pattern to Y's comings or goings that Clarence could find. Sometimes he was in the park; sometimes he wasn't. Clarence tried not to think about it and just put his head down and pushed forward in the storm.

The park itself was really just a green field that led to a green hill that led down to the road that ended at the apartments. A basketball court and some swings sat in the middle of the field, and at the top of the hill the picnic shelter and restrooms were splattered with words Clarence had heard, more than once, springing from the mouths of the porch-hanging girls. He slogged his way toward the park and tried to see, through the whipping curtain of rain, what he was dealing with. He could hear the swings clanking and clattering in the wind, but everything else was a blur of water and color.

The restrooms, in particular, were the special property of Y, and he knew that the restrooms were on the left, at the top of the hill, but try as he might, he couldn't make out their shapes in the storm. Pavement bled into grass which bled into treetops which bled into the gushing river of the sky. Clarence's routine was to cut a wide loop down the hill, traveling away from the restrooms, never looking in their direction unless called upon directly by Y himself. Today, though, it was hard to get his bearings.

He decided to just veer right and hope for the best. He could feel the slope of the hill under his feet, but it was now just a sea of mud, and the windbreaker did nothing to keep the whipping rain off his face or out of his eyes. He fought to keep his balance, and to keep his delivery close to his body under the jacket, and then "ITTY!" tumbled through the rain and wind, right down the hill and into his ears. He kept on moving, picking up speed. If he couldn't see Y, then maybe Y really couldn't see him. As he ran, the rain began to slow, and way up ahead a few thin slivers of light showed in the clouds. He kept on moving, cursing Johnnyprice and making promises to himself.

"Yo, little man . . . I'm talking to you!" Y's voice followed Clarence, but Clarence kept his eyes fixed on the hill below him as it flattened into a muddy soup. The street that led to the apartments was just up ahead, and he clutched the notebook tight and kept running. He ran for what seemed like a long time, unable to think or hear much of anything until, finally, he reached the apartments and cut left, hoping to disappear between buildings. As he puddle-jumped into the complex, his breathing settled, the rain eased, and he let himself finally stop to make sure all five bags were still in his folder. They were, and as he glanced back, he saw no one at all.

He hurried with his deliveries, grabbing bills and moving on. He needed to get back to his corner of the neighborhood, to the door of the Kwik-Bi-Handi-Mart, where Mr. K would spin on his stool and smile, his eyebrows dancing above his tinted glasses. *Oh, you are soaked to the bone!* he would surely say. *You must have some tea, sir! I will make it at once!* Clarence could almost feel the warmth of the rose-rimmed cup against his lips. Though little clouds of steam rose from the street, he realized he was bone-cold and, suddenly, so very tired. When he finished his last delivery, he shuffled down the steps of the apartment building, lost in his dream of comfort and tea, and then he heard it. A car engine revving up behind him and then easing into an idle. Revving up again. Idling again.

"Why don't we take a little drive so you can dry out, Itty?" Y's voice shouted, though Clarence knew he wasn't really asking a question. "Come on—let me give you a ride. I'll drop you over by the Kwik-Bi, or wherever you want. Johnnyprice doesn't need to know this happened. I just want to talk."

Clarence stood still, his back to Y, understanding that the few ways he had a choice in this matter were far outweighed by the ways he didn't. He stood there next to the curb and readied himself for whatever was coming, knowing he'd end up in that Lexus one way or another. Truth was that a little part of him was almost glad Y had showed up. He couldn't think of anyone who Johnnyprice despised more than Y, and he couldn't think of anyone who Y despised more than Johnnyprice. And right now he pretty much despised Johnnyprice himself, so there it was. The truth of the matter. "So, you coming or not?" Y leaned farther out of the car window and flashed him a smile. "I don't have all day here, little man."

Clarence moved slowly toward the Lexus, but he lifted his eyes and fixed them beyond the car, on the apartment building on the other side of the street. Bass beats blared from an open window where a woman stood in a yellow housecoat, smoking a cigarette, watching the sky clear. For a moment, he kept his eyes on the woman as he walked, thinking he wasn't going to look Y in the eye, that he wasn't going to give him that much of himself. Whatever it was that Y aimed to take from him, he didn't have to give him his eyes.

As he got closer to the car, though, his mind started to change. *Superhero,* he thought. *Make me a superhero.* He was learning that men used their eyes as power; even Mr. K's were fixed and powerful behind his glasses, no matter who was looking back at him. As he walked around to the passenger side of the Lexus, he remembered what Ra's al Ghul had said to Bruce Wayne about fearing his own power, and about how that power was part of his anger. For three long years Clarence had pretended he wasn't angry, because he wanted to keep on being the sweet boy his dead mama had loved. But he couldn't be a boy anymore, not if he wanted to survive.

"Superhero," he whispered as he opened the car door. He knew his clothes were soaked and he'd be sitting on Y's expensive leather seats, but he didn't care. *Superhero*, he demanded, and then he turned his head and looked directly into Y's tiny black eyes. "So, what can I do for you?" He hardly recognized his own voice—the throatiness of it, the manly certainty. He casually looked around the car, as if it was nothing.

Inside, the Lexus was soft, shiny, and smelled strongly of cologne—maybe men's, maybe women's, he couldn't tell. He only knew it stank like church on a Sunday morning. Next to him, Y adjusted the volume on the stereo, turning it down so Clarence could hear him working his tongue against the roof of his mouth. *Clack, shmack, clack, shmack; clack, shmack, clack, shmack*. He was just buying time. The usual. Clarence already knew what Y was going to ask him, anyway, and he already knew his answer.

"So, Itty," Y finally offered. "How many deliveries today?" Clarence didn't answer, but he didn't look away from Y. He kept his eyes steady. *Superhero*, he thought, and he blinked once, then once more, but he never looked away. Y was the first to turn, toward his window, and he sat there for what seemed like a long time, just sucking his teeth. Clarence found himself smiling way down deep, but his face didn't move. Y had looked away, not him. It was a good sign, whatever it meant.

Y began to drive. Clarence wasn't surprised when he

made a left onto the gravel service road that led into the woods behind the apartments. He wasn't surprised when he drove in far enough that the gravel turned to dirt and the road became so bumpy that at one point Clarence bounced forward, almost hitting his head on the dashboard. "I'm taking the long way, you know, so we can talk awhile. You know what I'm going to ask. So why don't you go first, Itty? Why don't you give me an answer before I even ask the question?"

"I want to know about money," Clarence said, keeping his eyes on the side of Y's face. "And I don't want to be fucked with. Not even by you." The words spilled out of his mouth, like they'd been waiting. Just waiting. Y nodded and let his right hand dangle over the side of the steering wheel, like he didn't have a care in the world. He licked at the corner of his sad little mustache. "Sounds fair, Itty. And me and my boys, well, we're like brothers. You commit to us, and we commit to you. If you're with me, I've got your back, 24-7. You down with that? You want to join the family?" Clarence shrugged. Shrugging was also a man thing, a gesture that bought time while making it look like you didn't need it.

"Maybe," he finally said. "I might be able to do that, if the money's right."

"Oh, the money will be right," Y said with a smile that was half real and half made of air. "It's about time you looked out for your own damn self."

BETWEEN

••

Y DROPPED HIM OFF back at the park, and Clarence walked home slowly, letting the afternoon settle into his skin. The rain had stopped, and a smear of sunlight sat low in the dusky sky. When he got home, the kitchen would be full of fake grins and lies, the way it always was. When Johnnyprice heard what he had to say, he'd be plenty pissed, and if Johnnyprice got pissed, his dad would get pissed, and if his dad got pissed, well—all he knew was that he'd say what he had to and be gone before either of them had a chance to stop him.

As he walked, he kept thinking, *Superhero*, like he always did when he was scared. Problem was, he was pretty sure no superhero would ever partner with a villain like Y, and no superhero would go home and speak the words Y had told him to, and no superhero would enjoy spitting out those words as much as Clarence knew he would. But the fact still remained: he wasn't a superhero. He was nowhere close yet. He was just a kid who wanted to get even, who wanted to make a decision for once. And Bruce Wayne had been an awful man before he found his way back to the other side. Didn't he deserve to be awful for a little while? Hadn't all the bullshit he'd endured earned him that right?

When he arrived at the back porch, the inside door was open and the screen door stood ajar. He stopped and stood outside, watching his dad and Johnnyprice at the kitchen table, sharing a forty. The radio was on, but the men weren't listening to it; they were too busy with their own voices as they bickered about dogs, and about how to find the dog that could finally beat Black and take Y down a notch. Johnnyprice sucked from the forty and said, "Damn, I've got to see somebody, somehow put that asshole in his place. Killing my dog. Stealing my business. Thinks he owns this whole damn neighborhood now, and he's barely old enough to buy a damn beer."

Clarence's father shook his head. "All true, Johnnyprice, but it's the same old sad story day in and day out. You're always bitching about the dude, but you don't do shit. You know that. You don't do a thing, and then you wonder why you're not making any money or why he's got the meanest dog or why every young dude in the neighborhood wants to be just like him. And here we sit, sharing a forty, no less, drinking from the same damn bottle." Johnnyprice sprang up from the table and closed in on Clarence's dad, his wall-of-muscle body pressing in close.

"Well, let's just get one thing straight, Rowley, and maybe you'd better take some notes. You've got nothing without me. The roof over your kid's head, the food in your bellies, the forty in your hand. All from me. When you finally start putting some money in the pot, well, that's the day you get to have a fucking opinion." The men were so deep into their argument that they didn't hear Clarence enter the room. They didn't know that he held a package in his hand or that the package was from Y.

Clarence paused for a moment, reminding himself that Y had promised to have his back. If Johnnyprice or his dad messed with him, he'd mess with them back a lot harder. Slowly, like he had all the time in the world, he walked over to the table and dropped a tiny plastic baggie next to the forty. "Y sends his greetings," he said, looking Johnnyprice in the eye and tightening his mouth into a line. "Said he wanted you to try a little bit of his product as a goodwill gift. Said it might explain why your business has been off lately."

Johnnyprice reached over and turned off the radio, never taking his eyes from Clarence. Clarence stood straight and still, never taking his eyes off Johnnyprice. Each of the three sent out signals through their eyes, their nostrils, their muscles, their parted lips, their sweating skins, the hot tips of their twitching fingers. For a long while none of them moved, but the air in the room jerked all around them, like a downed wire after a storm. It was Johnnyprice who finally broke the silence.

"I'm sorry you had to hear us talking like that," he mumbled, as if guilty, hanging his head in a manner that Clarence now recognized as an act. He could see that Johnnyprice was trying to pull him in, to earn his trust, but there was no trust left to earn. He wouldn't know how to get it back, even if he wanted to. Clarence kept his mouth pulled tight and his eyes on Johnnyprice's eyes. "We were just playing around, talking smack like we do. It wasn't real or anything. Won't be nothing but a thing."

Clarence remembered hearing the same words at the dogfight. *Nothing but a thing.* But Nasty's open throat had been real. The blood had been real. From across the table, Johnnyprice offered a questioning smile that invited Clarence to smile back. He didn't.

"Enjoy your crack, bitches," he said, just like Y had suggested, and he was surprised by how easy it was to talk like the men he was growing to hate. Being forced out in the storm by Johnnyprice had changed him, and being given a choice by Y, being treated like a man—well, that had changed him too. Johnnyprice wasn't the boss of him anymore, whether Johnnyprice knew it or not. Clarence kept his eyes straight ahead, away from the men, as he left the house by the back door, the way he'd come. He took to the street, knowing it would eventually lead him to Mona, knowing he wanted company but also knowing that the one person he couldn't look in the eye—not yet—was Mr. Khabir. Mr. K would see he was different, that he'd stepped out onto a wire he'd have to walk alone. Mr. K would see—and fear—all that might happen if he stumbled. If he fell.

When he left the box-of-gray, it was well past eight, and the last light of evening tumbled toward the dark tangle of Friday night. Even on the side streets, cars were out, cruising, pumping bass, stopping in front of houses where people stood around at the curb, smoking and bullshitting under the streetlights. Clarence walked his normal walk, glad to have left the men and the box-of-gray behind him, glad to know they were probably still sitting there, slack-jawed at the table with Y's crack right in front of them. When he finally reached Gina's house he stopped and drew a long deep breath. Being a man took so much energy. So much focus.

He leaned against the fence as his mind wandered, taking him back to his eighth birthday, when his parents had surprised him with a trip to the circus. A man in shiny blue tights had glided back and forth along a tightrope for what seemed like forever, moving with the grace of a fancy ballerina on a stage. Clarence remembered that the man had held a long pole across his middle, and that his mama'd said that the pole helped the wirewalker keep his balance. He looked down at the toes of his sneakers and let the memory guide him. Mona and Mr. K: they would be his balance. He would hold on to them. For as long as they'd let him, he would hold on to them.

He made his way quietly through the front yard, and it was only moments before Mona's great moon of a head appeared in the dimly lit living room window. He knew she could see him, and he knew she could feel him seeing her. He wished he could let her out, but Gina didn't want her out after dark, and Gina would be home from work soon anyway. So he just stood still for a moment, sending Mona the only thought he had. *Help me*, he said in his mind, and then he crept around back, into the wild overgrown yard, which tonight felt safer than anyplace he could imagine. *Please, Mona. Help me not to fall.*

Twigs and dead leaves crackled under his feet as he sought out the yard's darkest corner, where a huge doghouse disappeared under a drooping long-armed tree. He shimmied in, back end first, and then rolled onto his side, curling up so just the top of his head stuck out onto the grass. And there he lay, smelling Mona's beautiful stink all around him, fighting off sleep but finally letting it take him, knowing that inside the house from some window, somewhere, Mona would watch him into the night.

As he slept, he stumbled upon a dream, and in the dream he was seated around the kitchen table with his father, Johnnyprice, Y, and a few other men from the neighborhood who used to show up for Johnnyprice's parties back when the money was good. The radio was playing, and the mood in the room was light and easy. Clarence found that there was a bottle of beer in his hand, and that he was drinking from it. One of the neighborhood men pulled a deck of cards from his shirt pocket and began to deal.

As Clarence picked up his cards from the table, he realized he didn't know how to play the game, and a wave of panic broke through his body. He drank heavily from his beer like the other men but found it didn't help. In front of him, he held seven cards but didn't know what to do with them. He stared down at them and inwardly asked them for clues. Nothing happened. He stared at them some more. He drank from his beer. He bided his time, tried to look indifferent. He made his mouth into a straight line, realizing his heart had a mind to escape from his chest.

Across the table, Johnnyprice and Y exchanged glances and sucked at their teeth in unison. His father sat at the head of the table, watching him, looking ashamed. "Well, go ahead and bid, man," one of the neighborhood men said. "Let's get this game rolling."

Clarence could feel himself fading, growing dizzy, unable to find a way to do what the man had asked him to. "I thought you said you had a player here," the neighborhood man said to Clarence's father. "I thought you said you had a man who could bring something to the table."

"I thought I did too," his father muttered, shaking his head like he always did when Clarence was around. Across from him, Johnnyprice leaned over and put his arm around Y's shoulders, whispering something in his ear. Then they both laughed, and Clarence noticed that Johnnyprice had wet, painted-on hair, just like Y. They kept laughing, almost choking on their laughter, and Clarence felt himself growing hotter and dizzier, felt the room growing larger than he knew it really was. Then suddenly, behind him, he heard the kitchen door slam and the quick click of heels glide across the floor toward the table. It was a familiar sound, though he couldn't quite place it. And then he smelled her.

"Just what do you think you're doing with my child at a poker table, feeding him beer, no less? In the middle of the night. My child belongs in bed." And then he felt her small soft hands on the back of his neck, making little circles against his skin with her fingers. "These men," she said to her son, and he knew her eyes were accusing each of them individually. "May you never be like these men." With these words, she gently lifted him from his chair as if he was much smaller than he really was, as if he was a tiny thing, maybe just a baby, and she carried him down the hallway to his room, shutting the door against the noise in the kitchen.

"My Clarence," she said as she laid him in bed and sat down beside him, looking into his eyes and smiling. She looked at him for a long while, and then she leaned in and kissed him on the tip of his nose. She smelled like baby powder and freshly washed clothes. Just like she always did.

"I miss you, Mama," he said, and she gently laid her hands across his eyes and started to hum.

"Sleep, child," she said, then continued humming. Clarence could feel his body letting go, easing into rest.

"But I'm not a child now, Mama. I'm finally a man," he mumbled, and suddenly she pulled him up into her arms so they were face-to-face, almost nose to nose. Her hot-chocolate eyes pleaded.

"It isn't time to be a man," she whispered. "Not like this. Not like them. Can't you please be a boy for just a little bit longer?" Clarence laid his head on her shoulder and tried to memorize her face.

"Okay, Mama. I will," he said, and he waited until she smiled. He watched carefully, recording every part of that smile, the way her lips parted just a bit at first, how her eyes squinted like she was looking into the sun.

"You promise?" she asked, and he knew he would say anything to keep her smiling.

"I promise," he whispered. It didn't matter if the answer was true. It might be true, or it might not be. He didn't know yet, and right now the truth didn't matter.

What mattered now was that his mama was happy.

— — —

He awoke to a damp, colorless dawn. He raised his head, looked out at the yard, and wondered what he was supposed to do now. This day was not like the other summer days that slid into each other in a dull, familiar blur. This day stood out all on its own, different from any others. It called for a kind of attention he didn't know how to give. He had to go home eventually, he knew that. But what then?

He dragged himself from the doghouse and onto the wet grass. Gina might be waking up soon, and he needed to be well on his way before she left for work. As he passed the back door, he heard a thud, and suddenly Mona was up on her hind legs, looking out at him through the door's small glass window. "Hey, girl," he said, and for a moment he forgot about the day before and the day to come, completely lost in her sweetness. He walked over to the door and put his hand against the glass of the window. Mona ran her cold-cut tongue over the glass, and Clarence put his face up against hers so the two of them were nearly eye to eye. "Big dumb dog," he said as she licked at the glass in front of his face, but what he was thinking was that his heart felt big in his chest, that for this moment, he felt light.

As he left the yard, he carefully clicked the gate lock shut, checked his pocket for his key, and waved at Mona, whose head was a pale blur in the living room window. He walked to the curb and looked down the street to the right, but the Kwik-Bi wouldn't be open for almost an hour yet. For a few moments he just stood there, still and empty, until he felt himself turning to the left, toward home, dragging feet against pavement, the sky still slate above him but lightening at the rooftops. An early morning mist coated his skin as he hoped he'd never reach the box-of-gray, even as he moved closer to it. From a block away, he could see that all the lights were on, including the porch light. His dad never left the porch light on, and he'd counted on a dark house, his father passed out in front of the TV, snoring. His dad wouldn't touch him, now that Y was involved; this much he knew. Still, he'd hoped for more time to figure out what the two of them were to each other now, if they were anything. Maybe they'd always been nothing since his mama'd died.

As he neared the house, he wondered if he should work

his mouth into the hard straight line he'd hidden behind more than once just yesterday. But he was barely awake, the dream of his mother was too fresh, and though his face was damp from the mist, he knew it was also wet from tears he hadn't expected but that fell anyway of their own accord. Once again he smelled her baby-powder skin, felt her soft hands against his eyes, heard her speaking his name as he stood there in front of this house that used to be hers, that seemed to suffer her absence like the people who lived there.

He was still standing in the street when his father walked out and looked up at the sky. He took the steps slowly and then stopped in the yard, head tilted, watching the murky morning brighten, not knowing he was being watched. Clarence had never really looked at his dad from a distance, or at least not that he could remember. He'd pretty much stopped looking at his dad a few months after his mama died, when he realized life was easier when he disappeared into corners, drifting silently through the house as if made of breath.

Standing there in the ashy dawn, his father looked much smaller than Clarence remembered him. His clothes fell loosely on his body like grown-up clothes on the body of a child. Clarence said nothing but just stood and watched. He was waiting for a feeling to arrive to guide him, but nothing came. The life beneath his skin just wasn't responding today. It was like it was sleeping. Or maybe dead.

By and by the sky grew dirty white with light, and his father caught sight of Clarence and turned to face the street. He made no other movement other than to raise his cigarette to his lips. Clarence stood exactly where he was until a passing car forced him forward to the curb, where he stopped again and stood once more. "You're probably hungry," his father finally said, letting his cigarette fall to the street, and though Clarence had no appetite at all, he answered with a "Yeah." His father shoved his free hand into his right pants pocket and rifled around for a moment.

"Here," he said, pulling out a few crumpled bills. "Go down to the Kwik-Bi and get us some biscuits. It should be open by now." His father held out the bills, and Clarence walked over to take them. He didn't know why he was obeying. He didn't know why he didn't just walk away. He kept his eyes on his father's outstretched hand, away from his face, and he kept looking at that hand, long after he'd slid the money into his own pocket. In the end his father seemed satisfied. He made a low sound in his throat, turned away, climbed the porch stairs, and entered the house.

— — —

Clarence walked toward the Kwik-Bi, his body full of dread. He really wanted to see Mr. K, but he was afraid of Mr. K seeing him. Still, his father wanted biscuits, and he knew the biscuits were more of a message than a meal, his dad's way of saying something he couldn't say with words. After last night's face-off in the kitchen, Clarence just didn't have the heart to say no to the sad skinny man who'd waited up for his son. He could *work* for Y, yes, but he didn't have to *be* like Y. He needed to take small careful steps on the wire, minding his balance.

Before long he ended up at the store's front door but found it locked. For the first time ever he'd managed to show up before Mr. K opened the store. He sighed, then smiled. He couldn't help but be grateful. He needed Mr. K, but Y's stink was still on his conscience, and he knew Mr. K would smell it.

Just then, though, right when he thought he was in the clear, Mr. Khabir passed by the glass door, a mop in his hand. Clarence froze. He held his breath. Mr. K turned toward the door, smiled wide, and pulled his keys out of his pocket. "Why are you up so early, Clarence?" he asked as he opened the door and offered a tobacco-stained grin. "On a Saturday morning, no less. This I have never seen!" Clarence shrugged and headed past him into the bleach-and-bacon smell of the store. He kept his eyes on the linoleum floor.

"My dad wanted me to get a couple of those biscuits you make for breakfast. If they're ready and everything." He walked over to the counter and leaned forward on it, putting his weight into his elbows, hoping that if he kept his eyes on the television, Mr. K would forget to make eye contact. "I can wait if you need me to. I've got nowhere to be."

He could feel Mr. K standing behind him, there by the door, weighing and assessing. Clarence knew that Mr. K's left hand would be on his hip and that his eyebrows would be arcing into the light, then falling back into the shadow of his huge tinted lenses. *Please, Mr. K*, he thought, closing his eyes as tight as his fists on the counter. *Please just let me be. Give me some time.*

Behind him, Mr. K's loafers went *click-click-click*, then stopped. "Well, the bacon is in the pan in the back as we speak, so if you don't mind waiting, you will have your sandwiches sooner than later this morning." He walked from the door back to his mop and resumed his work, whistling along with the oldies on the radio. "And you can sit on my stool if you like, while you are waiting!" he hollered from over by the newspaper stand. "You will hurt your back leaning forward in such a way. Choose any channel on the television—it is no matter to me."

Clarence thought better of it but slid in behind the counter anyway. There was more to look at back there, more places to cast his eyes when Mr. K returned and wanted to make conversation. If he could make it out of the store without Mr. K's eyes meeting his, he would be all right, at least for the moment. Soon he would find a way to switch faces when he needed to, to pull his mama's Clarence forward, hiding the Y-boy behind the good boy. But that was a job for another time. Right now he would sit on Mr. K's personal stool and keep his eyes busy.

Once seated, he realized it was an unusually high stool, much higher than it looked from the other side of the counter. Mr. K often said that from it, he could see everything that went on, even in the farthest corners of the store. As Clarence sat, he tried to see what Mr. K saw, but the back ends of most of the aisles were out of sight, and he wondered how Mr. K's vision was different from his own. No one got away with stealing while Mr. K was at the Kwik-Bi counter. When it came to his store, Mr. K had superpowers, and everyone in Mayfair Heights knew it.

A few minutes passed. Mr. K finished mopping, and then suddenly he was gone. Clarence could hear water running in the kitchen at the back of the store, and his eyes started to wander, bored of the squawky weather lady on the black-and-white. On top of a filing cabinet, in an orange ceramic bowl, sat a collection of pennies and random loose stamps. Next to them, on the right, a piece of paper was taped to the cabinet, reading, *Banned from Store,* followed by a list of names and descriptions. He'd seen some of the dudes on the list at the dogfight, and a couple of them had been at parties in the box-of-gray, back when Johnnyprice was in the money and living large.

Next he opened the deep lower drawer, just because it was there. He wasn't thinking he shouldn't; he wasn't thinking at all. The drawer was there, and he had hands. At the top of the drawer, a framed photograph sat on top of the phone book, and in it, a woman smiled brightly. Her dark shining hair was pulled back from her forehead, and her lips were the color of caramel candy. Two girls sat next to her: one on either side.

Clarence picked up the frame and ran his fingers across the glass, noticing how happy each of them looked—eye happy too, not just mouth happy. The real thing. He could hear Mr. K whistling back in the kitchen, and Clarence could see that this woman and these girls gave him a reason to whistle. He'd never seen Mr. K's family in person, and he wondered if they still lived back in the country that Mr. K came from, wherever it was. He wondered when they'd be joining him in Mayfair Heights, and if Mr. K missed them, like Clarence missed his mama.

Farther down in the drawer were stacks of paperwork, and an old calendar with a kitten on the front. Digging deeper, he found a smashed box of Oreos, and behind that box, a gun. It wasn't like he hadn't seen a gun before. It wasn't like his dad hadn't shown him how to use one, more than once, but his dad and Mr. K weren't the same sort of men. He stared at the gun and then looked back at the banned list taped to the filing cabinet. Then he shut the drawer, turned back to the television, and waited for Mr. K to show up with breakfast.

Before long he heard the *click-click-click* of Mr. K's loafers moving up the center aisle from the kitchen. When he rounded the corner, he was carrying a tray. On that tray were the two foil-wrapped biscuits Clarence had ordered, but next to the biscuits were the lady-cups from a few nights before. Clarence hadn't planned for this. What he'd planned on was a paper bag, a quick money swap, and a straight line out of the store's front door. Instead there was tea. Mr. K had made him tea.

Mr. K laid the tray down on the counter, picked up one of the lady-cups, and gently blew into it. "The other one is for you," he mentioned between exhalations. "The one with the circle of roses, just like before." Clarence knew his dad was waiting for him, and he also knew that if he drank tea with Mr. K, their eyes might meet and Mr. K might See. Him. Clearly. But Mr. Khabir was the only truly good man Clarence knew, except for a couple of his teachers at Stonewall Jackson Middle. Mr. K walked straight and true like the circus man on the wire, though he didn't have to. He wasn't on a wire, but walking like he might be was just his way.

Clarence glanced down at the lady-cup, checked out the store to make sure no one was around to see him take a sip, and then wrapped his whole hand around the side of the cup and lifted it. Mr. K's eyebrows quivered. "No, no . . . you must grasp the handle like this, sir, the way you did before." His long neat-nailed fingers looped around and through the handle with ease, and Clarence copied him, like he had the other night, though today he felt nervous about it. Mr. K had raised the blinds on the front door and left it unlocked, and if Y walked in right now, well . . . he didn't want to think about it. He drank quickly from the cup, then returned it to the tray, keeping his eyes on the circle of roses. "Thank you," he said. "For the tea, I mean."

Mr. K lowered his own cup onto its saucer. He paused. "It is my pleasure, Clarence. But now I must ask you for a favor. You see, there are some things I need a bit of help with here at the store. Small things. Just a little something here and a little something there." Here came another pause. Clarence knew Mr. K was waiting for Clarence to look at him, to give him his eyes, but that wasn't happening today. Clarence would listen, but today his eyes were his own. "A little mopping, a little putting of the items on the shelves—this is all I require. Might you help me then, or you will consider it, at least?" Clarence wrapped his fingers and thumb around the lady-cup handle. He lifted the cup. He didn't drink.

"Well, my dad . . ." flew out of his mouth, but he quickly remembered that his dad and Johnnyprice didn't own him anymore.

Mr. K nodded. "You know that I know your father, as well as his friend, the one who uses the two names as the one name. And I knew your mother as well, you know." Clarence's mind went fuzzy. Something caught in his throat, like a sticky piece of candy. "You are having your mother's eyes, you know." Clarence didn't look up, but he nodded, because it was true about his eyes. For months after her murder he couldn't look in the mirror for more than a second at a time.

"I'll help you," he said to Mr. K. There was nothing else *to* say. And though he was still staring down at his cup, he could make out the shape of Mr. K adjusting his glasses—up down, up down—on the meaty bridge of his nose, just considering it all, Mr. K style. "You must understand that I cannot pay you," he finally admitted. "You are still too young for the working and the paying; it is against the laws, you know. This would simply be a visit, with you stopping in here and stopping in there, just like that, you see. You would be putting a few things on the shelves, and then you would be taking a few things home, just for you. For no one else. It would be like that, Clarence. A visit between friends."

"Sounds good," Clarence replied, without even stopping to think about it. He knew an opportunity when he saw one. Like Bruce Wayne, he needed to learn to walk between worlds, between what regular people called right and wrong. In one part of his life, he couldn't afford to do the right thing, at least not for a while. In another part, he could, and so he had to. It's what his mama would have wanted. Mr. K could be his Alfred, his teacher. Maybe even his friend.

— — —

He entered by the side door of his house and stood there for a moment in the kitchen, listening for the TV sounds in the living room, where his father would be sprawled on the couch, flipping channels. This morning, the kitchen felt real and imaginary at the same time, taking him back to his dream in the doghouse. He closed his eyes and tried to get back to his mama's baby-powder smell, but all he smelled now were the egg sandwiches in his hand and the three full ashtrays over on the kitchen table. With his eyes closed, he tried hard to remember what it felt like to be carried from the card game down the hallway to his bed, but in awake life, his body was a gawky, awkward mess, and he couldn't get back to the dream sense of being tiny and light in his mother's arms.

In the living room, his father was already laid out, just the way Clarence knew he'd be. Legs propped up on the coffee table, spread. Ass sunk into the pillows that used to live on his father's bed, back when he used to sleep in his bedroom.

Cigarette sucked down to a long trembling ash in his right hand. Empty coffee cup, now ashtray, trembling in the palm of his left. "I got breakfast," Clarence said, and he walked over and placed one of the biscuits on the coffee table.

"Good enough," his father mumbled, gazing down at the sandwich and nodding. This sudden motion caused the cigarette ash to drop into his lap, where he stared at it for too long and with too much focus, like he was deciding on its punishment, or what—or whom—might be punished in its place.

Clarence took a few steps back, in the direction of the window. Then he stopped and watched as his father's eyes became angry, then blank, then sad, then scared, then blank once more, holding back everything. Clarence looked away— as was his habit—up at the smoke-yellowed wall above his father's head. A piece of their past was being projected there as a memory movie, and he watched a little version of himself sitting at the kitchen table with a much younger dad than the one he had now. A song about a love train played on the radio, and before he knew what was happening, he was up in the air, suddenly in his mama's arms, being danced around the table in circles. Looking over her shoulder, he could see his dad following along behind them, making goofy, fish-mouthed faces as he danced. The freckle dust on his nose made him look even younger than he was, almost like a kid.

"Thanks for the sandwich," his current dad said now, and then he dropped the cigarette butt into the coffee cup and looked up, straight at Clarence. "Why don't you sit down for a while now. Go ahead. Sit on down."

Clarence chose the chair that had long ago made its way from the kitchen to its current home in front of the living room window. Sometimes, when Johnnyprice was out conducting business, his dad sat in that chair for hours, just staring at the street. Clarence took his time, unwrapping his biscuit, hoping his father wouldn't ask him to come closer, that he wouldn't look him in the eye again like that, when he hadn't seen it coming. Fortunately his dad seemed busy with his own sandwich and with the news story on the TV. It was a story about dogfighting, people claiming that their dogs had disappeared from their yards, then policemen warning the public, saying that dogfighters often grabbed unattended dogs for bait.

"What do they mean by bait?" Clarence asked, and then realized he didn't need an answer. Mona. Gina's yard. The lock on the gate. He got it now. No one needed to tell him.

His dad slowly shook his head. "You know, I never wanted to have this conversation with you. Doesn't feel right. None of this feels right." Time passed while pretty-people commercials danced by on the TV. Clarence gnawed at his biscuit but found it hard to swallow.

"Drugs. Dogs. Your mom would have put me out on the street." His dad watched the screen. Clarence watched the screen. "But Johnnyprice and me, we aren't bad men. You know that, don't you?" Clarence nodded and chewed, like he was off somewhere deep in thought, but he wasn't thinking. His dad had asked a question, and Clarence thought he had an answer. The words would come, or they wouldn't.

"You sure about that?" he finally said. He knew he was smaller and faster than his father, and if his dad got mad, Clarence would be out the front door before his father's ass even left the couch. "I mean, I was eleven years old, delivering so-called medicine to sick people. I was a good kid. I thought I was doing something good. Then, when I realized what I was really doing, I told myself it was still okay, I mean, it had to be okay, right? If your dad wants you to do it, it's got to be okay, and I really had no choice one way or another, anyway. Right, Pops?"

His dad's upper lip twitched just the tiniest bit. The rest of his face sat stiff and still as a mask. A heavy silence filled the room, in spite of the chattering television. "We needed the money, is all. We were broke, and we needed the money." His dad's voice had faded down to almost nothing. Clarence had barely heard him over the TV.

"Well, why didn't *you* run the crack for Johnnyprice? You stopped working, and you had all the time in the world on your hands. You barely even left the house. So why'd you let him send me out instead? Why couldn't you be a man and make your own damn money?"

His father just sat there and sat there and sat there, like someone trapped in a wheelchair after an accident. "I couldn't," he finally said. "I couldn't do anything after she died. I still can't do one fucking thing for myself, much less take care of my own son." Clarence watched his father look away, toward the window. He'd spoken the truth, and Clarence knew it, but the knowing brought no peace. "Please don't leave like that again," his father added in a low, flat voice. "You had me worried."

Don't make me, Clarence thought, but he didn't have the heart to say it. There would be no pleasure in it, and no point.

IN

••

THE STREET THAT LED to the park looked the same as it always did on weekends, but as Clarence walked it, he knew he was different. Today he walked along as a calm observer of the house with the red towels for curtains, no longer worried about whether some housebound freak might be peering out from the shadows inside. The trampy porchhanging girls seemed to be talking trash from a great distance as he passed, and for a moment he had a good mind to walk right over and talk some trash back. He didn't care enough to make the effort, though, so he just kept walking while their voices trailed off, like the buzz of little bees.

When he got to the park, he didn't slow down to think, and he didn't cut his usual path down the side of the hill, away from the bathrooms. He walked right across the basketball court, knocked three times on the men's bathroom door, and then ambled over to the picnic shelter to wait. In his own sweet time, Y foot-dragged out of the bathroom, tugging at the back of his jeans. Clarence studied him as he walked over to the picnic table, and he found there was nothing worth noting. Y looked like every other low-life gangsta in Mayfair Heights, except that his pencil-thin mustache made him look silly and weak.

"'Sup, Itty?" Y shrugged and grinned. "You been thinking about our conversation?"

Clarence shrugged back. "Yeah. I've been thinking about it, and I'm officially done with Johnnyprice. If I'm going to be running, I may as well make some money." A group of Y-boys were clustered over on the basketball court, kicking at asphalt and tugging their own jeans. Oily waves of heat shimmied off the blacktop around them.

"So you've made up your mind? We got a deal?"

Clarence shrugged again. "Got to take care of myself. Those two don't do shit for me. They've been using me for years. So, yeah. We've got a deal." He sat down on the picnic table's bench and leaned way back, letting his elbows rest behind him on the tabletop. He knew he probably looked like he was trying too hard to seem relaxed, but he wasn't. Oddly enough, he wasn't trying at all, but it wasn't because he actually felt relaxed. Relaxed was a feeling. He felt absolutely nothing until—in a strange, sudden flash—he remembered having tea with Mr. K that morning, and for a moment he felt dizzy. Lady-cups. Crack. Teetering between.

Walk the wire, he told himself, tilting his head back and

meeting Y's eyes. *Walk between, and don't look down.*

When he went home, it was briefly, with seven ten-dollar bills plus a five in his pocket. His father and Johnnyprice were perched on the front porch, drinking and smoking like they always were, before they took the party into the kitchen. Clarence walked toward them and nodded, keeping his eyes on the door. "'Sup," he said, never slowing down.

"Come on over here," Johnnyprice called, his voice breezy in the style of any Saturday dusk. The rest of the street's sounds were breezy too. Laughter and hollering rose from porches and backyards, subwoofers growled, car stereos howled, whole families were spread out on stoops, holding paper plates, sinking into the heart of the weekend. Life was going on all around the porch, but life wasn't the same. Johnnyprice would realize that sooner or later. Or he wouldn't. Clarence didn't really care.

"Come let me have a word with you," Johnnyprice called out again, but Clarence didn't stop, didn't even glance back.

"No," he simply stated. He opened the door. He walked through the living room, down the hallway, and into his room. He wasn't in a hurry, not even when he locked himself in. He was moving at his own pace, not theirs, not anyone's. For a moment, he stood very still in front of his closet, and then he opened its door, pulled out his mama's big-buckled bag and, as always, pulled it up to his face, searching for her baby-powder scent. He found what was left of it, inhaled deeply, then found himself wondering if she knew how he'd changed.

"Forgive me, Mama," he whispered, and then he felt, for a moment, like he might cry or just turn around and leave. Instead he pulled out her driver's license, closing his eyes as he flipped it over in his palm. He let his eyes open up as he slid the license back into its plastic window, picture side down, just staring—for what seemed like a long, long time—at the curlicues of her signature. There, in a back corner of his mind, he could almost see the graceful, gold-ringed fingers that had once held the pen that had written the signature. "Bye, Mama," he whispered as he carefully tucked six of his seven tens into the cash compartment of her wallet. "It won't be for long. I promise."

He left his bedroom and walked back down the hallway, through the kitchen, then passed through the living room to the front door. He knew he could just as easily leave by the back door, but that would send the men on the porch the wrong message. He faced the front door, took a short, quick breath, and then opened it wide, saying nothing to them as he passed. He took his sweet time with the steps, refusing to hurry. When he hit the street, he turned left, heading in his usual direction. The men sat silently behind him, and he imagined their faces as they watched him. For once they seemed to be at a loss for words.

When he got to Mona's house, he saw that Gina's car wasn't on the street, so he used his key and let himself into the yard. Though he'd been alone with his Superdog many times, the first moments always left his heart racing. His routine was to slide into the yard slowly, stop, close his eyes, and then wait for Mona to come to him. He'd stand motionless, listening to her huge feet pounding the ground as she galloped in from the backyard, and then he'd shiver as the cool wetness of her nose danced along his arms and, eventually, his face. When she finally licked him, he'd open his eyes and reach out to touch her great moon of a head, always lingering on the especially soft stretch of fur right between her ears.

This was the way it happened this Saturday evening, just as always. The difference was that moments after Mona bounded around the corner of the house, she was followed by Gina, who wasn't full-on running but who definitely seemed to be in a hurry. Gina was barefoot and wearing low-riding shorts and a tiny white top that showed most of her tan flat belly. Certain other not-so-flat parts of her body popped and jiggled as she moved. A little gold ring dangled from her belly button, and for a moment Clarence couldn't look away from it. Gina sure looked different when she wasn't in her Bar-B-Q Palace uniform, and he wasn't sure he liked the way she looked, all in all. She looked a lot like the porch-hanging girls, and this wasn't the way he wanted to think about the person responsible for Mona's safety.

Gina shifted her weight from one foot to another in a nervous sort of dance. Her lower lip flitted about with a mind of its own, and from time to time she'd pull it into her mouth and chew on it for no reason. This was not the Gina who'd asked him to look out after Mona, the one who'd given him his own keys and who'd sat on the back porch between double shifts, too tired to move. This Gina was like the first one he'd met, the one with the red sneakers that wanted to take flight. She was fast and jittery like the first Gina, just more amped-up and a lot more skanky. "I'm locked out!" she finally yelled at Clarence. "I'm locked out of my house, and I need to get in! Quick!"

"Oh," Clarence said as she continued to dance. He couldn't think of anything else to say, but then he remembered her car. "Well, where's your car? Maybe your keys are in your car."

"Long story, the car. Anyways, I need to get into the house, big-time. Right now. So can you help me? Will you help me, Clarence?" Gina kept her eyes fixed on the street beyond Clarence's shoulder as the words sprinted out of her mouth. "You've got a key, right? Don't you have a key? Don't you?" Suddenly Clarence understood what was happening. Gina was coming down from a crack high. Sometimes, when he made his deliveries, the customer would come to the door, yammering and twitching, and Clarence would just nod and slip away down the hallway.

He used his key to let them into the laundry room, which was where Gina kept Mona's food and water bowls. A big bag of doggie treats was stashed under the sink, and Clarence loved to sit on the laundry room floor, feeding them to Mona one by one. But today wasn't about Mona or treats. Today was not a regular day. Behind him, Gina was busy deadbolting the back door and pulling down the shade. When she turned to him, her eyes were animal wild, and then she started to cry.

"Is he out there?" she whimpered. Her voice was tiny and uncertain now, like the voice of a child. Clarence could hear a car revving its engine out on the street, its subwoofer growling. "It's him. I know it's him, Clarence." Like Gina, Clarence recognized the engine's roar: it was definitely Y. At this point there was nothing to do but follow Gina into the living room, over to the big front window with the purple mini-blinds. Outside, the car still thundered. "I'm too scared to look. I can't. I just can't. Will you look, Clarence? Will you please just take a look for me?" Because she was a woman and because she was crying, Clarence knew he couldn't say no. He lifted up one of the blinds, but just barely so that his right eye was close enough to see out.

It came as no surprise to see Y's car pulled up next to the curb, but Clarence wasn't ready for what he saw next. Y had gotten out of his car and now stood next to the tall fence, his bony wrist thrust right through the chain link. His girl-nailed fingers scratched between Mona's ears, and then he casually looked up and waved with one hand, still rubbing the patch of fur between Mona's ears with his other. Clarence dropped the blind and forced himself to breathe. How had they locked themselves into the house and left Mona outside?

"Is it him? Is it Y?" Gina wiped her nose with the back of her hand. Wet makeup ran down her cheeks. *Of course it's Y,* Clarence thought, and for a moment he wanted to punch her. He knew he had a lot of punching stored up somewhere, and Gina could stand to have some sense knocked into her. Instead he found himself just watching her as she trembled there next to the window, completely lost. Completely alone. There were people who might need to be punched, but Gina wasn't one of them. Not yet.

"I'm going out there," he said flatly, and then he walked right past her to the front door. "And if anything happens to Mona, I'll have your ass myself." He was surprised at how easy it was to speak like a grown-up, at how much those words felt like power. Gina stood there trembling while Clarence flipped on the porch light.

"I'm so sorry," she gurgled into her wet hands. "I don't know what I'm doing anymore, Clarence." Clarence nodded, then opened the door and ambled down the sidewalk, moving casually toward the street. He'd had his share of pathetic adults. The only thing he cared about at the moment was Mona.

Y stood on the other side of the fence and leaned forward, toward the house. One of his hands clenched the chain link as Clarence approached. The other hand waved. Clarence couldn't hear his teeth-sucking over the Lexus's subwoofer, but he could see it going on as Y pulled back his lips and showed his grill. "'Sup, Itty," he said, nodding and rubbing Mona between the ears.

"'Sup," said Clarence. He fixed his mouth into a line, pretending he didn't see Y's hand on Mona's head. The hand on her head was about power, he knew that much, and if he didn't react, Y didn't get what he wanted. He was playing the men's game now, and that game was easier than he'd thought it would be. It was like playing a part in a movie where all the lines had been written for him, a movie he'd already seen a hundred times before.

Y's eyes wandered from Clarence over to the house.

He licked the tip of his long pinky nail and ran it across his sad little mustache. "I've come to pay Gina a little visit. She around?" Y's words sounded innocent enough, but Clarence wasn't buying them. "She left her car keys at my place. She can't get far without her keys, you know."

Clarence simply nodded, keeping his face under control. "I wouldn't know about any of that," he answered. "I just help her out with the dog. You, I work for, so why don't we keep what's between you and Gina between you and Gina." Y looked at Clarence, then glanced beyond him, back at the house. He shook his head. Clarence thought, *Superhero*, and refused to blink.

"Well, damn, if little Itty isn't growing up all the sudden." Y glanced down at Mona and showed his teeth, pretending to smile, and Clarence felt himself go hot. This time, though, he made sure his face didn't show it; he could feel that his face was as dead as a stone. "Next Friday at four then," Y finally said. "You and me in the park. There's someone I want you to meet."

"A'ight," Clarence agreed, and then Y turned and walked his walk back to the Lexus. Clarence stood perfectly still as Y drove away. He didn't move or even breathe until Mona licked at the tips of his fingers, reminding him it was time to move on.

— — —

When he arrived at the edge of the park that Friday, he stopped at the curb to assess the situation. There were no Y-boys out today, no one hanging by the bathrooms or kicking at the asphalt of the basketball court. Down to the left, though, over by the picnic shelter, Y leaned into one of the shelter's support beams, and a supermuscly dude with short spiky braids sat on a picnic table, staring out at nothing. "'Sup?" Y called to Clarence, giving him a nod. "Come on over. We been waiting for you."

Clarence did as asked, and as he walked, he readied himself. He envisioned himself as Bruce Wayne facing Ra's al Ghul, and used his mind to create a force field around his body. He vowed to give up nothing he didn't want to give, reminding himself that he was no one's property, and he'd never be property again. He was a free agent who was ready to get pissed if he needed to, and while he was still figuring out what his version of pissed might look like, he knew that for any dude, it was part real anger and part bluff. He knew he had plenty of the real part, and he could figure the rest out. If the skinny asshole up ahead—who'd never even made it to high school—could bluff, an honor roll student sure as hell could do the same.

Y straightened up as Clarence approached. "Itty. My little man," he said with a frozen grin, walking over and laying a hand on Clarence's shoulder. "Come meet Demario.

He's one of my Big Boys, you know . . . one of my right-hand men." Clarence slid out from under Y's hand and made his way toward the dude with the braids. Y followed; Clarence could hear the slide-shuffle of his walk *shoo-shoo-shoo*ing just behind him.

"Hey," he said when he got to the shelter. "I'm Clarence." He fidgeted for a moment, not sure if he should offer his hand. Demario rose from the picnic table, strolled over, offered his hand first, and Clarence took it, trying not to react to the fact that Demario's long strong fingers all but swallowed his own. He let Demario move his hand around in three quick steps, like the other Y-boys did, and then he pulled it back in close, sliding it deep into the pocket of his jeans.

"Nice to meet you, Clarence." Clarence looked up into Demario's face and nodded. He liked that Demario had called him by his given name, that he hadn't followed Y's lead with Itty. He liked the possibility that like Bruce Wayne, he might finally be turning his suffering into power.

"Nice to meet you too," Clarence mumbled, and then he felt Y's hand on his shoulder again. There was really no getting around it—like Johnnyprice, Y would have to believe he was in control. Clarence just stayed put and took his time with his breath: in and out. In and out. He strengthened his force field while he waited for Y to make the next move.

"So . . ." Y said, and then he paused, walking around Clarence and casting a glance at Demario. Demario glared at him, narrowing his eyes, and Y sucked his teeth, narrowed his own eyes, and glared back. The air between the two of them throbbed like it often did back in the box-of-gray, before the men's inside anger made it out of their mouths. Clarence took a few big steps back. If something was about to go down between them, he didn't plan on getting stuck in the middle of it.

"So I'm going to be your Big Boy," Demario finally chimed in, turning away from Y to head back toward the picnic table. He stopped and glanced back at Clarence. "Come on over and sit with me, right? I don't bite. Much." Clarence walked slowly toward Demario and realized that the *shoo-shoo-shoo* of Y's walk was no longer following him. His stomach quivered as he realized he was walking alone toward an older boy who was almost twice his size.

Demario ambled back over to the picnic table and stopped. "Here you go. Have a seat." He pointed at the tabletop and then sat down on one of the benches. Clarence appreciated the fact that Demario was giving him the highest seat, but he knew there was no reason to trust the gesture. He took his time getting over to where Demario sat and then climbed up onto the bench next to him, gradually taking a seat on the edge of the table.

From where he sat, he had to look down to see into

Demario's eyes, which turned out to be the same exact color as his mama's. He'd never known anyone other than his mama or him with such pale-cocoa eyes, and all bluff in him vanished as he blinked, swallowed, and hoped Demario hadn't seen him fumble. "'Sup," he finally said, faking swagger. "So, what's this Big Boy thing you two were talking about?" Demario laid his massive hands, palms down, on the table. Clarence noticed that either one of them would fit nicely around his own neck.

"Well, Y has two types of boys in his family. We're all like family, you know. I don't know if Y told you that." Demario smiled, just slightly, and Clarence tried to see behind it, into the lie. "And the older ones, well, we look out after the younger ones, the ones Y calls his Little Boys. We show them the ropes, teach them what they need to know about Y's business, and about survival. Y was my Big Boy a long, long time ago, and now I'm going to be yours. You cool with that?"

Clarence had no idea whether he was cool with it, but he knew he'd better *get* cool with it, real quicklike. All that family stuff—well, he knew that was bullshit. He'd been down that road with Johnnyprice, and it didn't surprise him that Johnnyprice and Y read from the same sad script. But Demario's eyes were like his mama's. And Demario was tall, with lots of meat on his bones. A boy called Itty could use a big guy with some meat on his bones, especially as he headed into high school. "How old are you, anyway?" Clarence asked the Big Boy, his palms on the table. "You still in high school?"

Demario nodded. "I'm old enough," he said. "I'll be a senior at Lee High." Clarence nodded himself but didn't know what to say next. He waited for Demario to continue. "Well, Y said you'd be starting at Lee this year, said you might need a little support, you know, a little protection." Clarence didn't like the fact that Y seemed to know everything about him when Clarence had told him nothing, but he knew Y was right. He was tiny for his age. He was vulnerable. He could use all the protection he could get. "But are you sure you want in on this, brah?" Demario lowered his voice and looked back over his shoulder at Y, who stood off at a distance, nodding and smoking. "This isn't for play, not with Y, and not with me. This isn't some chump operation like your Johnnyprice's. You need to be all in, or you need to walk away. Now."

Clarence reminded himself to strengthen his force field. He knew what Demario was saying, and he could feel his answer taking shape. He was where he was. He knew what his options were, and what they weren't. At least right here, at this moment, he'd be making his own decision, for his own future. At least for once, the men in his house had no say in the matter.

"I'm in," he finally said, and he felt the chill of his words as they started to harden in his belly, like a puddle in winter. Demario turned back to Y and nodded. Y smiled.

DOGS AND HEROES

BUSINESS WAS GOOD WITH Y, far better than it had been with Johnnyprice, and true to his word, Y paid much better than Johnnyprice ever had. By the end of the weekend before high school started, Clarence had almost five hundred dollars stashed in his mama's big-buckled purse, including what he'd saved from his years as Johnnyprice's runner. Every night after dinner, he'd retreat to his room, lock the door against Johnnyprice and his dad, sniff around in the handbag for traces of his mama's baby-powder smell, and then pull out his money and count.

He didn't know what he'd ever do with it except buy snacks, sodas, and DVDs from the Kwik-Bi, but spending the money wasn't the point. Every night his father sat at the kitchen table with Johnnyprice, drinking and bitching about money, and every morning his father laid himself up on the sofa, watching the morning shows instead of looking for work. Once in a while, he'd get up early enough to make it to one of the daywork operations back behind the Walmart, but mainly he sat, ate, drank, and whined, and this was the reason Clarence counted his money at night.

He wasn't going to be like his father.

He wasn't going to be the kind of man who pimped out his own son to pay the electric bill.

But Sunday night—the night before his first day of high school—entered his body like a bad case of the flu. He rolled about and fussed in his superhero covers, unable to find sleep, and it wasn't just that it was hot in his room. It was hot in his room from June to October, and his dad had sold the window unit in his bedroom the year after his mama had died. Hot was the way it was for almost half the year in Jackson City, and he was used to it, for the most part.

Tonight, though, bellyaches rode rolling waves of heat that had nothing to do with the temperature in the room. One moment he would suddenly be hot enough to scream, and the next he'd realize he was suddenly shivering. There was nothing to do but hug his pillow tight and hope for the best, because sometimes, when his nerves got the best of him, he would suddenly have to vomit, and he hated to vomit. He especially hated to vomit when other people were around, especially people he knew would judge him, like the two men yammering in the kitchen, down the hallway.

Eventually midnight rolled around, and then 12:30, and then at exactly 1:13 a.m., according to his digital watch, he

could feel himself getting mad, and his anger made him temporarily forget his nerve sickness. He had to be up at seven in
the morning, and the so-called grown-ups in the house were
carrying on like it was a Friday night. It was almost as if they
were making noise on purpose: the sports radio sounded
louder than usual; their voices sounded louder than usual;
and it seemed like nothing had ever been funny until this
particular Sunday night in August.

The more they laughed, the madder he got, and on some
other night, he would have just left through his window and
started walking. But tonight ... tonight was different. He had
a right to some respect after the way they'd used him since
his mama'd died. Tonight he would refuse to escape from
their noise. Tonight they'd see that the house rules were
changing. Before he even knew what was happening, he was
up and out of the bed, stomping his way down the hallway, in
his underwear, straight into the kitchen.

"Can you ever, for a single minute of any night of any
week of any year, just shut the fuck up?" he screamed at
them as he exploded into the room. Almost in unison, the
two men looked up from the table, and he suddenly felt sick
again. There, just a few feet away from him, his dad stood up
from the table and picked up his beer can. He drank from it
slowly. He belched and then licked his lips.

"Go back to your room and lock the door," he said, loud

enough that he could be heard over the radio but not loud enough to be considered yelling. "This never happened. Lucky for you, we're going to pretend like this never happened." Clarence heard the actual words, but he also heard the message that lay beneath his father's words, which was, *Please don't make me hurt you*, and then he remembered his dad waiting up for him, lost in the ashy dawn. He remembered their talk over biscuits and the weight he visibly carried in his thin, meatless bones, so he turned and walked away from the men, back down the hall. His anger was strangely gone, replaced by a fierce longing for all he'd lost. Down the hall, in the kitchen, the radio suddenly went silent, then the men went silent, and he crawled back under his covers and whispered, *Superhero*, until he slept.

—   —   —

By the end of his first day at Robert E. Lee, he knew he'd walked straight into the truth of what he'd suspected all summer long: he just wasn't ready. He simply wasn't tall or built or cool or cocky enough to survive the teenage tornado that was Robert E. Lee High. That morning he'd walked into an entire student body that pitched and whirled as if tossed by the wind. For every average-looking student, there seemed to be ten potential Y-boys or porch-hanging girls, but he soon learned that none of this mattered, at least not yet. He had Demario, and Demario moved through the teenage tornado like a bull in a summer breeze.

When he'd walked up the school's front steps at 7:45 a.m., Demario had been there, waiting. When he'd wandered into the lunch room and felt everyone's eyes burning holes into the tiny boy with his hands in his pockets, Demario had suddenly walked through the double doors and given him a fist bump. "Hungry?" he'd asked, and then he'd walked Clarence through the food line, paid for his lunch, and led him to a table on the edge of the cafeteria. From that table, they'd had a full view of the entire room, and Clarence could feel people watching them but pretending they weren't. Eyes darted, bodies leaned into tables so mouths hidden by hands could whisper in private. Finally a couple of dudes wandered over, very casually, like they'd arrived at Demario's table by accident.

"This your boy?" they'd finally asked, and Demario had nodded, laying his massive hands on the table and giving them a look that sent them walking in the other direction. Like the three dudes walking away, Clarence found himself afraid of that look, and he hoped he'd never give Demario a reason to look that way at him.

He left his first day of school full of a little hope, a little fear, and a lot of questions he didn't dare ask, not even of himself. Demario walked him as far as Barton Street and then stopped and looked left, in the direction of the park. "Not too bad, right?" he asked, crossing his wide, muscled arms over his chest.

Clarence shrugged. "I guess not," he said. While he meant it, he knew there were many, many more days to come.

— — —

The store door jangled as he opened it, and Mr. K looked up from his stool and grinned. "First day of school," Clarence mentioned as he stopped in front of the counter and pretended to look at the *National Enquirer*. "Just stopping by, you know, like we talked about before. You need any help today? I could sweep up or put some things out on the shelves." As Clarence glanced up from the magazine, he could feel Mr. K trying to read him, though he couldn't exactly be sure, on account of his tinted glasses. Clarence went back to pretending to read, and Mr. K just sat there, still and silent until he suddenly hopped up and raised his hands, turning their palms toward the ceiling.

"Well, you have arrived at the perfect time, my friend. There has just been a delivery. The boxes are in the back. . . . Here, I will show you." Clarence followed him down the far right aisle to the combination kitchen/utility room. Two big boxes—one with FOOD CLUB stamped on the side and another that said POWDERED MILK—sat in the storage closet next to the stove. "A box cutter is there on the counter, Clarence, but first, we must take some tea. What a day for you—the first day of the high school! You must share with me its story!"

Clarence walked over and picked up the box cutter. He carefully opened the boxes while Mr. K settled into his tea-making. Once the boxes were open, he rolled the grocery cart from its corner over by the door to the back of the room, parking it next to the closet. As he lifted each box into the cart, his mind searched for a way to tell Mr. K the truth about his day without telling him the things he didn't need to know. "I may as well run these out front while the water boils," Clarence mentioned as he rolled the cart back toward the door. "I'll be done in time for the tea."

As he worked there in the center aisle, the unpacking and shelving became a rhythm that started to soothe him. It felt good, just doing a thing because it needed to be done, turning a can so its label could clearly be seen or finding the neatest, most pleasant way to display the boxes of powdered milk. Here, in the Kwik-Bi, life instantly became simple. Moments came and went, came and went, came and went, and they were just moments, light and clean. Never anything big to gain or lose.

When it came time to tell Mr. K the story of his day, he decided he'd just keep it simple, like their time together. He would tell Mr. K a *true* story but not the *whole* story.

For some reason, Mr. K believed in him as a person, just as himself, and Clarence knew that now, he'd have to tiptoe the wire strung between his Kwik-Bi self and his Y-boy self each time they were together.

On his way back to the kitchen, he passed Mr. K *click-click-click*ing up to the counter with the two cups of tea. Clarence gave him a lip smile: no teeth, no conviction. It felt strange, knowing that at school that day, he'd been a scared freshman and a Y-boy and a secretly good student rolled into one, and that in just a couple of minutes, he would be sipping tea from a lady-cup. Just the idea of holding such different boys inside his body and mind made him tired.

"So, listen," he said as Mr. K sat down at the counter. "I've got to be honest here. If someone walks in that door, I'm hiding this teacup. Period. I mean, I like the tea and everything, but I've got to survive around here, and you know. Well."

Mr. K nodded from his stool behind the counter. "I understand, Clarence. This is my neighborhood too. We all find our ways to survive here." Once again he and Mr. K understood each other, and Clarence climbed up onto the other stool, checked the front door and windows, and then blew gently down into his cup of tea. "So my day at school . . . was . . . interesting." Mr. K nodded. Clarence knew that Mr. K would wait as long as it took. "I mean, not bad, really. I've got this older friend named Demario now, and he was looking out for me today, and I decided my favorite class will probably be English again, my usual. You know I made honor roll all last year at Stonewall Jackson, right? So I think things might be finally getting better for me, Mr. K. I really hope so."

In front of him, Mr. K sipped his tea. Clarence squirmed inside his skin, eager for Mr. K to break the silence. "Things around us, Clarence . . . they sometimes get better, and they sometimes do not. We cannot always control them. We, on the other hand, can *always* get better, and in getting better, the things around us *become* much better, even when nothing has changed at all. So in this way, yes. I agree. This may indeed be a good year for you, sir."

Clarence took his time walking home from the Kwik-Bi, glad he had one more stop before finally entering the box-of-gray. As usual, Mr. K had given him something to think about, and he needed a little time to let it sink in. Up in front of him, on the left, Gina's house came into view, and he felt something skitter across his heart. He was about to see Mona. Magical Mona. He picked up his pace, quickly let himself into the yard, backed up against the privacy fence, and just waited.

His ears sensed Mona long before he saw her, and as he listened to her coming, he closed his eyes and imagined her as a white pony, big enough to ride right out of Mayfair

Heights, into whatever world lay beyond its borders. "Girl!" he shouted when she threw her weight against him, plunking her front paws down onto his shoulders. He backed up and braced himself against the fence and then opened his eyes, looking straight into the baby blues that looked back. "You're the best girl ever, aren't you?" he cooed, letting himself fall to the ground as Mona collapsed on top of him. He rolled over onto his side and rubbed the palm of his hand along the wide bridge of her nose, and then up between her ears, the softest spot of all. In no time her huge mouth fell open in a huge sloppy grin. "I love you, Mona," he said without even thinking about it first, and then he felt scared and quite suddenly, sad. If he loved her, well, knowing what he knew . . . he couldn't bear to think about it.

"Let's get you fed, girl," he said, pushing himself up off the grass. Mona trotted by his side as he walked to the back of the house, and he couldn't help but imagine what it would be like to have her by his side wherever he went. He pictured her walking with him into the box-of-gray, filling each dark corner with sunshine. He pictured her lying there next to his bed, the tips of his fingers grazing her forehead as he drifted off into peaceful sleep. Now, together, they climbed the stairs to Gina's back door, and as he pulled her food off the shelf over the dryer, he couldn't help but close his eyes and make a wish. *May we always be together*, he sent out to whatever powers could make it so.

Like always, Mona ate slowly and carefully, not like other dogs that seemed to suck in their entire meal as if they were simply taking a breath. First she smelled her food, and then she simply licked it for a while, creating a watery gravy with her tongue. When she tired of that, or when all the gravy was gone, she gently took the food into her mouth, in the tiniest of bites, and then chewed. And chewed. And chewed. The whole process took forever, but Clarence never got tired of watching. He watched her now, and while she ate, he talked.

"I'm in high school now, Mona," he said. "Still shooting for straight As. I think I already told you I made honor roll last year at Stonewall Jackson." He listened to himself and recognized the same words he'd just spouted off to Mr. K, and this time he could hear the way they sounded like a TV ad for himself—shiny and phony—even if they were true. He wanted to tell her that he also had a real job, and that he was making good money so he could take care of himself, but that would mean telling her that he was still running crack, and if he told her that, he'd have to tell her he was working for Y.

Y. She knew Y. He wondered if she knew Y had a dog named Black who'd killed another dog named Nasty, and then he forced himself to stop wondering, as the same old nervous heat began to sizzle beneath his skin. "I've got to go, girl," he finally said, and before he'd even said good-bye, he was through the back door and locking it after himself. He kept his head down as he walked back along the side of the house to the front gate. He kept it down as he clicked the gate's lock back into place, and he only lifted his head when he heard someone call his name. Except for his teachers, only two living people called him by his given name anymore: Mr. K, and now Demario.

And yes, there it was—the sound of Y's Lexus revving up behind him. Clarence turned and faced the street. "'Sup, Clarence?" Demario shouted, hanging his head out of Y's passenger window. "You want a ride?" Behind Demario, inside the car, Y's face sloped into shadow. The top half was still bright with day, while the bottom half disappeared into darkness.

"Itty!" Y's voice called from the driver's side of the car. "How's Mona doing, my man?" Suddenly Clarence felt too many things at once, and he pulled himself deep inside his body, praying that all the feelings would pass. He looked at Y and felt rage. He looked at Demario and didn't know what to feel. He thought about Mona and felt fear. And he was headed toward the box-of-gray, where he had to make himself feel nothing. "Now, you've met Miss Mona, haven't you, D?" Y asked Demario now, from the shadows. "I bet she and your girl would just be the best of friends, don't you think?"

Demario didn't turn to look at Y, but his face took on the same expression it had with those three dudes in the Lee High cafeteria. Demario kept his eyes on Clarence, and Clarence watched those eyes become as hard and dead as Y's eyes, as hard and dead as Clarence's own mama's eyes as she lay crumpled on the kitchen floor. He couldn't tell if the expression was meant for Y or for him or for the both of them, and he didn't want to find out.

"Nah—I'm good on the ride," he muttered as he passed the car and faked a smile. Demario nodded, Y revved the engine, and Clarence slid his hands into his pockets and walked on.

BOOK 2
AUTUMN

INITIATIONS

· ·

THE BEST PART OF Clarence's school day quickly became Ms. Angelique Moffett's English class. He liked the way Clarence Feather sounded coming from her mouth, like it was an important name that deserved attention. Every day, he walked into her class and knew she saw the best Clarence he could be. He was almost positive that she looked straight at him when she talked to the class, and while this had made him nervous at first, he'd learned to keep his eyes on hers. He wanted her to know that he really saw her, too, in all her black-coffee darkness plus those funky green-framed glasses that made her look like a cartoon character. He wanted her to know that the space between her front teeth made her unique, and that her square fingernails—always painted bright orange to match her lipstick—added a snappy edge to her "nice teacher" image.

In just a few weeks' time, he'd realized he felt happy when she was happy, and he waited for the moments when something would please her, when she would clap her hands and rise up onto her toes, balancing there like a sparrow on a street sign. Unlike her students, Ms. Moffett didn't have to play it cool—she *was* cool because she most definitely was *not* cool. But while Ms. Moffett was the sweetest little bird of a woman, she was tough, too, in her own way. If she had to, she could hold her own. He'd watched her do it on the first day at Lee High. On that day, in all his classes, the students had taken it upon themselves to test each and every teacher, trying to find their breaking points. Ms. Moffett's class had been no different; even the good students at Lee were borderline badasses. The boys in the back of the room had huddled together and then shouted out, "Little Miss Muffet!" asking if they could meet her pretty little spider and do a little dance on its head. Ms. Moffett had just smiled and gone about her business. When the class showed up for school the next day, though, she wasn't alone. A man with a bushy black mustache sat on the edge of her desk, next to an aquarium full of gigantic hairy spiders. "This is Mr. Hammershine, from Earth Sciences down the hall," she'd announced. "He's agreed to let us meet his friends. Who wants to hold one?"

At first all the badasses in the class had swarmed around the aquarium, taunting the spiders, but no one ever mustered the guts to actually pick one up except for Ms. Moffett, who soon had them crawling all over her bright-green dress. "I keep them in my handbag, you know," she said, sliding one into her shiny orange purse and winking. After that, the badasses mainly left her alone, and only called her Miss Muffet behind her back.

Every morning, as he dressed himself for school, he thought about Ms. Moffett, and about the small, warm world of her classroom. When he was in that world, he didn't feel like a wirewalker—he just felt like a good kid who made good grades and wanted to do the right thing. He could slide in a few rows from the front, scooch right up against the left wall, and just sink into the open space of his own mind, free to be the boy his mama'd raised, the boy she'd loved.

On Friday, at the end of the first month of school, Ms. Moffett returned the essays the class had written about their first reading together, *Lord of the Flies*. The prompt had been: *Write an essay that compares at least one theme in* Lord of the Flies *to your own observations of life*. Clarence was both excited and a little bit nervous to get his comments back. Eighth grade at Stonewall Jackson had been easy for him, especially English. Mrs. Danielson's class felt more like elementary school than the last year of middle school: he simply did what came naturally to him and was given As, just like that. He'd worked hard on his first paper for Ms. Moffett but knew he really had no sense of what an A might look like in high school. Now, as he watched her return papers to six other students and then walk over to his desk, a wave of heat broke inside of him, traveling all the way out to his fingertips. He briefly looked up at her and then away, up toward the ceiling, sending out a wish. *Let it be an A. Please let it be an A.* He had to get As no matter what, because As proved he was still the good Clarence. Without As, he was just another Y-boy who would grow up to be like his dad or Johnnyprice or even worse, like Y himself. As could help guide him on the wire. Like Mr. K and like Mona, their weight helped to balance the weight of his life as a runner.

"Clarence," Ms. Moffett said now as she stood over him and laid the paper facedown on his desk. He stared at her hand as it lingered there for a moment. He couldn't bring himself to look up at her again, and for the entire period, he didn't touch the paper. Not once. It was only when he was finally home and safely locked in his bedroom that he pulled it out of his backpack and dared to take a look. Instead of a grade at the top, there was a collection of words, and the words said this: *Dear Clarence, I would like very much to talk to you about this essay in person. Please drop by my classroom right after school, when you can.*

Clarence found it hard to sleep that night, in spite of the fact that the men in the kitchen were quieter than usual. Their voices were muffled, and Clarence found himself trying to pick out words and sentences, strangely curious about what they were saying, and why. Maybe they were just keeping their voices down on account of it being a school night, but tonight their voices sounded strange and slithery, like the voices of girls who spoke to each other behind their hands. They made him feel nervous, and alone.

He rolled over to the side of the bed and told himself he was thirsty, that he needed a glass of water, and then he climbed down and slid into the *Dark Knight Rises* pajama bottoms he'd left on the floor next to the bed. The sticky heat of late summer still lingered in the house, but for some reason, Clarence didn't want the men to see him in his underwear, not tonight. He would rather be labeled a Batman-loving sissy than enter the kitchen in nothing but his briefs again. Slowly he walked over to the bedroom door, opened it, and took a deep breath as he walked out into the hallway. Down at the end of the dark corridor, boxed in by the doorframe, the kitchen was washed in a golden glow, and if he walked slowly—and squinted—he could make out the shadow of a woman moving in and out of the square of light.

Sing to me, Mama, he thought, and soon the faintest melody drifted into his ears, and then came the lyric of that old song she loved, that she used to sing to him as she sat on the edge of his bed and gave him pep talks about his size, or about the fact that he was so different from the other boys he knew. *You're the best thing that ever happened to me*, she sang now, and he stopped and backed up against the wall, letting each syllable soothe him, and soon he'd drifted so deep into the song that he jumped when he felt an actual hand on his arm. He opened his eyes, and there stood his dad, right in front of him. "You okay?" his dad asked. Clarence nodded, though he really didn't know what he was at that moment.

"I just needed a glass of water," his voice said, but the rest of him was still lost in his mama's voice.

"You kind of looked like you were dead," his dad muttered, and for a moment Clarence saw a darkness pass across his father's face, something like fear. "But then I realized that someone who's still standing probably isn't dead, and so I touched you. Just to be sure." Clarence nodded, and his dad nodded, and then his father walked away down the hall, toward the bathroom.

"Mama," Clarence whispered, and he squinted and looked back toward the kitchen's glow, but his mama was nowhere to be found. Soon he found himself shuffling down the hallway and into the kitchen, wandering over to the sink, and then mindlessly pouring himself a glass of water. He stood there, just drinking it. He didn't turn around. He wasn't even sure why he was there. He just went on drinking until the glass was empty, and then he stayed there for a moment, waiting for something to happen. He'd come down the hall for more than water, but he no longer remembered what had driven him.

When Johnnyprice finally spoke, Clarence jumped, just a little. He'd forgotten he wasn't alone. "You know, your dad and me . . . we were just trying to help you way back, when you started running. We didn't mean you any harm." Clarence didn't feel much of anything about this statement, one way or another. It was a lie—everything Johnnyprice said was a lie—and Clarence knew that whatever part of himself had once been open to this man had long since grown over and sealed itself shut, a thick tough scar replacing a wound. "G'night," he muttered, and then he felt Johnnyprice's hand on his shoulder, and Johnnyprice's breath in his ear.

"You working for Y, you know that's the ultimate betrayal, boy."

Clarence had to admit that throwing in the whole "boy" thing, the old keep-the-kid-in-his-place tactic, was a crafty move. It had been a while. He waited for a feeling—anger, sadness, something, anything—but nothing came. "Sure, Johnnyprice," he finally said quietly, turning and walking away toward the hallway. "Whatever you say."

— — —

The door closed behind him with a *screech-screech-screech*, then a bang. Ms. Moffett looked up from her desk and smiled. The little gap between her teeth made her look young, almost like a kid, though she was probably old enough to have her own kids. "Come on over," she said quietly. "Pull up that chair. I'm so glad to see you, Clarence." Clarence did what she requested but kept his eyes away from hers as he slid the chair up next to her desk. He fought his nerves and tumbling belly by staring down at his hands—specifically at the tiny crescent moons poking out of the skin at the bottom of his thumbnails.

"So," he heard Ms. Moffett say. "Let's talk about your essay first. Did you bring it with you?" Clarence nodded and slid the essay, facedown, across the desk. "And you can look at me, Clarence. It's all right. This is a wonderful essay. There's absolutely nothing to be nervous about." Clarence let his eyes slowly rise until they met Ms. Moffett's. "I just wanted to pick your brain a bit. . . . This essay says so many interesting things about *Lord of the Flies* and, well, other things. Don't worry. It's definitely an A. But are you willing to talk to me a bit about it?"

Clarence nodded and felt his stomach start to settle. "So you liked it?" He couldn't help but ask this question. For some reason, he desperately wanted this woman's approval. The only opinion that mattered more to him was Mr. K's.

"Lord, yes!" Ms. Moffett's gapped teeth slipped into view again. "It really got me thinking. So let's start with the title:

Is Good Really Good? I think I can see how you came up with that, but I'd like to hear your thoughts about it."

Clarence shifted in his chair. He looked out of the window behind Ms. Moffett, into the parking lot. A group of older dudes was gathering around a shiny black car with tinted windows, parked over next to one of the outer curbs. "Well, when I look around me, I don't see anything that's all good. I mean, most of us start out wanting to be good, but then things happen. We're good when it doesn't get too hard, when it doesn't come down to our own survival."

He looked back out at the parking lot. Demario was leaning back against the shiny black car, a cold blank look on his face. "But if you take good people and make things hard enough, you know, well, they might still be good inside, but they might end up acting like they aren't. Like how if you beat a dog too many times, it might eventually bite back. That was the way Bruce Wayne was, you know, when Ra's al Ghul found him. Bruce was pretty much just an angry lost dog, doing what it took to protect himself." Clarence looked away from the parking lot, back down at his hands. "And that was the story in *Lord of the Flies*, too. They came to the island as boys, but it didn't take much to turn them into animals. The boy who stayed good . . . well, he ended up dead."

Ms. Moffett nodded. Clarence looked beyond her green-framed glasses, straight into her eyes, and in them, he saw a glimmer. Some kind of recognition. "I hear you," she said. "I really do." Then she sat there quietly for a moment, barely nodding. It was strange how different kinds of people nodded in different ways, for different reasons. His dad nodded instead of actually talking. Y nodded, all smuglike, to make people think he knew something they didn't. Mr. K and Ms. Moffett nodded because they were listening, because they were trying to understand. One gesture, many messages. "So, in your essay, you said you related to Simon, to being stuck on an island that's going crazy all around you."

"Yep." Clarence glanced back down at the little moons rising in his thumbnails. "But I also said I related to the beast, and to the boys when they wanted to kill it. Same way with Bruce Wayne and Ra's al Ghul. They both were good, and they both weren't. I think it might be that way for most everyone. Like I said in the paper: maybe nobody is just one kind of person. Maybe we can't be."

"And yet you say that we all have a Simon in us, and that part of our job is to keep him from getting killed." Clarence's eyes traveled back to the shiny black car, and he noticed that his mind was with Demario, out in the parking lot, at the very same time it was in the classroom with Ms. Moffett. Suddenly he felt empty and dizzy, full of nothing. He held on to the edge of the desk and looked back into Ms. Moffett's eyes, but he didn't speak. There was nothing more to be said.

He just nodded—slowly, briefly—like his father had taught him when the words wouldn't come. He waited for Ms. Moffett to speak again, but she was already busy with another thought. She was staring down at her orange fingernails, like he'd been doing with his own, just minutes before.

"Clarence," she finally said. "I'm going to ask you to do me two favors, and I want you to understand that you don't have to agree. If anything about either of these requests makes you uncomfortable, you just say no thanks, all right? Do you promise to be honest?"

Clarence nodded again. "Yes. I promise, Ms. Moffett." He said this, all the while knowing that Ms. Moffett would have to ask him to do something really crazy for him to turn her down. He'd only known her for a month, and yet he already felt like he owed her. She'd given him so much, and he couldn't imagine what he might give her in return.

"Well." She paused. She let out a sigh. "I would really, really love for you to read this essay at the school's Fall Fest assembly in October. Our principal is really pushing writing skills this year, and he asked all the teachers to keep an eye out for exemplary student work. Your essay, well . . . it is exemplary, Clarence." She leaned back in her chair and smiled. Clarence studied the little gap between her teeth and felt himself already starting to nod as Ms. Moffett clapped her hands like she did sometimes in class. "Oh, Clarence! This is wonderful!" she exclaimed, and then she paused. There was more.

"I have another favor to ask you as well. Mrs. Danielson over at Stonewall Jackson contacted me about a mentoring program there. The idea is to pair a ninth-grade student here with a seventh- or eighth-grade student there. She brought up your name in particular as a possibility—the program is seeking strong students who have recently left Jackson and know the ropes. What do you think? Might you be interested?" Clarence's first though was of Demario, his own Big Boy "mentor," the one standing out in the parking lot next to a car with tinted windows. Maybe he wouldn't have needed a Y-boy mentor if someone had been around to mentor him a few years back. Maybe a mentor would have realized he was running drugs—not medicine—and steered him in another direction.

"Sure," he said quickly, and he meant it as surely as the words he'd written in that essay. "I'll do it, Ms. Moffett. Tell Mrs. Danielson she can count on me."

— — —

As he left Ms. Moffett's classroom, he heard someone calling his name. He didn't have to turn around to know who it was—it was Demario, with that deep, booming voice Clarence had come to both value and fear. "Clarence!" he called again, and Clarence could hear Demario's feet smacking the floor behind him. "Slow up, brah! We need to talk!" Clarence slowed down, but he didn't look back. The conversation with Ms. Moffett was still so fresh. He didn't know if he could shift gears from good student to drug runner so quickly. He wasn't even sure that he wanted to.

"Where you been?" Demario asked as he fell in next to Clarence. "I was looking for you. Thought maybe you'd left without me."

"I had to talk to one of my teachers before I left," Clarence murmured. "You know how it is." Clarence felt Demario's hand on his shoulder, pushing him over to the left side of the hallway, past the few students who were still making their way out of the building. He was suddenly nervous. This guy was on a mission.

Demario pushed Clarence toward the back of the school, and soon they were alone in the hallway. Demario slowed down. "Where we headed?" Clarence asked as Demario led him to the right, down one of the side halls. "I mean, school's over. Shouldn't we be going the other way?" Demario didn't answer. He took a few more steps, and then he stopped and faced Clarence.

"Look," he said. "Last chance. You sure you want to work for Y, I mean, for good? I mean, what exactly is it worth to you?" Clarence slid his hands into his pockets. This was not good. He was all alone with Demario at the back of the school, and now Demario was asking questions about commitment.

"Well, you know, I just really want to take care of myself. I don't want to run for Johnnyprice anymore. I know that much."

Demario nodded, then looked up at the ceiling. He nodded again.

"You know, I get that, brah. But you know, somebody's always gonna be doing something to you one way or another. Life's not clean. It isn't easy. It all comes down to what you're willing to allow in order to get what you want and need. You want to be your own man, but what's that worth to you? Is it worth a little pain?"

Clarence took a few steps back from Demario. "What do you mean, pain?"

Demario shrugged and looked up at the ceiling again. He sighed. "Well, you've been hurt at some point, right? Physically, emotionally—somewhere along the line you've been hurt." Clarence nodded. He'd been hurt, all right. "But most of the time, you didn't want to be hurt; it just kind of happened. I mean, you didn't choose that pain, did you?" Clarence shook his head, and Demario looked down, straight into his eyes. "The thing is that sometimes, as you get older, you make a decision. You decide to exchange a little pain for profit, meaning, you let yourself suffer temporarily to get something as a result. You willingly pay the price. I guess I'm telling you that working for Y comes with a price. This has been a tryout up until now, whether you knew it or not. Today's the day you pay that price, if you decide to stay."

Demario ushered Clarence over to the little staircase that led down to the boys' locker room. Clarence knew that the locker room was where the so-called athletes of the school hung out, but he knew that other things went on in the locker room too, things that had nothing to do with school or sports. That first week at Lee, he'd quickly realized that the parking lot, the boarded-up concrete building on the other side of the football field, and the boys' locker room were the same kinds of places. Demario stood two steps below him and once again looked him straight in the eye. "So this is where you become part of Y's family, or you don't. It's your choice. If you decide to stay, I can tell you that you'll feel some pain in that locker room, but I can also tell you it won't last long."

Clarence didn't know what to do. Without his own money, he was nothing; he would just go on being owned by his dad and Johnnyprice, even if he was no longer running for them. And the fact remained: since his mama'd died, everything in his life had been bought by crack. Food, clothes, shelter, anything extra—whether the men at home had paid or he'd paid himself, everything had been paid for with drug money. At least with Y, he'd be making a choice. He'd be an employee, not a slave, and he'd have Demario. He didn't think he could make it at Lee High without his Big Boy, and he wasn't ready to quit school. School was the one thing he was good at, really good at.

Clarence finally nodded, and then Demario said, "Well, go ahead and open the door, brah," and Clarence entered a darkness that was blacker and thicker than any he'd ever experienced. He felt himself gasp, like he'd been punched in the gut. Suddenly Demario's hand was no longer on his shoulder. Suddenly he was on his own.

He didn't dare move; he could tell he wasn't alone. He could hear people breathing, then someone clearing his throat, and as his eyes adjusted, he could see the glowing tips of lit cigarettes brightening as they were sucked. "These are your brothers," he heard Demario say, and then a flashlight blinded him. "I'm your Big Boy, but everyone in this room is your brother. You don't need to know who they are yet. You just need to know they exist and that you're almost one of them."

Just like that, Demario grabbed his left hand, and he felt a piercing heat in its palm, like a red-hot nail being driven into its center. Orange cigarette tips quivered in the blackness, but the hand on his wrist didn't move, and the pain didn't stop. "Don't scream," he heard Demario say, and then he felt a strong arm wrap itself around his shoulder. "Just take the pain—it's almost over." Demario pulled Clarence in close, like Johnnyprice used to do back in the day, when his father couldn't, or wouldn't. Clarence said nothing. He just kept on breathing.

"It's just pain," he heard Demario whisper, and Clarence bit his lower lip as hard as he could stand. He found himself counting—one, two, three, four, five—and then on ten, Demario let go of his wrist. Clarence sank into Demario's arms, and Demario let him stay there for a moment, and then he stepped away. Clarence was alone.

The locker room stayed black for what seemed like a long time as little by little, feet shuffled off in different directions and doors opened and closed. Muffled voices lingered in corners and then disappeared, and Clarence knew that the rest of the Y-boys were gradually leaving the locker room. "How's the hand?" Demario asked from somewhere in front of him, and then the locker room lights flickered on, though only a few actually worked. The lamps themselves were just long low-hanging metal boxes. A few dying bulbs sputtered here and there, and Clarence could see that he and Demario were the only ones left. "So go ahead, brah. Take a good look at it. It's just a wound. Wounds heal." Clarence sat down on the bench, letting his eyes fall until they found the raw, bloody center of his outstretched hand. "But this is for real, you know. You're one of us now." Demario leaned up against a locker splattered with red and black paint. He stretched out his arm, showing Clarence the palm of his own left hand. It had the same mark, only healed over, with a shiny pink outer layer.

"So I'm officially a Y-boy?" Clarence had been watching Y's boys walking their shuffle-slide around the neighborhood since before his mama'd died, and while he hated Y, he hated being powerless more. Y was a prick, but he'd built a following, and as his mama used to say when she pushed him to make friends at school: *There is strength in numbers, Clarence. Don't try to go it alone.*

"For better or worse, that's what you are." Demario pulled at one of his braids and his eyes drifted, like Mr. K's eyes did behind his tinted lenses, when he was thinking hard about something. "But you mind your business, brah. Keep your mouth shut and your eyes down. You feel me? My brother's no joke." Demario's eyes found Clarence's again, and Clarence felt himself holding his breath. Demario was Y's brother. He hadn't seen this coming.

Mouth shut. Eyes down. This he knew how to do, and it was all he *could* do, at least for now. He looked down at the mangled center of his hand. It was done. He'd been marked.

He was a Y-boy.

ENTRANCE AND EXIT

THE BOY MS. MOFFETT wanted him to mentor was named Billie Wade, a seventh grader who apparently suffered from two kinds of trouble. "Trouble in school, and trouble in general," Ms. Moffett informed Clarence as they sat together in the Stonewall Jackson lunch room after school. "And I have to be honest with you, Clarence. From what everyone here tells me, he isn't a nice boy." She glanced down at the piece of paper in her hand and shook her head. "Not a nice boy, but maybe a boy with some good in him, down deep. You of all people know the difference between nice and good."

Clarence nodded, keeping his burned hand in his lap, in a painful fist that would hide his injury. He understood, all right. Nice was easy. It was like washing your hair, brushing your teeth, and sliding into a clean set of clothes. It was nothing more than dressing yourself up and looking pretty for the world. Anyone could wear Nice, even his dad and Johnnyprice sometimes. Even Y, if it meant he'd get what he wanted. But Good? Good might be buried underneath all that Nice, though for most people, himself included, Good was a lot harder to come by.

From across the table, Ms. Moffett's orange lips formed a weak smile that looked like it took some effort. "So I'm having him meet us here. Mrs. Danielson will be walking him over; he should be showing up any minute now. Any. Minute. Now." She adjusted her glasses, then adjusted them again, then removed the orange tip of her pinky nail with her teeth.

"Are you nervous, Ms. Moffett?" Clarence asked, though he realized, just after he'd spoken, that it might not be a question a kid should ask his teacher, not even in high school. Ms. Moffett didn't seem bothered, but it did take her a while to answer.

"I am," she finally said. "I'm asking a lot of you here. Are you sure you want to do this, Clarence? Would you honestly tell me if you didn't?" Now he was the one who needed some time to answer. Would he actually say no to her about anything, this Ms. Moffett, who made him feel normal and happy and maybe even Good sometimes? He didn't have an answer to that question, so he offered the truth as he knew it.

"What I know is that I want to do this," he said, and he smiled at her without even thinking about it. "That should be enough, that I want to, right?"

"Clarence." She reached over and laid her tiny hand on

his for a moment. "You are a wonderful boy." Clarence knew that from that moment on, he'd have to keep giving her reasons to believe that. Like Mona and Mr. K, Ms. Moffett saw things in him that he didn't. Clarence wasn't sure if those things were actually there, but he knew Ms. Moffett already helped him, on the daily, to walk safely on the wire that ran between his selves and his worlds. Whether she knew that or not didn't matter. He needed her.

A few minutes passed in silence, and then Ms. Moffett lifted her hand to her lips as over on the far wall, the double doors swung open, creaking on their hinges. Clarence turned and looked into the unblinking blue eyes of a tiny blond boy, his hands shoved deep into his pockets. *He keeps his hands in his pockets, just like me,* Clarence thought. *He's afraid.* He looked Billie up and down, amazed. This boy was even smaller than Clarence had been in seventh grade. It didn't seem possible.

The boy didn't smile. He didn't say hello. When he finally spoke, he said, "What the fuck are you looking at?" and Ms. Moffett reached over and squeezed Clarence's arm, as if to remind him that he could back out if he needed to. But Clarence had seen this boy last year, when Billie'd been in the sixth grade. He'd run into him more than once in the bathroom during recess. What he knew was that boys who snuck off to the bathroom during recess were afraid of something—

he knew because he'd been one of those boys himself.

He turned back to Ms. Moffett and asked her to leave them alone for a bit. "Really," he said. "Just let us hang out."

Ms. Moffett rose slowly from her seat, taking small quiet steps over to where Billie stood with his back against the wall. "I'll be right outside if you need me," she said, glancing back at Clarence. Clarence nodded and then looked over at Billie. "Hey," he said. "I've seen you in the bathroom, I think. Or somewhere around here. I'm Clarence Feather. I used to go here, but now I'm over at Lee High."

The top half of Billie's body pitched forward slightly, like he was about to attack, but his feet stayed still. Rock-heavy still. "Yeah, I guess I've seen you around," he said to Clarence, pulling his body back into a straight line. "But just so you know. I'm only here right now because I have to be. Just so you know. I've done this before." Ms. Moffett glanced over at Clarence and raised her eyebrows in a question. Clarence motioned toward the double doors.

"Go ahead," he said. "We'll be fine." She sighed and then walked out, leaving the two of them alone, facing each other across the long metal table.

"So. Clarence. You going to save me? Is that why you're here?" Billie started laughing quietly, but Clarence could see that his eyes weren't laughing. His eyes were hard and glassy, like a doll's eyes.

"Well, are you looking to be saved?"

Billie didn't seem ready for this question. "No," he finally said, but he'd paused just for a second. Clarence heard the pause, loud and clear, and it meant something. Just after that pause, Billie pulled his hands out of his pockets, then seemed to realize he didn't know what to do with them. He fake-punched the wall, gave it a little kick, then pretended to laugh again, cramming his hands back into his pockets. Clarence just sat there, watching him. There was nothing else to do. Eventually Billie walked over to the lunch room table and just stood there, doing something stupid with his mouth. "What?" he asked. "What are you looking at?"

"Nothing." Clarence sat quietly, wondering when Billie was going to blink. "And by the way. Me neither." He let his hands drop to his lap and made himself still and calm. "I'm not looking to be saved either," he said, hoping that Billie was a liar too.

— — —

Clarence finished his weekend run for Y and quickly made his way back to the box-of-gray. Two older Y-boys had stayed a couple of blocks behind him all the way back from the park, so he decided to hide his weekend's pay in the house before he went to see Mona, just in case. Despite what Demario said about Y's "family," Y's boys didn't seem to see him as a brother. He didn't even know who most of the boys were, but the few he'd actually seen up close wore the hard flat expressions of boxers gearing up for a fight. Johnnyprice and Y had sported the same expressions the day of the dog-fight, and he'd seen the same expression on Demario's face many times. "Mind your business," Demario'd said back in the locker room on initiation day. He wasn't going to lose his money to any of his so-called brothers.

When he walked into the kitchen, Johnnyprice and his father were sitting there, looking guilty, their hands palms down on the table. It was clear that the pile of cash between them had brought on the twitchiness and sudden smiles. "What's up, little man?" Johnnyprice said, all teeth and ly-ing eyes. "Why you home so early tonight? Shouldn't you be off with Y, or that dog of yours?" Clarence's father sat next to Johnnyprice, wide-eyed and silent.

Clarence looked down at the money on the table, and his father stretched and yawned, mumbling something about having to use the toilet, just like he used to do when Clar-ence was running for them. Always leaving when things got real. "So," Johnnyprice said, once the bathroom door closed.

"So . . ." said Clarence. "What you got there?" He looked down at the money on the table and cocked his head toward the pile. "What's going on here, brah?"

Johnnyprice kept his eyes on Clarence's eyes, away from

the money. "Hey, you're not the only one in this house who has money that needs counting, you know. Or had you forgotten that? Did you think you were the only one making money anymore?"

Clarence shook his head. He folded his hands across his chest. "I don't care about you or the money you make anymore." His hands fell, palms first, onto the tabletop. They made a smacking sound, and Johnnyprice jerked, just a bit, in his chair. Clarence liked the way his hands sounded on the table. He liked the way his voice sounded today, and the way his words were making Johnnyprice squirm. If Y had any value beyond money, it was in the effect his unseen presence had on Johnnyprice. Clarence knew that when Johnnyprice looked at him now, he saw Y, and for the first time in his life, Clarence was glad for Y's influence.

"Now, I'm not going to go back to my closet and find anything missing, am I?" he pretended to ask. He knew he was pushing his luck with Johnnyprice, but he needed to see how far he could push, even if it meant he would pay for it later. He'd still been a kid when his mama'd died, and these men had taken the last years of being a kid away from him. But he wasn't a kid anymore. He wanted Johnnyprice to see that, up close and personal.

"Don't move," he said to Johnnyprice. He could hear his dad fiddling around in the bathroom down the hallway, pretending to be busy. Clarence stomped down the hallway, straight into his room. He ran over to the closet and yanked its door open, looking in at his mama's big-buckled purse, tucked way back on the floor, under his few hanging clothes. He picked it up and opened it, unsurprised that it was empty, and then he ran back down the hallway to the kitchen, where his father now stood next to the table, shaking his head. Johnnyprice sat at the far end of the table, his palms face down on the money. He said nothing.

"Give me the money," Clarence said calmly. "It's mine. I earned it. Get up and walk away." Johnnyprice simply shook his head. "I said, *get the fuck up now*, Johnnyprice." Clarence heard his voice getting louder all on its own. It felt exciting. And dangerous. Like walking too quickly on a wire. Johnnyprice just kept shaking his head.

Clarence heard one of the kitchen drawers slam shut behind him, and then he realized his dad was no longer standing at the end of the table. "Walk away," his dad's voice said suddenly from somewhere behind him. He hadn't seen this coming. "Walk away, Johnnyprice. We're done here." Johnnyprice did as he was told, standing up and walking slowly, carefully, down the length of the table. What in the hell was going on? Why was his father ordering Johnnyprice to get up and leave the money, and why was Johnnyprice obeying him?

Clarence turned around as Johnnyprice slowly left the kitchen, slamming the back door behind him. His dad let his right hand slowly drop to his side, let his gun just dangle there like a mistake, and Clarence walked over to the same drawer his father had just opened to get the gun. He pulled out a thin plastic grocery bag and balled it up in his fist. "I'm taking my money now," he spat, and while a tiny part of him thought he should thank his dad for getting rid of Johnnyprice, nothing could change the fact that just minutes before, his dad had been next to Johnnyprice at the table. Clarence remembered that not so long ago, Johnnyprice had stood right behind him in this kitchen, whispering into his ear about betrayal, and he wanted to whisper the same words in his father's ear now. *Ultimate betrayal.* Instead he pulled the bag of money in closer to his chest and headed for the door.

He walked fast, with his whole body, with no thoughts about where he was going or where he'd end up. As he passed Gina's house he slowed down, hoping Mona would run out to greet him, wishing for her giant pink eraser nose pressed up against the fence, making him forget. He slowed to a stop and just stood there for a moment on the sidewalk, but no Mona: only the dark shapes of people showing against Gina's blinds and music streaming from the open windows. He kept on walking.

He was passing Vernetta Wilmer's house when he noticed that one of the cars parked on the street was Y's Lexus. In a split second his mouth filled up with the salty taste that meant he might be sick. He imagined Mona in that house with Y and his boys—with people who watched dogs kill one another for fun—and then he remembered he was now one of those boys. He tried think up something to comfort himself, but nothing came until *You will protect her* drifted in, out of nowhere. He nodded, hugged the money tighter, and walked on.

When he slipped into the Kwik-Bi, Mr. K was ringing up a block-shaped woman in tiny pink curlers. She was laughing, and soon Mr. K was laughing too. Clarence ducked in quickly behind her, hoping Mr. K wouldn't see him, but deep down, he knew better. He knew he was dealing with the eyes of God. It was only a matter of time.

He ran all the way to the back of the store, sliding left into the store's bathroom. As always, it smelled of bleach and stale blunts. Seemed like everything around Mr. K smelled of bleach or funny cigarette smoke. There in front of him, a long curving crack opened like a hand right in the center of the bathroom mirror, and Clarence just stood there, looking at it, noticing how, in its reflection, his head seemed to be resting in its palm. He closed his eyes. He let himself stop a moment, then a moment more, still hugging the grocery bag, its plastic sticking to the sweat on his arms. He hadn't realized he was sweating, but he could see it now as he opened his eyes, gathering there above his upper lip.

"Are you all right in there?" Mr. K called from the other side of the door. "If you are robbing me blind, I will have your hide," he joked. Clarence faked a high girly sounding laugh, but his voice cracked right in the middle of it. "Hey there, now." Mr. K's voice grew quiet. "You come out now, Clarence," he instructed. "You please come out and tell me what it is that is wrong."

Clarence said nothing. He had nothing to say. He was grateful when he heard the bell sound at the front of the store, meaning someone had entered. "You come up front please and talk to me, sir. Are you understanding what it is that I am saying? I will be waiting. You will see that everything will be all right." Clarence closed the toilet lid and sat. He had no intention of talking to Mr. K, not tonight. On any other night, sure, but if he talked to him tonight, what words would he use? And if he had no words, what was the point?

He waited until he heard Mr. K asking a man at the counter a question about cigarettes, and then he quietly opened the bathroom door and crept down the little hallway to the back door of the store. He could feel Mr. K's eyes behind him as he pushed the door open, though he knew there was no way he could be visible. Mr. K's voice followed him as he ran out into the night. "I will be waiting for you, my friend!" he yelled, and then the door closed with a clack, and Clarence stopped and stood in the speckled light of the alley, wondering which way to go.

All around him, Friday night made its noise. At any given moment, he could hear the sound of a car door slamming shut, its stereo a low moaning throb against the asphalt as the driver pulled away. On weekend nights, Mayfair Heights vibrated. Usually the vibration started in the street itself and then crept up into Clarence's body, filling him like the warm buzz of the television, but tonight the vibrations didn't help. There was no way he could carry around a bag of money all night. Not on these streets.

He put his head down and, without thinking, slunk away from the Kwik-Bi, keeping to the alleys, his arms locked tight across the bag of money. He wasn't even thinking that he'd have to pass back by Gina's house. He wasn't thinking at all. He was just doing until he found something else to do, and in the shadows, he finally started to feel comfortable, like he could slow down and take a minute to breathe. And so he did slow down, kicking at an old tennis shoe, then at the broken pieces of a bottle next to it. He nodded at an old drunk dude hunched over something that looked like a paint can. "'Sup?" Clarence said. The drunk dude grunted but kept his head down, and Clarence thought about his father. He wanted to look back one more time, wondering if he could imagine his father on that can, but he didn't have the nerve, so he just turned away and kept on walking. Walking was what he knew how to do.

He heard the music before he was even close to Gina's house, and then he remembered the party. And Y. And Mona. Next he remembered the little shed he'd come across not long ago, way back behind the house, in the thin strip of woods that ran between the alley and Gina's new fence. He'd been scaling the back fence, looking for a ball he'd thrown too hard and high for Mona, when he'd noticed a rusted roof peeking out through the trees. At the time he'd figured that the shed had been there since way back in the day, when that little mess of woods was probably still part of Gina's mom's yard, or maybe even before that. He bet he could find that shed now, and if he did, he'd have a place to pull himself together and make a plan.

When he got close enough to hear Jay-Z rapping, he stopped and peered into the trees over to his right. Heavy vines hung like knotted hair from the branches, and the house's lights were just flickers in the thick dark leaves. It sounded like Gina's house, so he pushed his body forward into the woods, holding tight to the bag of money, trying to keep his balance without using his arms. He took tiny careful steps so as not to trip in the bramble, squinting against branches that scraped his face.

Soon the lights of the house glowed more clearly in front of him, and he let them guide him. He was clearly in the right place. The woods were filling up with the sounds of bass and laughter, and he knew if he kept walking toward those sounds, he'd eventually run into the shed, and he did. His left shoulder slammed into one of its metal walls before he even saw it coming, and he lost his footing, falling headfirst into a web of thin knotted vines.

With one hand, he held on to the bag of money; with the other, he pushed himself up onto his knees. He crawled along slowly, peeling back layers of overgrowth as he traveled, until he finally laid his hand on a metal wall. He knew if he got lucky, he'd be able to feel his way to the door, and if he got really lucky, that door would be unlocked. Soon he found the door and banged his shoulder against it one, two, three times until it finally gave. He stumbled into a dark metal box that smelled like dirt and old wet clothes. The only light came from a small broken window on the wall closest to the alley. He was finally safe. For now.

Beyond that window, distant streetlight drifted in through the little woods, and he could make out the shape of his hands, as well as the white plastic bag he held between them. He stared at the bag, not really seeing it. He was suddenly so tired. He couldn't believe how tired he was. He couldn't believe he was alone in Gina's shed, with a bag of money in his hands, and he couldn't believe that his dad and Johnnyprice had planned to take that money right out from under him. He couldn't believe he was a Y-boy with his own Big Boy, and that his Big Boy actually seemed to care about him, and he couldn't believe he was now Billie's mentor, as if he'd earned the right to be a role model for somebody else. He couldn't believe this and he couldn't believe that, and the list kept scrolling in his mind until he felt himself sinking to the concrete floor and, once there, he realized there was no energy left, not even enough for sitting. He rolled onto his side, pulled the money in tight, and within seconds he was asleep and dreaming.

In this dream it was a Friday, and he was making a run for Y. He had his notebook pressed to his chest and a bag of Andy Capp's in his jacket pocket. A hot breeze beat against his face as he walked, and the sun was white and bright, making everything around him seem like too much of what it already was. The trees were too green, the cars too shiny; the glare on the windows of the apartment buildings blinded him like noon light on snow. He kept his head down and his eyes on the pavement in front of him, but that didn't help. He could feel the light even when he wasn't looking at it. He could feel it in the back of his throat: a blistering, spreading fire.

In the dream, he stood at Fat Terrence's door and formed a fist to knock. Fat Terrence was one of Y's regulars, and as always, before Clarence's knuckles met wood, the door opened and a hand reached out, palm up, waiting. But this outstretched hand wasn't massive and fleshy like Terrence's. This hand was small, thin-fingered, and gold-ringed like the left hand of his mama. "Clarence," she said, and Clarence looked up into her sad sunken eyes. "You came. You're a good boy, Clarence. You came to help me."

His mama reached out to him with both hands, and he could see the blood blooming up through the part of her shirt that lay over her chest. "Mama," he said as best he could, what with the fire in the back of his throat and the heaving of his chest. "I don't know what to do. . . . I don't know what I can do for you, Mama."

"Be a good boy, Clarence," she whimpered, and the blood continued to claim her shirt until there was no longer any shirt left. "Be good for your mama. That's all that any mama needs." Clarence covered his face with his hands and wept. He tried to swallow, but his throat was too hot, too raw, too dry. He fought to form sounds with his voice, and then the words came.

"But I don't know how to, Mama!" He was yelling now,

choking on his words and his tears. "Don't you understand? I'm trying to tell you that I don't know how to be good anymore! It's too hard; it's just too damn hard!"

Clarence had never yelled at his mama, much less cursed at her, and he quickly lowered his face into his hands, ashamed. His mama. His sweet dead mama. All she wanted was a good boy, the boy she used to know.

A long time passed before he looked up from his hands, and when he did, she was gone.

"Whatcha waiting for, boy?" Terrence hissed, waving his empty hand in front of Clarence's face. "Go ahead and give it up." Clarence laid the plastic baggie in Terrence's outstretched hand and fell to his knees, back into the comforting darkness of dreamless sleep.

SOLO

•••

EARLY THE NEXT MORNING, when the color of the
sky and the color of the streets became the same shade of
gray, Clarence snuck into his house while his dad slept off
his Friday night drunk. Part of him was glad his dad hadn't
waited up for him like last time, but another part of him
wished he had. Not because he wanted to see him, but because that was what a dad was supposed to do. A dad was
supposed to wait up for his son, even and especially if he'd
just tried to steal that son's money.

He had to drop that wish quickly, though. Thinking
about his dad would slow him down, and he reminded himself that he was just back for his essentials, nothing more,
nothing less. He didn't have a plan beyond simply collecting
his things and then storing them in the shed behind Gina's,
but he had to start somewhere. His money was safe for the
moment, buried deep in the brush outside of the shed. He
would think about his next move once he'd officially moved
out of the box-of-gray.

He headed over to the sink and pulled a big black trash bag out from the cupboard underneath it, making a list in his head, like he always did when he needed to accomplish something quickly. But he was tired and sad and angry and distracted, and this morning he just couldn't seem to focus. He needed to put his list on paper, some step-by-step instructions, so he tiptoed around what used to be his mama's kitchen, looking for something to write with, and on. The most he could find was a worn-down pencil and a paper towel. As he scribbled out his list, it occurred to him that his dad hadn't bought one single thing on it, and on this morning it seemed important to put that in writing. And so he did.

1. clean clothes and underwear (Mama bought)
2. pillow, sheet, and blanket, just in case (Mama bought)
3. backpack, notebooks, green ink (I bought)
4. portable DVD player (I bought)
5. DVDs (I also bought)
6. digital watch with alarm (I bought because no one never wakes me up for school anymore)
7. Mama´s big-buckled purse (she bought for herself)

He knew this was all he could carry without making a spectacle of himself when he crisscrossed the alleys back to

Gina's shed. He took a minute to revisit his decision: he was fourteen, and he was finally leaving. It seemed only right to lock this moment into his mind, and he felt himself stalling, not ready to take the next step. As he looked around the room, he tried to remember the time before this time, when the kitchen had been a happy place full of good smells and his mama's humming, and he could almost see it like it was happening right there, and then it *was*: right up there on the wall next to the pantry.

In his memory movie, his dad sat, his feet up on the table, listening to sports radio, jiggling the beer in his hand. His mama stood over by the stove, flipping something in a pan. He himself was in a chair not far from his dad's, working on some kind of homework. He couldn't tell what subject it was, but he had his face down close to the paper and was chewing his upper lip like he did sometimes, when he was having trouble finding an answer. "He gets his brains from you, you know?" his dad mentioned, and his mama turned around from the stove and smiled.

"No doubt about it," she said, winking, and then his dad turned and winked at him, and he winked back. It wasn't a very good wink—he must have still been learning. From his spot next to the kitchen table, he watched himself up on the wall, winking again and again until the picture faded and the wall became just a wall again. This is what they'd come to, all of them. This is what they were now.

Thinking about his mama's purse—and the trash bag—made him think about trash in general, and he remembered the way his dad had trash-talked Miss Vernetta Wilmer on that morning after the fight, calling her a nigger under his breath, which made his mama a nigger and him a half-nigger son who'd run crack so that two white men could make money off him, and then try to steal what he'd earned for himself. He knew his dad had never really meant his mama or him harm, or at least he thought he knew it. But was that even the point, whether he'd meant harm or whether he hadn't? Wasn't the point what people did, not what they'd *meant* to do?

But there had been a time before this time, when the kitchen had been clean and his mama had forced the men to smoke outside, just because. *Rules are rules*, she'd said, *and that's that. In a civilized house there are just certain things people don't do.* And the meals, oh, the meals she made back when he and his dad used to eat real food every day, whether they wanted to or not. The fried fish, the Brunswick stew, the fresh chicken sandwiches, the ham and eggs on Sunday mornings when the radio played hand-clapping music about Zion and the Promised Land, places Clarence had hoped to one day visit on vacation. His mama had packed his school lunches in this kitchen, always rolling the top of the paper bag down exactly three times to form a neat seal—never more, never less. Every morning, Monday through Friday, she'd wake up early before work, and Clarence would watch her thin gold-ringed fingers slide over one another as she made his sandwich, bagged it, and folded down the top of the bag exactly three times.

And then, on a Friday night three years back, she'd died in this kitchen, slipping from her chair at the table into a creeping red tide. A small hole was left in the window, smaller than an eye or even the tip of a finger. Seconds later, his father and Johnnyprice had blown in through the porch door, howling and falling to their knees beside her while her blouse filled up with blood. She was dead by the time the ambulance arrived. The men in blue pulled a white sheet up over her face before they took her, as if to help Clarence forget her before she was even gone. And now, he too was about to leave without saying good-bye.

He glanced down at his list lying there on the table. It was time to get moving. He dropped his mama's purse into the trash bag, got up quietly, and snuck back to his bedroom. There in front of him was his bed, his end table, his little dresser, his closet. He recognized the room, but it no longer felt like his. Technically everything in this house belonged to his dad, and in one way or another now, his dad belonged to Johnnyprice, just like he had. The gun in his dad's hand that night hadn't changed that. He returned to his list, slowly filling the trash bag, taking care not to bump his bandaged hand against anything hard, and then he tiptoed out into the hallway, where he stopped for a moment, listening for his father's snoring.

Instead of snoring, he heard another familiar sound: his father sobbing, very quietly, like a boy who didn't want to get caught being weak. Clarence sighed and threw the bag over his shoulders as he plodded back into the kitchen. There was no need to be quiet anymore. His dad wouldn't confront him, not now. He was too proud, too afraid of looking soft, and while some part of Clarence wanted to run back and weep with his father—to just let it all out and finally let go— everything else in him was already heading for the door. As he walked past the kitchen counter, a thought came to him, and he slowed down and then stopped. He turned around, walked back to the top drawer, picked up his father's gun, and dropped it into the trash bag. "Sorry, Mama," he said, hoping that this time, she wasn't looking.

— — —

According to his watch, it was 12:37 p.m. when he left the shed after unpacking. His trash bag of belongings was stashed behind a big rusted-out barrel in the corner, not that he had anything worth stealing. Most of his money—and his dad's gun—were safely buried beneath a deep thicket of briars; he had the scratches on his arms to prove it. The only thing left to do was to find something to eat. As he walked down the alley toward Chuckie's Chicken Hut, he tried to remember the last time he'd eaten, but he couldn't. So much had changed so quickly. All that had happened the day before felt like years ago, somehow.

As he wound through the web of alleys that would eventually lead him to Chuckie's, his stomach started dreaming about lunch. Fried chicken. Mac 'n' cheese. Hot rolls. Spicy greens. A bag of food big enough to take him through lunch and dinner, and maybe right into breakfast, if he needed it to. He figured he'd eat his lunch in the tiny patch of woods across from Chuckie's. He could use some privacy, some time to think about what to do next. He knew he had a place to sleep, if he needed it, but he could only hide out in Gina's shed for so long. The food would get him thinking straight, but for now he let all thoughts go, thinking only about the meal that lay ahead of him.

Fried chicken. Mac 'n' cheese. Hot rolls. Spicy greens. He played the list over and over in his mind, even found himself speaking the words out loud until their rhythm became a song, and that song carried him right up to the dumpster behind the Chicken Hut. From there, he crept along the side of the building to the front, peeking his head out to make sure he was alone. He wasn't ready to deal with people yet, and he sure as hell wasn't ready to run into his dad or Johnnyprice.

"Six-piece chicken," he said to the sleepy-eyed cashier who didn't hear him come in and had been leaning against the register, her eyes closed, until the moment he spoke. "And a large mac 'n' cheese. And give me some hot rolls too, please, while you're at it." He was just about to order the greens when he heard the front door open and felt himself flinch. Then he felt a huge hand drop its weight onto his right shoulder and give it a squeeze.

"Brah," a dude's voice said. "'Sup, Clarence?" Clarence's body relaxed, just a little, and he turned around.

"Hey, man. 'Sup." In one way, Clarence was glad to see Demario. Demario'd had his back so far, just like he'd said he would. But he was Y's brother, and like Y, he was impossible to read. Blood was loyalty, and Demario was Y's own blood, his real blood, even if they didn't get along.

For a few minutes the two of them just stood there, silent, until a chubby pink hand reached through the window holding a white paper bag. "Your chicken," the sleepy cashier mumbled, and Clarence turned and laid a twenty on the counter and then just stood there, staring down at the toes of his sneakers.

"Mind if I join you?" Demario asked from behind him. Clarence collected his change, but he didn't turn around. "Come on now. Grab your chicken and come sit with me." Clarence did as told, following Demario to a little orange table in the corner. Demario squeezed himself into one of the tiny chairs and laid his hands palms down on the table-top. Palms down, legs spread. This seemed to be his way. Demario glanced down at the tabletop, then back up, and Clarence could feel him trying to lock his eyes onto Clarence's eyes. "So, how you doing, brah? How are things at home?"

Clarence pulled out his chair and slid in, keeping his eyes on the bag of chicken. Demario was fishing; he could feel it. The only question: Was he fishing for himself or for Y?

"It's okay, I guess, if you like living with assholes." Clarence glanced up at Demario briefly and saw the faintest hint of a smile playing at the corners of his mouth. He'd almost never seen Demario smile. Smiling was a sign of weakness.

"Well, they're *all* assholes, every last one of them," Demario muttered, turning his head toward the window for a moment. "Trust me on that." Clarence couldn't help but wonder who was included in this group of assholes. Were Y and his Y-boys included? Was Demario himself? "But me . . . I've got my own place, you know. I've got to get a little space sometimes, get away from all that. So if you ever need a place to crash, it's cool, I mean, if you ever need a break from those assholes at home."

Clarence nodded but said nothing. It was odd, the way Demario was suddenly reaching out to him, just hours after he'd left home. It was like he'd been watching him or maybe even following him, and on one hand, that thought was comforting. On the other, it was creepy, even scary. Demario belonged to Y, no matter what he said about assholes.

Clarence was glad when Demario suddenly changed the subject. "So, how's that hand? Still healing up all right?"

Clarence nodded and shrugged, glancing down at the bandage. "I don't really need the bandage anymore. It's just to remind me to be careful with it, I mean; it still hurts if I knock it up against something."

"You're a smart little dude." Demario raised his hands above his hand and stretched. Clarence watched him and couldn't help but think: *You did this to me.* He knew he'd agreed to the initiation, but the burn on his palm—and what almost felt like a hug afterward—both things still felt personal. Both felt true, and both told very different stories about his Big Boy.

"So, you eating?" Clarence finally asked as he opened up his box of chicken.

"Nah, brah . . . just happened to see you through the window when I was passing by. Thought I'd pop in." Clarence nodded, then looked back at the food, concentrating hard on his box of chicken and hoping, for a moment, that his Big Boy would stay.

— — —

He ate his lunch in the patch of woods across from Chuckie's, just like he'd planned. The woods were really just a deep stand of skinny trees that hadn't been leveled as the city developed, but right now they felt secret, as if they belonged to him, like the little woods behind Gina's. He quickly peeled a chicken leg and arranged the skin in the box's corner, for later. Then he picked the leg bone clean and dropped the meat into a roll that he carefully dipped into the open container of hot sauce. Finally he took a big bite and chewed slowly, taking in the sweet softness of the bread against the grease of the chicken, the whole thing kicked up a notch by the heat of the sauce. Chicken and bread and sauce. A simple want he could satisfy.

In front of him, beyond the trees, passing cars were flashes of color and metal, splintered by the lean trunks of trees. As usual, lately, he found himself wondering where all those cars were going. Some of them would be stopping in Mayfair Heights, he knew, but some would keep moving

down the roads of his neighborhood on their way to someplace else. He knew about some of those places. He'd read
about them, had seen them on TV and the Internet at school,
and had even studied some of them in detail. The only places
he'd seen in person, though, were the few miles that had circled him since the day he was born.

Half a mile to the Kwik-Bi, so we'll walk it, his mama used
to say, if they needed bread or milk or cigarettes for his dad.
Over a mile to the Food Lion, so step it up, were her words if
they were heading out to make real groceries. *Almost three
miles to church, so we can't miss the bus*, she'd remind him as
they gathered their things and ran hand in hand toward the
stop across the street from the Kwik-Bi. She always gave him
the window seat, and he'd watch as the road snaked beyond
the apartments, slinking along the iron fence of the cemetery, then widening as they passed the Video Circus and
veering left toward the Weekend Flea, a parking lot full of
tables where people put their things out for other people
to buy.

From his window seat, he'd wait for the stoplight up
ahead, which meant they would be turning right onto a four-
lane highway with stores and restaurants stretching out as
far as he could see. Next they'd pass the Walmart, and his
mama would say, *Open all night*, and then three stoplights
up, she'd pull the bell cord, and the bus would stop in front

of the church, which sat in a half-vacant shopping center between a laundromat and a liquor store, in what his mama said was once a Dollar General. That church was where his world ended. Any traveling beyond that little strip mall happened in Ms. Moffett's class, his DVDs, or his imagination.

He sat in the little woods across from Chuckie's, sucked his fingers clean, closed his eyes, and just listened to the traffic over on Mayfair Heights Parkway. Half a mile to the Kwik-Bi, over a mile to the Food Lion. Almost three miles to the church, past the cemetery and the Walmart. He'd never much thought about the size of his world when his mama was alive, but hidden there in the trees, completely alone and lonely, he suddenly sensed the edges of his life and felt them pressing in on him. He no longer went to church or rode the bus with his mama for groceries. He hadn't even been on the bus in over a year. His son-pimping dad wasn't more than eight blocks away at this very moment, and over in the apartments, Fat Terrence waited, his hamburger hands ready for his next delivery.

Everywhere he looked, he saw boundaries. Boxes. Cages.

He pulled in a long deep breath and let it out slowly, trying to use the air inside to make some space in his tightening chest. As he sat and breathed and listened, he could still hear the cars moving in and out of Mayfair Heights, just like it was any old thing you might do on any old day. He imagined how those cars might smell, what stations their drivers might be listening to on the radio, how it would feel to gaze out onto a TV-style world where happy people said funny things until other happy people laughed: a shining world of loved children and brightly lit houses. No dogfighting, no crack, no box-of gray. No reason to walk a wire.

— — —

He sat between two buildings on Mayfair Heights Boulevard—just him, a bag of Andy Capp's, a can of Mr. Pibb, and a little colony of ants. Because it was Sunday, the bus would only be running once an hour, and the first bus wouldn't start until ten a.m. That was what the lady in the Mayfair Minimart had told him when he asked her to make change for him. Time wasn't a problem, though—he had all the time in the world to do whatever he wanted. No one would be expecting him home, well, *ever*.

From his spot between the community center and the TV repair shop, he'd be able to see the bus coming, but until then he was mainly hidden from view, like he wanted. He wasn't about to sit out on the bus stop bench where his dad, or Johnnyprice, or Y, or any other asshole might want to stop and make him their business. Technically his dad could force him home, even call the cops, though he couldn't imagine why he'd bother. It had to be easier for him now: no son around to demand he be more than he was.

The morning dragged along, and the moments passed like hours. To entertain himself, he laid down a hot fry, dribbled a few drops of Mr. Pibb on it, and then watched as the ant colony made the fry its own. He identified each visible body part as he imagined their invisible mandibles working at the spicy red dust of the fry: there was a thorax, an abdomen, some six jointed legs, and he could almost make out a few of their compound eyes. He wondered what he'd be able to see if he had compound eyes, and next he thought, *Superhero*, and then he imagined that superhero compound eyes would give him super-vision on the wire, allowing him to see exactly which step he should take.

He was finishing up his soda and hot fries when he saw the bus rounding a corner and heading his way. The lit-up sign above the bus driver's head said CUMBERLAND PARK. Though Clarence had ridden this bus many times with his mama, he'd had no idea where Cumberland Park was, and he had no idea now. They'd always gotten off at the Walmart, or at the Dollar General church, just a little bit farther up the line. Until his lunch in the woods across from Chuckie's, he'd never once thought about the fact that the bus went someplace else once he and his mama reached their destination. And until yesterday, he'd never wanted to know what that someplace else looked like.

He climbed up the stairs and handed the bus driver his money, like his mama always had. The bus driver nodded. "Hello," Clarence said. "I would like to go to the farthest place that this bus goes. And then I want to come back to this bus stop here. Would you like all the money now, or do I pay you some later?"

The driver seemed confused by the question. He pulled at his puffy pink chin with the tips of his fingers. "Reckon you can pay me half now and give me the rest later," he muttered. "But you're really just riding to the end of the line and back?"

"That's what I'm planning on," Clarence answered.

The bus driver kept working his chin like it was a ball of dough. Clarence could tell the driver had made a switch inside himself. He'd stopped being a bus driver and started being a grown-up; he was looking at Clarence's size and thinking that this was an awfully long way for a kid to go on his own. "So . . . your parents know you're doing this, then?" he finally asked.

Clarence shook his head and started walking toward the back of the bus. He was used to people thinking he was too young to do anything on his own, but on this day—after reclaiming his drug money and sleeping alone two nights in a shed full of squeaks, thunks, and skitters—the driver's question just rubbed him wrong. "Believe me, sir!" he yelled as he continued toward the back of the bus, row by row. "I'm old enough to ride, and my parents aren't around to care." He stopped and looked back. The driver's puffy gray eyes were framed by the square mirror above his head.

The bus was empty except for a bunch of grandmamas in church clothes, trying to keep ahold of their grandkids, most of whom weren't old enough to even form sentences. "Gimme!" they howled, as well as "No!" and "Mine!" and "Ouch!" and "Aaaaaah!" Watching them, Clarence found himself wishing his parents had given him a brother or sister, someone to sleep in sheds and ride buses with. He took a seat in the back and stared out the window, noting each of the landmarks he remembered from his trips with his mama. There went the Jewish cemetery. There went the Walmart. As they passed the Dollar General church, he squinted and imagined his mama standing in front of the glass door. Pale purple dress. Black high-heeled shoes. Big-buckled purse. Shoulder-length hair as dark and slick as tinted glass.

And then she was gone.

He slid in closer to the window and watched the life outside of the window change, then change, then change again. Strip malls became neighborhoods, then parks, then strip malls, neighborhoods, and parks once again. Schools and hospitals and car dealerships flew by; sometimes there was concrete and asphalt, sometimes great stretches of grass, and sometimes there were more trees than he'd ever seen in one place before, except for the woods behind Stonewall Jackson Middle. Sometimes he felt glad he was on the bus— he didn't want to mingle with the people he saw out on the sidewalks and in the parking lots. But sometimes he saw faces that were warm and open. He saw mamas and children, and boys a few years older than he was who weren't looking like they were the property of some low-life crack dealer, and he'd think: *Maybe they'd like me. Maybe we could be friends.*

As the bus motored on, he studied the shapes and patterns, the way the world unfolded again and again around its moving wheels. There was so much out there, and it was more than what he'd seen on TV or in the movies. This real world just kept on coming and coming, and he could see that all its pieces and people fit together into something bigger than Mayfair Heights, his dad, Johnnyprice, and Y. "Mayfair Heights," the driver suddenly called, and Clarence got up, walked to the front of the bus, and handed the driver another fare. "Again," he said, ignoring the questions in the driver's eyes. "I'd like to ride again, sir. Thank you."

— — —

In spite of a long, mostly sleepless night in the shed, he managed to make it to school on Monday. He'd made a promise to Ms. Moffett about reading his essay at the assembly, and he was going to keep it. After the first bell, though, he sat in homeroom and started to feel the truth of what was to come. Beneath his skin, every inch of him trembled, and his heart and stomach traded places so quickly, it was hard to tell which was which anymore. He watched the clock behind the teacher's head, unable to hear anything she was saying. Robert E. Lee was not the kind of school where people wrote essays, much less read them aloud in front of the whole student body. What had he been thinking when he'd agreed?

Sure, he knew he'd agreed because the idea made Ms. Moffett happy. At that moment—when he'd been sitting across from her, looking out at the shiny black car with the tinted windows—he'd needed to see himself as good, and he'd needed Ms. Moffett to see him as good. He'd hoped that the weight of his goodness to her might balance some of the badness of being a Y-boy and grant him a few more safe steps on the wire. The problem now was, Ms. Moffett wouldn't be the only one sitting in that auditorium.

He pictured himself standing there at the podium, looking out into a wide, wild sea of porch-hanging girls, Y-boys, boys who hated the Y-boys, and boys who hated the boys who hated the Y-boys. At Lee High, no one really had friends, or nobody seemed to, anyway. Kids traveled in packs, but if a different pack had something better to offer, they'd simply leave one for another, all loyalties forgotten. Even some of Y's boys were pack-switchers during the school day, protecting their interests when they needed to.

Suddenly Clarence's hand was in the air, and he was asking for permission to be excused. He was up and moving before he'd even finished his request, running for the bathroom. The stomach storm came and went with fury, leaving him stumbling from the stall to one of the sinks along the wall. He glanced briefly into its dirty mirror, splashing water on his face but refusing to let his eyes linger on his smeared reflection. He didn't even bother to towel himself off before he left the bathroom; he just walked out then made a left, walking straight back down the hallway, toward homeroom. Then right past homeroom. Then straight ahead to the side door of the building, the one that led out to the parking lot. He wasn't trying to hurt Ms. Moffett. He wasn't trying to do anything wrong.

He was just admitting the truth of his limitations.

He chose a route that would bypass the Kwik-Bi, taking him briefly along the woods behind Stonewall Jackson Middle, then putting him out just below Bedford Street. Though he wanted nothing more than to stop in and drink tea with Mr. Khabir, he forced his mind away from that want. He'd passed three nights in the shed since leaving through the Kwik-Bi's back door, and he knew he wasn't yet ready to return. He just didn't know what to say to Mr. K. No matter how much he missed their conversations—and the bleach smell of the store, and the *click-click-click* of Mr. K's loafers, and even the flowery little lady-cups—he still wasn't ready to face him. He hung his head and took the long way to Gina's alley, making sure he was alone before he slunk into the little woods toward what, at the moment, was home.

As he sat down on the sofa cushions he'd pulled from a dumpster, he found his eyes drawn to the little window on the far wall, the one part of the shed not tucked completely into shadow. Dust floated above and around him in the watery light, and a granddaddy longlegs crawled back and forth across a crack in the glass, trying to find a way out. Part of Clarence wanted to pick the spider up, open the shed door, and set it free into the woods, but he realized that the spider was his only company. "Hey there," he said, but he couldn't think of anything else to say. He looked down at the DVD player next to his backpack and hoped it still had some juice. He wondered which movie in the Dark Knight trilogy was right for this particularly pathetic day.

He was loading up the DVD player with *The Dark Knight* when he heard footsteps moving toward the shed, in from the alley side, through the woods. Dead leaves crunched and crackled; twigs snapped all around him until the footsteps stopped right outside, just beyond the shed door. He pulled his breath into his chest and waited. There was nothing to do but wait. Nowhere to go, no way to escape. Like the granddaddy longlegs in the window, he was trapped.

Slowly—so slowly—the door creaked like a door in a scary movie until quite suddenly, it burst open. "Boo, motherfucker!" someone yelled, and then a form stepped into the shadows. Once Clarence's vision adjusted to the light, he could see that there, right in front of him, glittered the icy-blue eyes of Billie Wade.

"What is this shit?" Billie asked, walking into the shed and looking around. "I saw you walking along the woods behind my school, so I left and followed you. What the fuck are you doing, dude? Aren't you supposed to be the good one out of the two of us or something?"

Clarence didn't know how to answer this question.

"It's a long story," he offered.

"I've heard that before," said Billie. Then neither of them did anything much. At this moment, in a rusted-out shed in the woods off an alley, there really wasn't much to be done. Billie slid his hands into his pockets and shrugged. Clarence glanced back up at the granddaddy longlegs. "So," Billie finally blurted out. "What the hell, mentor? You living in here or something?" Clarence didn't know what to tell Billie, so he told him the truth.

"Kind of." He looked down at the DVD player on his lap.

Billie pulled his left hand out of its pocket and pointed at the ceiling of the shed. "Either you're living here or you're not. I mean, there isn't any *kind of.*" He put his hand back into his pocket and slowly turned around, taking the shed in. "So you're skipping school, and you live in a shed. I mean, *really*? This is my role model?" Clarence wanted to get mad at Billie, but he couldn't. Billie made a good point. Who was he to be anybody's mentor? He was the one who needed help.

He ignored the comment and simply pushed the play button on the DVD, asking Billie if he'd like to sit down. "If this thing powers up, I'm going to watch *The Dark Knight*," he said. "Want to watch it with me?"

Billie squinted as he checked out the floor of the shed. "This thing clean?" It was clear he wasn't looking for an answer, that he was just talking to talk. "Because I don't want to get any diseases from some skanky shed floor." Clarence just stared at him, wondering how such a bitter old man could live in the body of a twelve-year-old boy. Billie stared back, his blue eyes slippery and cold. "I guess I'll sit down for a minute," he finally said. The movie had already started, and he no longer seemed interested in Clarence at all. "You know, Batman is a badass, but not as badass as the Joker," he suddenly declared, settling in and leaning forward toward the screen.

"Maybe," Clarence said. "But Batman has a harder job. It's easy just to kick people around all the time. Batman has to be a badass *and* good at the same time. It's a thin line, you know? Only a few can walk it, I think. Maybe it's just a superhero thing."

Billie looked up from the screen, right at him. "Umm . . . what did you say?"

"I said it's easy to kick people's asses. Anybody can do it. Bullies are everywhere, and they're pussies." For a moment the two boys' eyes locked, and Clarence could see a crack in the ice of Billie's gaze. There was something there, an opening. And then it was gone. Billie coughed, but the cough was forced, just a way to end the moment before. Both boys looked back at the screen, but no one spoke again.

By the time the movie was over, the light was as bright as it ever got in the shed. Clarence knew it was coming up on lunchtime, and he felt he should at least give Billie something to eat. Then it occurred to him: he should probably send Billie back to Stonewall Jackson, but he wasn't sure how he could, given the fact that he wasn't in school himself. Seemed the best he could do was make sure that Billie got fed, and that he was safe for the moment. Anything after that was a blank. "I've got some leftover chicken from Chuckie's," he mentioned, rolling over to the other side of the cushion-bed and reaching for his most recent Chuckie's bag. "Do you want a piece, maybe?" In spite of the fact that they were both skipping school and that Billie now knew he lived in a shed, Clarence was grateful that Billie had come looking for him. As far as he could tell, no one else had.

He handed Billie a good-sized thigh, along with a napkin and one of the moist towelettes that came with the meal. "Biscuit?" he asked, and Billie nodded, though his eyes said, *I don't need this, you know.* Billie's eyes. Clarence didn't know what he saw there, but he knew he'd seen it before. He handed Billie a biscuit, and they both started eating—not speaking, not looking at each other—just sitting quietly there in the half-light, enjoying a meal.

Finally Billie broke the silence. "So you live here, then?" he asked, but this time it sounded like a question, not a judgment. "So you've, like, run away or something? Or else your parents are dead?" Clarence nodded and chewed his bite of chicken, biscuit, and sauce.

"My mom is dead, yeah. And my dad. Well, he's as good as dead."

Billie studied the inside of the shed while he ate. He took his time. He chewed off another chunk of chicken and then started talking with his mouth full. "There's one good thing about this shed, though. No one can fuck with you. That's all right, you know, not being fucked with. I wouldn't mind some of that for a while."

As soon as Billie admitted this, his eyes froze over, as if he'd been caught. Clarence dropped his own eyes to the chicken in his lap, letting Billie pull himself together in private. Billie had clearly said something he hadn't meant to, and he needed a way to take it back. "So I'd better be going now, you know." He stretched and faked a yawn. "If I'm back at school by last bell, I can lie my way out of this whole thing. But thanks for the food. And the movie. I guess I'll see you later, or whatever."

As Billie got up, Clarence felt a weight settling into his body. Soon he'd be able to let Mona out and roll around with her in the grass for a while, but what happened after that? The thinning light, the setting sun, the darkness, the footsteps in the alley while he tried to sleep. What would happen tomorrow, and the day after that, and the day after that?

He said good-bye to Billie and then headed over the fence into Gina's yard, tossing the ball for Mona as the sun slid across the sky. He tried not to think about Gina, or about the last time he saw her, all jittery and crazy-eyed, or about the way she'd flown into the house without even speaking to her dog, or about the way she'd left, shoving a fifty-dollar bill into Clarence's palm and muttering, "Thanks," as Y's subwoofer growled from the street. That had been the day after the party, the day after he'd moved into the shed. He hadn't seen her since.

As Mona finally hunkered down next to him in the sunlight, he laid his head on her warm back and tried not to think about what would happen to her if he weren't around. He tried not to think about the fact that the boy-man who now owned Gina also technically owned Mona. The sky above them swayed, clouds came and went, and soon the sun dropped into the treetops. He missed Gina, and her sweetness, and the sadness she couldn't seem to shake. He knew Mona must miss her too, and he wondered if Mona lay awake at night, thinking about all she'd lost, like he did.

Dusk fell, then darkness, and he rolled over and spooned Mona, dreading the lonely hours ahead of him. "Don't worry, girl," he said, as he finally pushed himself up off the grass. "I won't let anything happen to you. Don't you worry." He started walking toward Gina's back door, and soon Mona was by his side, trotting along next to him like his own personal pony. She followed him into the utility room, where he filled up her water bowl slowly, not wanting to leave. He looked around the utility room, then up the steps into the kitchen, knowing that while Gina's house was mainly empty these days, he would have to stick to his routine. He could chance a quick shower once in a while, while letting his DVD player charge up, but that was as long as he could safely let himself linger. "G'night, girl," he finally said, locking the back door as he left. Mona raised herself up on her hind legs on the other side, putting her front paws on the window glass between them. Clarence put his own hands onto the glass, and they just stood there like that—paws to hands—as he willed himself into the long black night.

REVELATIONS

....

THE DOORBELL CHIMED, AND Clarence walked into the Kwik-Bi, with a clumsy grin and what he hoped looked like a swagger. Truth was that he was almost nervous enough to puke, but he'd decided he would rather face Mr. Khabir than go back to the shed. After he'd said good night to Mona, he'd spent the next hour walking the alleys and thinking about how he'd manage the lie he knew he had to tell to Mr. K. He didn't want to lie; he'd stayed away from Mr. K for that very reason. But he'd learned that a few days alone was an awfully long time. Mr. K was his only friend in Mayfair Heights besides Mona, and maybe Demario. Mr. K was his only real friend who wasn't a dog. He'd decided he'd explain his behavior Friday night with a story that would be part truth and part fiction. It was getting easier to walk the wire, to stay surefooted in the in-between.

In front of him, Mr. K watched the black-and-white TV, his back turned to the door, and Clarence knew, if Mr. K was interested in the show, he'd be turning around in exactly ten seconds. If he wasn't interested, he'd turning around in under five, so if Clarence was going to change his mind and make a run for it, he needed to do it. Now. Mr. K spun around on the heel of his worn but always polished left loafer and said, "There you are," very quietly, as if he'd been waiting.

Clarence meant to reply with an easygoing chuckle but suddenly found himself coughing, for no reason, instead. He just kept on coughing, too, like he was really sick, and even though he knew he wasn't, he couldn't stop himself. He didn't know why. He just couldn't stop, and he turned back toward the glass door and coughed into the palms of his hands, watching his own reflection like he was watching someone else on TV.

In the door's reflection he also watched Mr. K walk up and stand behind him. He just stood there behind him as Clarence coughed and coughed until he was almost choking, and then Mr. K lifted his hands, placing one on each of Clarence's shoulders. "Stop the coughing," he said softly. "You are all right. It is all right now, Clarence." Clarence watched this happen; he heard Mr. K's words and felt his hands there on his shoulders, but it didn't seem like it was happening to him. The cough was coughing itself now, fed as it was by his nerves, and he was just along for the ride.

He'd thought he was ready to do this. He'd thought he was steady on the wire, but he couldn't feel it supporting him anymore, and he couldn't see which way to step.

"There now," Mr. K whispered, and he leaned down and pulled Clarence in close, like he meant to squeeze the cough right out of him. But he didn't squeeze too tight; he just held him. He held him like he meant it, but not like he meant it too much. He held him like Clarence sometimes held Mona when she slept out in the backyard, when he lay right behind her and let his arms make a circle around her shoulders. Not too tight, or she wouldn't be able to breathe. Just close enough that if she woke, she'd know she wasn't alone.

"That is it, then," Mr. K said, finally letting go. He took a couple of steps back and waited until Clarence turned around to face him. When Clarence's eyes finally met his, he nodded while Mr. K's right hand drifted over the frames of his tinted glasses, down the bridge of his nose, then across the map stain on his cheek. "They are looking for you, you know."

Clarence suddenly felt tired.

"Who?" he pretended, leaning back against the glass door, which creaked open an inch or two, making the bell chime again. As soon as he heard that bell, he jumped right toward Mr. K, tossing his head in midair to look back. His feet hit the floor in a tangle of sneakers, socks, and bony ankles, and he was on the linoleum at Mr. K's feet before he realized he was the one who'd made the bell ring.

"Dear Clarence, you are nothing but the—how do they call them?—the jitters." Mr. K squatted and cupped his hands under Clarence's elbows, raising him to his feet. Clarence appreciated the fact that Mr. K didn't look at his face as he lifted him, that his friend let him be soft in private. "All right then," Mr. K said once Clarence was steady on his feet. "I will make you some tea now. The way you like it, with the milk and the sugar and the extra cinnamon. In the meantime, you watch the television and keep an eye on my store. There are tissues on the counter."

Clarence hadn't realized that a few tears had escaped from his eyes and made their way onto his cheeks. He could feel them now, though, and he wanted them gone. He grabbed one of Mr. K's tissues and rubbed hard at his face, like it was filthy. He couldn't afford to be weak like this. It simply wasn't an option. He could hear Mr. K behind him, locking the front door and pulling down the shades on the tall glass windows, the *click-click-click*ing back toward the kitchen where, each day at dawn, he made his own dough for the morning biscuits. "Don't take anything!" he yelled as he turned right at the end of the aisle and disappeared.

Clarence could hear the heels of Mr. K's loafers tapping the floor back in the kitchen, and he turned down the volume on the black-and-white so he could listen to the sounds of banging pans and running water, of the refrigerator door opening and closing, all the shuffling and bustling of another person doing something nice for him. "You are hungry? You are wanting an egg sandwich, Clarence?" Mr. K called. Clarence used his sleeve to wipe his nose and then turned his attention to a colorless Homer Simpson drinking a colorless beer at a colorless Moe's Tavern.

"I'll take one if you're having one!" he called back. Then suddenly there was a pause, a long dead silence, and for a moment Clarence felt like he was alone again, that Mr. K had just walked out and left him. But just like that, the silence was broken by Mr. K's musical voice and the tinkling of cups and spoons. Thank God, Mr. K was still there. Thank God that someone like Mr. K even existed.

"I will be having a sandwich as well." Mr. K's voice traveled up the aisles. "There was no time for the lunch today. The people, they never stopped the arriving today!" Clarence could hear the teakettle hiss. The fridge opened and closed, opened and closed. "But you keep those grimy mitts off my register, you there. I'm watching you, you know."

"You know you don't have anything I want, don't you?" Clarence tossed this comment across the first aisle, sending it spinning over the cat litter and Vienna sausages, past the dairy cooler and into the kitchen, toward the sounds of bacon sizzling in a pan. It felt good throwing around the sass with this man. He knew a different conversation was right behind this one, but it wasn't time, not yet. Now was the time for play.

"You say I have nothing, and yet you are back." Mr. K was on point tonight, and Clarence was glad that one thing in his life was in its place.

Before long, Mr. K returned, carrying a cookie sheet as a tray. He delicately placed the egg sandwiches and the lady-cups of tea onto the counter, taking the stool that was usually Clarence's. They ate silently at first, watching *The Simpsons* without really watching, taking little bites here and there, waiting for whatever would happen next. Mr. K lifted his cup and spent a long time blowing down on it before he finally took a single sip, wiped his lips with his pinky, and spoke.

"Your father and his friend say you are staying at your grandmother's house. They said you left a note to this effect on Friday, the day you left." He shifted the cup to his left hand and fingered his glasses with his right. Clarence watched him and was glad, for once in his life, that his dad and Johnnyprice had lied, even if it was just to cover their own asses. What he wasn't glad about was the fact that they hadn't also lied about when he left the box-of-gray. Now Mr. K had a way to link Friday night in the Kwik-Bi to the Friday Clarence had left home. "They came by yesterday, wanting to know if I had seen you. When I said I had not, they went back out front and loitered about, smoking their cigarettes and arguing with the young man with the little mustache and the many boys."

Clarence wondered if Mr. K knew he was now one of those boys. He kept his eyes on his plate and forced himself to swallow.

"You are liking it better at your grandmother's, then?"

Clarence nodded, but he didn't look up. "It's all right, I guess," he answered. Sitting there on the stool across from Mr. K brought Friday night back to him hard and fast: taking back his money; walking straight down the right aisle to the Kwik-Bi's bathroom; staring at his own strange face in the flower-cracked mirror; sneaking out the back door before Mr. K could ask him any questions. He suddenly felt small and naked. Though he'd practiced his lines many times on his walk, he found he had nothing at all to say.

Suddenly a fist pounded against the door of the Kwik-Bi, and Mr. K hurried over and slid back the shade a couple of inches. "I am closed for the next hour," he said, and a voice on the other side demanded: "Yeah? Well, I need some smokes."

"The truth is that I have just been robbed and the police are on their way, so I am going to need some time, sir." There was silence, and then Clarence heard the man's shoes slapping the pavement, moving away. Mr. K had been robbed three times that Clarence knew about. No one in the neighborhood would have a reason to question his story, and almost no one would want to be around when the cops arrived.

Clarence could feel Mr. K's eyes on him as he sat back down at the counter. Not his outside eyes, which were looking at his cup of tea, but his inside eyes, the ones buried deep beneath his skin. Clarence could feel them locked on him, searching. "So, you are back then, Clarence? I will be seeing you again from time to time, after your high school?"

Clarence knew this was not a simple question. He had to be careful about how he answered. "Well, my grandmother picks me up from school," he suddenly lied. "She lives in another neighborhood, you know, one you have to drive to. She and my dad are fighting about me. So it's hard to say when I can come by. I guess I'll just have to see what happens." As far as he could tell, he'd covered all his bases with this story, and the last part of the answer was even the truth.

Mr. K nodded and sipped his tea. "I see then," he finally said. "But I wonder if she would let you stop by to say hello now and again, if you might ask her this for me. Quite frankly, I would like the company, sir."

One of the fluorescent lights on the ceiling crackled, flickered, then went out. Mr. K glanced up and then turned his eyes back to Clarence, looking straight at him for the first time since he'd arrived. "I would not have to tell your father about your stopping in, you know, if he and your grandmother are fighting at this time. Maybe it would be best if I said nothing to anyone."

Clarence could feel a door opening somewhere in the situation, and he felt that Mr. K was opening it on purpose. Mr. K was giving him a way in, and a way out. "Well, that could work, I guess," he finally agreed, but he kept his voice flat, as if he had no interest in the situation's outcome at all. Just two men chatting over egg sandwiches. Whatever, whatever. "I'll run it by her, see what she says. Who knows."

"Very good, then," said Mr. K, but the way his lower lip curled into his mouth, then uncurled, told Clarence that he knew more than he was letting on. "Who knows," he said, then he said no more. And with this, the two of them went back to their egg sandwiches and *The Simpsons*. The fluorescent light above them flashed back on, and they both glanced up briefly, then kept on eating.

"Mr. K," Clarence heard himself saying between bites, though he knew he should just keep his mouth shut and keep on eating. Mr. K looked away from the TV and tilted his head, and Clarence heard his own voice continue. One part of him kept talking, and another listened nervously, knowing it was a bad idea. This happened sometimes, and somehow the talking part was always faster than the listening part. "You said you'd like some company here at the store. I was just wondering . . . are you afraid? Are you afraid of being alone here or something?"

Mr. K smiled weakly. His head sagged a bit on his shoulders. "I am not afraid of being alone, Clarence. But sometimes I am lonely." His caterpillar eyebrows rose up over his tinted glasses, adrift.

"But you have your family, right? So you're not really alone; I mean, you have people who love you. I've seen their picture. They look so happy." As soon as he spoke, Clarence knew he'd said too much. He wouldn't have seen the photo if he hadn't been snooping in Mr. K's private drawer.

"Ah. My family. You have seen my family, then." His face grew very still. The face itself was there, but the life underneath it had vanished. Clarence watched that face and wondered where Mr. K had gone. He had no choice but to wait until he returned; he always returned. Eventually. "My family, dear Clarence, is a conversation for another time," he finally said, coming back into his body, just like nothing had happened at all. "Eat your sandwich now; it is getting late. I will make you another if you're still hungry."

— — —

Clarence decided to go back to school on Tuesday because he didn't think he could take another day of being alone. He also went back for Ms. Moffett—he'd made her believe in him and then he'd let her down, and his regret, in addition to everything else rattling around in his mind, kept him awake most of the night on Monday, after he'd left the Kwik-Bi. The biggest reason he went back to school, though, was for Billie Wade. He'd been thinking about Billie since they'd met in the cafeteria, and Clarence had realized that whatever he was feeling, Billie was feeling worse, and that in spite of the ways Rowley Feather had failed him, Billie's dad—whoever he was—was in a category of his own. He'd seen the marks on Billie himself—marks made with more than fists, made with things that were sharp. Or hard. Or hot. Or heavy. He just hadn't known what he was seeing at the time.

He wasn't yet sure if Billie remembered it, but he'd been alone with Clarence long before Clarence became his mentor. It was in the springtime the year before, just a couple of months before summer break. Clarence had walked in on Billie in the bathroom during recess, as Billie was wiping one of his ribs with a paper towel. Clarence could see that big patches of the skin under Billie's shirt looked like the skin of a lizard: rough, ridged, and bluish-green. Billie dabbed at the bloody corner of one of those patches with a paper towel, and Clarence figured he'd fallen on the playground and opened one of the wounds. When Billie looked up, Clarence knew he'd seen too much.

"What the fuck are you looking at?" Billie'd hissed, and Clarence had no idea what to say back. He didn't even know what he was looking at, not yet, so for a second or two he and Billie had just stood there, staring at each other, and then Billie pulled down his shirt and walked out.

Billie was hard and foul-mouthed, especially for a kid his age, but Clarence knew he was a trash-talker because he was scared. Clarence had seen enough to know this. Billie was scared like most of Y's boys and Johnnyprice and his dad, and all the other neighborhood dudes who talked shit because they thought they had to. Clarence was going back to school for Billie because Billie needed him. He didn't know exactly what he'd say to Ms. Moffett once he got there, but if he didn't go back now, it would get harder, and time would pass, and if enough time passed, he might never go back. His mama would roll over in her grave.

He woke up at dawn on Tuesday morning, all on his own, without the help of his watch alarm. His mind was restless, on the roam. He switched on his flashlight and just lay there, trying to work up his nerve. He'd earned Ms. Moffett's respect, made a promise, and then bailed on her. What kind of person did that? It wasn't like he couldn't have just politely turned her down, told her he hated public speaking, and let that be that. But she'd been so complimentary, and at that moment he'd felt brave and capable and good. He'd seen himself through her eyes, but here, in this shed, there were only his own two eyes, and those eyes saw what he really was. Still, he knew all superheroes were flawed. Like him, they traveled along the line between good and evil and didn't always do the right thing. Eventually though, they faced what they'd done, like Bruce Wayne faced himself in Tibet. Clarence was the Wirewalker. It was time to make things right.

— — —

Robert E. Lee's front hall was a swarm of howling, bug-eyed teenagers being unsuccessfully herded by howling, bug-eyed teachers. Nothing new here; this was any old morning in high school. He kept his head down, his eyes on the gold-tile floor, and he set his mind to the task of shrinking into himself, of making himself invisible. He disappeared into the crowd as he passed the cafeteria, and then stayed close to the railing on the steps up to the main floor, imagining his inside self as a wisp of smoke rising above the hallway even as his outside body hunkered down and kept on moving. He could be two things at once: he knew this; he experienced it all the time. He could be tiny and the size of the whole world. He could be solid and made of nothing but air.

Just before he got to homeroom, he stopped for a sip from the water fountain. Within seconds he felt a hand on his shoulder. A small light hand, not unlike the hand of his mother but attached to a different smell. It wasn't clean sheets and baby powder; it was more like the honeysuckle that grew on the alley fences behind his dad's house. It was Ms. Moffett's smell. The water from the fountain hit his lips, but his lips did nothing.

"Clarence Feather," Ms. Moffett said, letting her hand rest on his shoulder. "I'd like to have a moment with you before you go to homeroom." And then it came. The stomach, the heat rising to his head. It was a good thing he hadn't had breakfast.

He turned slowly and wove his fingers in and out of one another, making awkward shapes with his hands. He cast his gaze down at Ms. Moffett's hands—at her orange fingernails and the three silver rings on three of her fingers. "Look at me, Clarence," she said. "Please look at me when I speak to you." Instead he looked out into the hallway, to the left, then to the right. The swarm of bodies was thinning as students ducked into their classrooms before the sound of the first bell. Down on the right, he could see the exit door at the end of the corridor, the one he'd left through just the day before.

Slowly Clarence raised his eyes. He had no choice. Ms. Moffett deserved that. "I talked to your homeroom teacher," Ms. Moffett said, and he swallowed again. "She said you were here yesterday, but that you'd left class suddenly. I handpicked you to read at that assembly, you know." Clarence nodded while Ms. Moffett checked the almost empty hallway, then the clock on the wall. "You should also know that Mrs. Danielson called me. Apparently Billie Wade left school yesterday morning as well. I have a feeling you might be aware of that. You were due for a mentor meeting that afternoon." Here it was. This was the whole truth. He could run or he could stay.

"I'm sorry, Ms. Moffett," he said, and he meant it. "I thought I could read at the assembly, but I couldn't. I just couldn't. It's hard to explain. I just had to get out of here." Ms. Moffett nodded, but she didn't speak. "And Billie, well, I guess he saw me on my way home. But I didn't plan on any of that. I planned on going to the assembly. That was my plan all along." Ms. Moffett looked back up at the clock on the wall. Just a couple of minutes before first bell.

"Well, what happened then, Clarence?"

"Well, I haven't been feeling so good," he heard himself say. "I got sick that morning. Really sick." It felt good to tell the truth. He hoped Ms. Moffett would see that truth and accept it. Ms. Moffett's eyes inspected his face, searching.

"Well, are you feeling better now, Clarence? Is everything all right?" He knew the question she'd asked was bigger than the words she used to ask it.

"I am, Ms. Moffett. I'm definitely better now." He studied her face, unable to tell exactly what she was thinking, but the skin around her mouth and eyes loosened a bit, like she might smile, or cry.

"I'm glad to hear that," she said, and then she reached over and laid her left hand's fingertips gently on his shoulder, letting them rest there for just a moment. At first he pulled back, but then he forced himself to stand still and accept her touch. Though he was standing in a hallway in a school where teachers were mainly seen as enemies, he found himself grateful, and unashamed. "Clarence," Ms. Moffett almost whispered before she walked away from him, toward her own classroom. "I need you to do right by that Wade boy. If you can't do that, I need you to tell me now."

Clarence didn't have to think about his answer; his answer had already found him, long before he set foot back in Lee High that morning. "I will," he said, and he gave her hand a little squeeze. "I can do that, Ms. Moffett. I promise."

— — —

During their next peer-to-peer lunch, he and Billie sat together at the back of the lunch room, and Ms. Moffett sat over on the other side with Mrs. Danielson. The cool boys who were already learning how to walk the walk took up a whole table right in the middle of the room. Every now and again they yelled bullshit comments at other students, but they basically left Clarence and Billie alone, too busy with their own yammering to notice a couple of undersized losers sharing a plate of chicken tenders. Part of Clarence wanted to walk over and set them straight, to let them know he ran crack, that he had hundreds of dollars stashed away, and that he had a badass Big Boy watching his back. But another part of him hoped that they'd never meet anyone like Y and never have a reason to do anything but get good grades, graduate, and get the hell out of Mayfair Heights.

Billie stared at the chicken and didn't say much while he ate. He sat, hunched over, his body curled in on itself. "I'm glad you came back, man," he mumbled to Clarence, but he didn't look up from his lunch. "I'm really glad you're here."

This was a Billie Clarence hadn't seen yet. This was a Billie coming apart. "Hey," Clarence said, trying to get him to look up. He nudged Billie in the arm with his elbow, and Billie flinched. "Billie, man. Are you all right?"

Billie hung his head and exhaled slowly, closing his eyes. He didn't speak. He just kept pulling air in and pushing air out, loud enough that Clarence could hear it clearly from where he was sitting. As Billie's breathing quieted, Clarence sensed a familiar feeling rooting itself inside of him, a knot tying itself up in his gut. A boy in pain wasn't anything new. Another boy in pain because a grown-up was fucking up. "So just follow my lead, okay?" Clarence whispered. "We're going to get up and go to the bathroom now, Billie. Just follow me as best you can. There's no hurry." Billie pushed himself up from the table and slowly trailed behind Clarence. When they got to the double doors, he guided Billie over to the right side, toward the wall. "I'll be right back," Clarence said. "I just need to let the teachers know where we're going."

When he returned, he led Billie, and they took their time getting down the hallway—Billie because he couldn't seem to move any faster, and Clarence because it was his job to take care of Billie. As soon as the bathroom door closed, Billie collapsed against the wall by the first sink. When Clarence tried to use his arms to support him, Billie moaned and pulled away. "Show me, Billie," Clarence whispered. "It's okay. . . . Just show me."

It took a while for Billie to lift his shirt. Once it was up, Clarence saw that the flesh underneath did not look like the flesh of a boy. It wasn't the color of a boy. It was speckled with many colors—pink, red, brown, black, blue, yellow, green—and it had many textures, but few of them seemed to be the texture of human skin. Clarence looked at Billie's body and felt the way he did when Y talked about Mona, like when Y'd stopped his car in front of Gina's house and reached through the fence to scratch her on the head, all the while dreaming of her in the fighting pen, of her white fur splattered with blood. He recognized this feeling as anger, but it was more than anger—a whole lot more. That *more* took shape as a knowing inside of him, and the knowing told him that he'd do whatever it took to make sure this didn't happen to Billie again.

"Okay, Billie. You can pull your shirt down." Clarence went over to the sink, wet a paper towel, and then gently wiped Billie's damp colorless face. "Should we tell Ms. Moffett or Mrs. Danielson?" he asked, knowing the teachers would be waiting for them down the hall. "I mean, I bet they can help you. Somebody's got to help you, Billie."

Billie's raised his eyes, and those eyes pleaded with Clarence. "You ever been in foster care, Clarence?" Clarence shook his head. "Well, I have. Twice. So no. Don't say anything. You have no idea, Clarence. I mean it. I've got to handle this on my own." Clarence wanted to give Billie something, anything to comfort him, but he couldn't find the will to speak. *You're not alone*, he thought, and then he put his hand on Billie's shoulder, guiding him back down the hallway, into the last ten minutes of lunch.

— — —

That Friday, after the mentor meeting to make up for Monday's miss, Clarence decided to follow Billie home from school. Billie crossed the playground and then the baseball field, but where Clarence usually made a right, Billie made a left. He walked along the edge of the woods until he reached the back side of a dead-end street. Across that dead end, through a high row of bushes, another collection of houses began, and Clarence thought they looked a lot like the houses branching out from the box-of-gray, only without the twisted tree or the pile of metal in the artists' yard. He stayed far behind Billie, ducking behind trees when he thought he needed to, but he really didn't need to at all. Billie's head was down and his shoulders were hunched, like he was walking into a mighty wind. He forced himself forward against it, and Clarence could see that Billie wasn't worried about what—or who—might be behind him. It was what lay before him that was the problem.

Billie's street also made Clarence think of the porch-hanging girls, the ones who called to him on his way to the park. The houses were all the same small squares with different-colored doors and shutters. Some had curtains in the windows, some didn't. Some had neat little yards with birdbaths and flowers; some were overgrown with weeds and scrub like his dad's yard and the back of Gina's. Way down the street, way out in front of Billie, a young dude walked a tan-and-white pit, keeping the chain lead pulled in tight next to his thigh. Maybe one of Y's boys, maybe not. He didn't really care one way or another.

About midblock, Billie slowed down and almost stopped

walking. He dragged his feet, kicking at gravel on the asphalt. He was stalling, and Clarence slid behind a tree, afraid that Billie might just turn around, head the other way, and find his mentor following him. And part of Clarence really wished he would. Part of him wanted to take Billie with him right now, but another part knew Billie wasn't ready. He thought of Bruce Wayne, of the hours and days and years he spent preparing to make just one important move. Bruce Wayne always had a plan. Clarence would have to wait.

Billie stopped in front of a white house with bright red shutters and a matching bright red door. Big yellow sunbursts of flowers bloomed in matching pots on the steps, and a pumpkin sat in one corner of the small tidy porch. The lawn was deep green, a shade of green Clarence had never seen in any yard anywhere in his neighborhood. As he peeked out from behind a row of low bushes, he could see that the grass was soft and silky, and he pictured lying down in grass like that with Mona, rolling around, the feel of that softness against his neck.

Billie shuffled into the driveway, sidling up next to a gleaming silver SUV without leaning against it or touching it. He just stood there next to it, staring up at the perfect little house. Clarence didn't know what to make of it. This was the nicest house he'd ever seen in his neighborhood except for the old man's, and the old man had nothing better to do than tend his yard all morning and then sit on the porch afterward, drinking coffee. Clarence just couldn't make the house in front of him line up with the image he had of Billie's dad, the man who had put those marks on Billie's body and who took great care to make sure none of them showed. If that was what Billie's belly and chest looked like, then what about his back, his legs? How could a man walk past a perfect green lawn and pretty sunburst flowers, then go inside to destroy his son?

The red door opened, and Clarence's stomach bucked. He was sure he couldn't be seen behind the bushes, but that didn't help. He wasn't afraid for himself: Billie stood there next to the car, completely alone, and Clarence wanted to dash out of the bushes, grab Billie's hand, and run away back toward the woods, but he couldn't. Bruce Wayne wouldn't. It wasn't the right time.

A blonde woman with her hair pulled back in a ponytail drifted onto the porch, a drink in her hand. She wore dark straight-legged jeans and a pink blouse that looked like it had just been ironed. Her pale fingers were long and slender with perfect red nails. She smiled like a model in a magazine. "How's my boy?" she called down to Billie, who dropped his head and pulled his shoulders forward again, bracing himself against whatever wind he'd already seen coming. Finally he raised his head, and the woman beamed down at him, like he was the best thing she'd ever seen. "How was your day, sweetie?"

She quickly bounced down the steps toward him, but he simply stood there, still as a stump, waiting. When she finally got to him, she put her drink on top of the car and then leaned down, taking him into her arms. She hugged him in the same way Clarence's mama used to hug him sometimes, like she hadn't seen him in days and like she might never see him again.

Clarence couldn't see Billie's face, but he could hear the sound he made—a muffled yelp like a dog being kicked. His mother dropped her arms and took a step back. "Oh, baby," she said, and she knelt down in front of Billie. She ran her perfect fingers through his hair. "It still hurts, then." Billie nodded, and Clarence pictured the colors beneath his shirt, all the bumps and scars, all the skin that no longer looked like skin. "Baby, I'm so sorry," she said, and she stood up and pulled her drink from the roof of the car, taking a long swallow as she gazed out over the street. "Jesus." She placed the glass back on the top of the SUV and slid her hands into the back pockets of her jeans. "What are we going to do, baby? It was so much easier when your dad was around. Things made sense then, don't you think?"

Billie didn't move. He didn't answer. His mother raised a hand and waved at a car that was pulling into the driveway across the street. She smiled like someone in a toothpaste commercial. "Hey there, Juanita!" she hollered, and the woman in the car waved back. Soon Billie's mom dropped her hand and reached for her glass, taking her time with another long swig. Clarence found that he really wanted her to stop drinking, for the glass to fall to the pavement and shatter into little bits. Instead she placed it back on top of the car and squatted in front of Billie, using her right hand to steady herself this time. "We're going to be all right, you know," she said to her son, and from where Clarence stood, it really looked like she meant it. "Whatever happens, Billie, we're going to be all right."

Billie laid his palm against the SUV as he took a single step back, away from her. Just a small step. Just a small hand on the side of the car. "Jesus—get your hand off the car, Billie, for God's sake!" Suddenly she reached over and grabbed his hand, balling it up like a rag in her fist. With her other hand, she wiped the place where his fingers had been. She wiped and wiped, and then it was like she suddenly woke up from a dream. She quickly dropped Billie's hand and looked at him, her eyes wide and confused. "Oh, Billie," she muttered, and she shook her head like she'd said those same two words a thousand times and was sick and tired of hearing them. Her blonde ponytail bounced and swayed in the last of the sunlight. "What are we going to do, baby?"

Billie slowly turned around and looked across the street at Juanita's house and then up at the darkening sky. Clarence wished he hadn't done that. He wished Billie hadn't shown him his face: the blankness of it and then, behind that blankness, a life giving up. Billie turned back around and forced his body toward the sidewalk, toward the house. "Come on, Mom," he said. "Let's go inside."

— — —

The next week at their peer-to-peer lunch, Clarence found it hard to look Billie in the eye. This didn't seem to be a problem; Billie wasn't looking at him, either. They sat there next to each other, not really together, just two people in the same place at the same time. Clarence couldn't understand how Billie managed to drag himself to school each day, much less make conversation. He knew he would have to be the one to reach out—it was his job as the mentor— but for the first time since he'd known Billie, he really and truly had nothing to say. He knew things now that he hadn't known before, and he didn't know what to do with them. It turned out that Billie's dad didn't live with him at all, that all those marks on his body came from his mother, from a woman. The woman who was supposed to take care of him, no matter what. Clarence couldn't get his mind around it, that a woman had done those things to Billie. Men were the bullies, not women. Women were supposed to protect.

He dipped his fry into the pool of ketchup he'd made on his tray, then dragged it around in circles, making curly red shapes on the plastic. He was trying to think of a way to connect. "Billie," he finally said, and he frankly didn't know where he was headed next. Billie nodded but didn't answer with his voice. "You live around here?" Billie nodded again. "Me too," said Clarence. "So maybe we could hang out sometime after school, not just for our meetings or lunches, you know, but just messing around on the playground or something. I mean, if your dad would let you. That would be cool if your dad would let you stay after school sometimes."

Billie turned his head and actually met Clarence's eyes with his. "My dad doesn't live with me. I thought I told you that."

Clarence shook his head. "I didn't know that. I thought . . . well, I thought—"

"You thought my dad did all this to me. That's what you thought, right?"

There was no use pretending. He'd seen what he'd seen. He'd wiped Billie's face with a cool wet towel. The two of them were way beyond nicey-nice chitchat. "Yeah, I guess that's what I thought. I mean, it's true. I did."

Billie didn't seem surprised. "I get you. You thought a lady couldn't do this to her kid, that only a man could do this. But you're wrong." They both fell silent. All around them, the lunch room pitched and rattled, a boat rocked by a sea of screaming children. Mrs. Danielson and two other teachers walked between tables, their arms stretched out at their sides, like they were trying to keep from tipping over. "Well, my mom, Clarence . . . she's special," Billie finally said, and he shot Clarence a devilish look, just a little bit of the old Billie, the bad Billie, the one who made Clarence feel he could survive if he had a little help.

"Billie." Clarence barely recognized his voice as it left his mouth. It was a low and serious voice. The voice of a grown-up. Maybe even a man. "I'm working on a plan. I've got your back."

"Better make it quick," Billie murmured, and then he smiled at Clarence, though his smile seemed made of wet paper, folding in on itself as soon as it appeared. "For real, though. My mom, well, I don't know. My mom is getting worse." And just like that, Billie left Clarence, left his body completely; Clarence could see it on his face. He'd traveled to his house, maybe later today, maybe a week or a month down the road. He was seeing the future, and Clarence was seeing him see it.

"I'll make it quick," Clarence answered. It was the only right answer, even if he didn't yet know how to make it so.

INTERVENTIONS

· ·

IT WAS HALLOWEEN AFTERNOON, and Mr. K still had everything out on the shelves, right in front, where the charcoal and beer huggies were in the summertime. There was candy, a few cheap costumes, and those plastic pumpkins for trick-or-treating, as if anyone in Mayfair Heights would open up their doors on Halloween, at least after dark. "Hey," Clarence said as he headed past Mr. Khabir toward the Halloween aisle. He knew that a costume was a big decision for a hero, but right now he had to work with what was available, and the Kwik-Bi sure wasn't any Walmart.

Judging by what was in front of him in the costume aisle, it looked like he would have to be a pirate, a clown, or a vampire, but none of them were right for the job. None them seemed heroic in the least, and all of them seemed way too young, now that he was in high school and a Y-boy. His other option was to be that caped guy from the movie *Scream*, but every Halloween night, packs of dudes traveled the neighborhood in that costume, popping out of alleys and doorways, tossing out screeches and howls when you least expected it. He deeply hated that *Scream* costume, and the guys who wore it.

But his mission wasn't about Halloween, or even about a costume. His mission was about Billie. And when he thought about it that way, he realized he could make the *Scream* costume work. The cape and hood would serve him well; he'd just toss the creepy melted-face mask into the trash and never look at it again. And he'd blend right into the mayhem that was Mayfair Heights on a Halloween night. No one would think twice about some kid in a black cape.

On the Halloween makeup shelf, a set of face crayons caught his eye, and he realized he wouldn't need a mask at all. He could create his own face, his very own hero face. He could be himself, only better. He picked up the costume, the crayons, and a tube of silver face paint. He walked up to the register and laid everything out in front of Mr. K at the counter.

"It is good to see you today, sir," said Mr. K. He reached out and shook Clarence's hand as if they were both grown-ups, both gentlemen. "You are looking well. It seems that things are looking up for you, no?" Clarence nodded. He wondered if Mr. K could see him balancing there on the wire. He bet he could. Mr. K had the eyes of God, after all.

"You are getting ready for the Halloween, then." Mr. K

placed the costume in a white plastic bag. "But this costume I do not like. Something about it. It is too much."

"Yeah," Clarence agreed. "But I'm just buying it for the cape. The cape's good." Mr. K seemed to like this answer.

"You will come on by tonight, and I will give you the candy. You must stop in and let me see you. I will have something special, even something for your dog."

"She's not my dog, Mr. K. I wish she was, but I just look out after her. She belongs to someone else."

Mr. K raised his shoulders, then let them fall. He sighed.

"So if I don't get by for the trick-or-treating," Clarence offered, changing the subject, "I was thinking I might come by later, you know, after you close. To help you with the floors and all. I know Halloween's a busy night for you." Clarence couldn't help but cast his eyes toward the blurry black-and-white TV while he spoke, though he knew one day he'd find the courage to hold Mr. K's gaze without looking away.

Mr. K turned his head toward the kitchen and waved at two men heading back toward the bait cooler. "You may come anytime, Clarence," he said. "Whenever your grandmother will allow it. And you don't always have to do the floors or the restocking of the shelves. Sometimes you can just stop in for tea, you know. I am your friend, not your employer."

Clarence shrugged and headed for the door. "Well, I'll

try to get back by around closing time and get those floors done. Get them bleached the way you like them. I'm spending the night with a friend tonight, right up the street. It shouldn't be a problem." He gave Mr. K a casual wave, all the while thinking: *He called me his friend. He called me his friend.*

"Be careful out there, sir," Mr. K said quietly as he opened the door, and Clarence nodded and looked back for a moment. "The Halloween night, well—you just be careful."

"Yep. I will, Mr. K." Clarence turned away, grateful that he, his dad, Johnnyprice, and Mr. K were all letting the grandmother lie be the truth, at least for now, and glad someone, tonight, would be thinking of him. He darted out the door as the store chimes sounded behind him.

He ambled down the alley behind Bedford, glad for the costume but knowing that while he planned to be a real hero tonight, not just a boy dressed up in a cape, something was missing. He stared down at the toes of his sneakers as he walked, letting his mind drift back to a warm evening in his mama's kitchen. His mama was staring down into a steaming pot, occasionally stirring it, humming something to herself, though her hum was so soft that it might have been mistaken for the whir of the ceiling fan. His father sat at the table listening to sports radio. The sports talk was of the

Redskins. The Redskins were his dad's favorite team, and as usual, his dad's favorite team was on a losing streak.

The little Clarence in his memory sat down next to his dad at his mama's table, right where he always did, on his right. He looked down at his spelling worksheet and tried to focus, but he was tired and fidgety, with a growling tummy and what his mama called the ants in his pants. Suddenly his hunger overcame him and he sprang up from the table to go check on supper's progress, knocking his dad's radio right off the table in the process. His dad froze, and the room went silent for a second or two, and then, "BOY!" his father spat, springing up from his own seat and blocking his son's path. His right arm flew up in the air, and his right hand formed a fist.

Over by the stove, Clarence's mama calmly lifted the pot and started walking toward the table. "Sit down, Rowley," she said, and Clarence watched his father's muscles quiver under his skin. But his father didn't move, and Clarence didn't move; they both just stood and watched as his mama walked, stopping an arm's length away from his dad. "Like I said," his mama said. "Sit the fuck down, Rowley," and Clarence could feel the hot steam from the pot drifting across the table. He looked into his mama's eyes and understood that at that moment, she was more powerful than his father. She was calm, but she was on fire. She was calm, but her kind of calm was dangerous. Anger. Real Anger. That was what had been missing.

His mama's love for him had tipped toward violence that evening in the kitchen, and many times Batman's devotion to his city became rage at those who wanted to destroy it. Billie's mom wanted to destroy Billie, and the Wirewalker wasn't going to allow it. Billie's words in the lunch room came back to Clarence as his mind's eye watched his dad backing away from his mama in the kitchen, the steam from the pot rising up like a wall between them. *Make it quick*, Billie'd said, and Clarence had promised. He knew he now held Billie in one hand and Mona in the other, and he could feel Mr. K's invisible hand steady there, on his shoulder. He wouldn't be alone out there in the darkness tonight. The power of these three others would guide him back along the wire, back to the light.

━ ━ ━

He sped along the edge of the woods, keeping his head down and his feet in motion. He expected to feel sick, to have his nerves attack his belly, but they didn't. He didn't know how this night was different from the other times he'd had to do a hard thing and had his stomach fight against him, but for some reason, tonight, his stomach was at peace. Maybe refusing to read an essay in school or avoiding Mr. K for so long were just cop-outs, lame ways to make sure he didn't fail. But tonight wasn't about him at all, and the memory of what lay beneath Billie's shirt had already become a wildness in his blood, a jacked-up feeling like running as fast as he could or laughing too hard or getting mad enough to punch someone. He didn't have a plan for what exactly would happen in the house, not yet, but he had something bigger than a plan. He had a mission: *Get Billie out.* And he had rage. He would know what he needed to do when he got there.

He entered the cul-de-sac and finally stopped in front of the house next to Billie's, turning away from the headlights of a car rounding the corner. He needed to find somewhere to leave himself behind, to officially make the switch to the hero. He cut into Billie's yard, sinking into shadows cast by the trees along the driveway. A little shed was right on the other side of the fence and he made a run for it, opened the door, turned sideways, and then inched into a gap between a lawn mower and a tall striped umbrella. If he stood very still, he'd have just enough room to slide the cape on over his clothes, and he didn't need any light to make up his face. All silver, with a big black *W* on his forehead: he could pull that off with his eyes closed.

The cape nearly swallowed him, and as he pulled its

massive hood forward, he could feel part of himself turn on while another turned off. He felt no fear. He had no weak thoughts, no thoughts at all, really. He pulled down the hood so it covered up his face completely, and then his world went black. Against that blackness he could see Johnnyprice and his dad counting his money at the kitchen table, Gina locking Mona in and forgetting all about her, Y grinning as he rubbed the fur between Mona's ears. He could see the open neck of Nasty as he went down in the pen. He glimpsed his mama there in front of his dad, the steaming pot in her hand, and he could feel her fierceness, her willingness to protect. And then Billie showed up. Billie with the pale blue eyes and the skin that didn't look like skin. Billie, who yelped when his own mother hugged him.

Just like that, the Wirewalker's rage caught fire, and he let it burn. He pulled back the hood a bit so he could see, and then he exited the shed and walked through the damp grass up to Billie's back door. In his left hand, he held a rag, and in his right, he held his dad's gun. He laid the rag flat against the pane of glass closest to the doorknob, like he'd seen his dad do when he locked himself out of the house. Then he quietly cracked the glass with the handle of the gun, used the rag to push the pieces out, and then, carefully, he slid his hand through the window to unlock the door.

He stepped into a laundry room that smelled like detergent and perfume. A night-light glowed in the outlet next to the dryer, and neatly folded stacks of laundry were lined up on a table on the far wall. The sound of a TV traveled to him from down the hall. He stood for a few moments, listening to it, to how normal it sounded. The sound of it almost made him think there was nothing wrong in the house, that this was just like all the clean, happy houses he'd seen on TV. But then the image of Billie's belly returned to him, and he reminded himself not to be fooled by appearances. He crept down the hallway, following the laughter from the TV until he reached the front room. He'd hoped Billie's mom would be in bed, but no matter. This was why he brought the gun. He didn't need to shoot it to make it useful.

As he made a right into the living room, Billie's mom was there, right in front of him, sitting on a red-and-white-checked sofa in front of a TV. Her back faced him, and her ponytail bounced as she laughed along with the TV show in front of her. Ice clinked in the drink in her left hand. She seemed so casual and light and free, everything Billie wasn't anymore, everything he couldn't be because of what she'd done to him. The Wirewalker felt his body fill up with heat, a heat so much thicker and hotter than the steam from his mama's pot, and he suddenly knew how it happened, how people hurt one another and then couldn't take it back. The heat needed somewhere to go, like how if he walked right over and pointed the gun at Billie's mom's head, and how if he pulled the trigger, how in that one moment the fire in him would rage, blaze out with the bullet, and then fizzle. Go out. But how after that moment of release, he'd have to live with what he'd done, every single day. Like Billie's mom. Like his own father.

He tiptoed closer and could see that Billie was stretched out lengthwise, his head in his mother's lap. With her right hand, she stroked his hair as she watched the program, and the Wirewalker thought Billie must be asleep. But when he took a few steps forward, he saw that Billie wasn't sleeping at all. Billie's eyes were wide open, but he wasn't looking at the television, or even at the Wirewalker; he was looking at his mother, and he was smiling. Clarence had never seen Billie smile. He'd never even imagined Billie happy.

Suddenly Billie saw the Wirewalker—and the gun—and his eyes flashed with anger and fear and a message that said: *No! Not like this! This isn't what I fucking asked for!*

NO! Billie mouthed as his mom took another sip of her drink. *NO!* he said with eyes that were now full of their own fire.

Straighten up on the wire, Clarence. . . . Steady now, he heard Mr. K's voice say from somewhere within him. *Find your balance and then step away. Step away, sir. Do it now.* Clarence started taking small steps backward: one, two, three, four, five. He was grateful for the noise of the television, drowning out any other noise in the room. As he kept backing up and the fire in him weakened, he could feel Mona waiting for him at Gina's, her blue eyes blinking. Who would have protected her if he'd actually pulled the trigger? What would he have destroyed—of Mona, of Billie, even of Mr. K—if he'd let the fire take what it wanted?

— — —

Once outside Billie's house, he stopped for a moment, tossed the gun into the hedge between houses, and ran. He took off toward the woods, toward the alleys that would lead him back to Gina's shed, whizzing along the edge of Stonewall Jackson's baseball field and finally slipping into the alley behind Bedford. Here he stopped, gulped air, and then heard sirens whining off in the distance. A different decision at Billie's might have meant that those sirens were coming for him, and a broken boy in pieces under a wire couldn't save anyone. But more important: Billie didn't want to be saved, at least not like that. As usual, life was way more complicated than even the Wirewalker could have imagined.

He found himself lingering in the alley as this knowledge settled in, bogging him down. In school he'd always learned that knowledge was a kind of freedom, but it was clear that knowledge could just as easily become a burden. It seemed that the more he knew about life, the harder life became. And he didn't want to go back to the shed. He didn't want to be alone, especially not tonight.

Where he'd normally make a right into the woods, toward the shed, he instead made a U-turn and walked back the way he'd come, back in the direction of the Kwik-Bi. He vaguely remembered saying something to Mr. K about doing his floors at the end of the night, but he was in no shape to see Mr. K. Mr. K would know. Everything. Mr. K would see right through him with his eyes of God.

The Kwik-Bi's parking lot was packed with cars and people—some in full costume, some simply wearing masks or hats, and some just dressed for a regular old weekend night. A few little kids danced around here and there, waving glow sticks and throwing candy at each other. While Clarence normally avoided crowds, tonight he found that he wanted to sink into the thick of the laughter and hollering. These were the sounds of life, not unlike the sounds in the box-of-gray, back when things were good.

He knew it was late, and that on Halloween, his mama would have never let him be out on the streets after dark. But he'd been a kid with a mama back then, and his mama was long gone. Helpless Itty was gone. Tonight his face was painted, he was wrapped in the Wirewalker's cape, and he'd considered holding a gun to a bad woman's head. Though his plan had been flawed, and though he wasn't anything close to a superhero—or even a man—he now knew he had a badass living somewhere deep inside him. Tonight he would go where he damn well pleased.

As he entered the crowd in the parking lot, he pulled himself deep into the cape again, hoping to go unnoticed. There was always the chance that his dad and Johnnyprice would be out and about, and he hoped to look like just another kid out on Halloween night, wearing a *Scream* cape, blending in. He glanced across the crowd, over at the Kwik-Bi's glass door, and Mr. K was just standing there, shimmering for a moment in the white fluorescent light. From that distance, he looked like an angel, some magical being lit up from within, and as he lowered the blinds on the door, closing up for the night, Clarence thought, *Thank you*, and then kept on walking.

Y was holding court with his boys over on the left, on the Bedford side of the parking lot, and for a moment Clarence thought about splitting. He couldn't handle Y tonight, and he didn't want to make another stupid move, like the one he'd made with Billie. But then he caught sight of Demario on the other side of the parking lot, and he remembered the offer he'd made in the Chicken Hut. Maybe after a couple of nights of decent sleep, he'd be able to see what should happen next, but regardless, this much he knew: tonight he wouldn't be going back to the box-of-gray, and he wouldn't be going back to the shed unless he had to. If he could find a way out—even for a night—he was going to take it.

Beyond him, over on his right, Demario was ambling toward a gleaming black car on the far right side of the parking lot, directly opposite Y, and he took his time, never once looking over at his brother. Clarence remembered this car from the parking lot at school, but whenever Clarence saw Demario around the neighborhood, he was always riding shotgun in Y's Lexus. "Demario!" he finally yelled when he knew he was out of earshot of Y. "Wait up! Hey, wait up!" He knew he was taking a chance. Demario was Y's brother. But Demario didn't act like Y or talk smack like Y. Demario was different, and he was Clarence's only shot at the moment.

Clarence glanced across the parking lot at Y, who was lost in his little world of bullshit and boys, and then he headed in the opposite direction.

"'Sup, Clarence?" Demario asked as Clarence approached the car's driver's-side window and shrugged.

"How'd you recognize me?"

Demario shook his head. "Brah. I know your voice. I know your size. I know how you move; I pay attention. It's my job." Clarence didn't know what to say next, so he said nothing. "So, what brings you out tonight, Clarence? Seems like you've been lying low lately. This party here, well, it sure as shit isn't lying low."

Clarence nodded. He knew he'd taken a risk by coming.

"Well . . ." Clarence moved closer to Demario and then turned his back to the crowd. "I've been thinking about what you said that day in the Chicken Hut, about crashing at your place, you know, taking a break from the assholes. I thought I might take you up on it. I mean, if the offer still stands. I could really, really use a break."

Demario nodded, then cast his eyes out over the parking lot, back toward where Y stood, holding court. "Hop into the car, brah. Go on and get in. This isn't the right place to have this conversation."

Clarence did as told, but for a moment, as he settled into the passenger seat, he reconsidered his decision. What did he actually know about Demario? What if the whole decent guy thing was an act? The reality, though, was that if he didn't stay in the shed, there was nowhere else to go. Gina had taken up with Y, so her house wasn't safe. And Ms. Moffett and Mr. K: well, they believed in him. He needed that belief. He wasn't ready to lose it. For now Demario was all he had.

Demario started the car and eased out of the parking lot, taking a right, away from Bedford Street. As Clarence watched Halloween winding down outside his window, he wondered what lay in store for him tonight. Then next week. Then the week after that.

"You ever been out of the neighborhood?" Demario asked as the scenery outside the car started to change. Many of the houses' little front yards were neatly tended now, streets were brightly lit, and in the glowing squares of the houses' windows, Clarence caught glimpses of lamps on tables, colored paint on walls that were decorated with pictures, home after home where people seemed to be living, not just surviving. Many of the porches were still decorated with lit jack-o'-lanterns, though according to Clarence's watch, it was well after midnight. In Mayfair Heights, no one put out real Halloween pumpkins anymore. Once darkness fell, they'd only end up smashed into bits in the street or up against the side of somebody's house.

"Yeah. I've been out of the Heights." He answered Demario without looking away from the window. "I took the bus a while back, and I stayed on it for as far as it would go. And then I rode again. I've been on the bus lots of times before, and I'd never done that, but that day I did it twice. For some reason I just kept on riding."

"Ahhh. You finally heard the call, didn't you? I was a little bit older than you are when I first heard it, but I heard it, all right. Here." Demario closed his right hand into a fist and thumped it against the part of his chest that covered his heart. Clarence turned his head and studied his Big Boy's profile. Who was this guy? Was he for real?

"So, we going to your place?" Clarence asked, changing the subject. He figured Demario was just laying down bullshit, trying to earn his trust, like Johnnyprice had so many times. He also figured they'd been driving a long time. He didn't recognize the landmarks, or even the look of the place. Demario turned down the radio, and Clarence knew that meant something. It all made him nervous.

"Well, I want you to see something. That's all. We'll go back to my place after that." Soon, the long stretch of changing neighborhoods opened up onto wide busy streets surrounded by tall glass buildings, rising up as far as Clarence's eyes could see. "Where are we?" he called back as he hung his head out of the window. This place looked a lot like Gotham from his Batman movies, or like the cities in his dad's cop shows. He'd never seen a place like this in person, not even on his bus ride out of Mayfair Heights.

"Well, we're downtown now. This is the heart of the city." Soon Demario pulled the car over, parking it next to the curb. "Go ahead and get out," he instructed. "Let's take a walk." As they made their way down the street, they passed people who were right around Demario's age, Clarence guessed, or maybe a little bit older. Some of them walked arm in arm, making chains of four or five that ran the width of the sidewalk. Clarence stayed close to Demario, not wanting a confrontation, but each time they'd get close to another wall of locked arms, those arms would suddenly drop, giving them room to pass. "Happy Halloween," a girl dressed like a sexy black cat giggled to Clarence as she stepped back, out of his way. "I love the silver face. *Terminator* meets *Scream*, right?"

Clarence didn't answer. Between Mayfair Heights and here, so much had changed so quickly. He'd completely forgotten his silver face. His memory of himself—in Billie's shed, getting ready to rescue him—was real. He knew that. But this street, these people, the gleaming walls of windows all around him—they were real too. He spun back around to look at the girl, who now walked backward, away from him, trying not to trip. She waved at him, and without stopping to think better of it, he waved back.

"Hey. Come on over here." He felt Demario's hand on his shoulder. "I want you to see something." Clarence followed him toward a tall sprawling set of steps. At their top sat a massive brick building filled with row after row of windows made of mirrors. "There," Demario said as they reached the front. He pointed to the words etched into stone above the doors. "Read that, and tell me what it says."

"Jefferson State University, Logan Hall. So this is a college or something?"

Demario nodded, keeping his eyes on the sign. "I plan to be here in the fall," he said. "I've got the grades, you know. And from what I've heard, you've got the grades too, brah."

Clarence looked back up at the sign and then over at Demario, Y's brother. His Big Boy. The dude who'd left a burn in the palm of his hand. He sat down on the steps and pulled the hood of the cape back, away from his face. He was suddenly hot and confused and very, very tired.

"Hey. Listen." Demario sat down next to him and fist-bumped his shoulder. "Let's go ahead home. I'll make up the sofa for you. We can talk more in the morning." Clarence nodded, then trailed along behind Demario, back to the car. What a crazy-assed day. The rescue plan, the Wirewalker, the sadness of walking away from Billie, and now this—whatever it was—with Demario. Nothing today had gone as planned, but it had gone. Somewhere. Maybe, come morning, he'd understand where he was.

CONFESSIONS

••

CLARENCE AWOKE TO BRIGHT light and a wet tickle along the back of his right hand. Where was he, and why was someone licking his hand? He opened his eyes and right there, next to the sofa, sat an enormous pit bull in a pink metal-studded collar. This pit was much bigger than Nasty or Black and was the color of the honey his mama used to put in her tea. Its golden eyes stared back at him, and he remembered where he was. He'd spent the night at Demario's, so this must be the dog Y'd mentioned in front of Gina's that afternoon, right after he'd asked about Mona. Dark bloody flashes of the fight night between Black and Nasty passed in front of Clarence's eyes. This wasn't good. This couldn't be good.

The pit kept staring, and then it was suddenly right up on him, its tongue slurping the back of his hand again, and then his forearm, and then Clarence felt its front paws land on his chest as its dripping tongue cut a straight line from the tip of his chin to the center of his forehead. He was terrified, but that wasn't all of it. He could also hear himself giggling. Even his fear couldn't seem to stop him. The laughter came on its own, like it did with Mona, and the fact that his face might be eaten at any moment just didn't feel as real as that laughter.

He scrunched his eyes shut and tried to roll over, toward the back of the sofa, and then he heard Demario's voice above him. "Come on, now. Let Clarence alone for a minute, girl." Clarence opened his eyes and looked up at Demario, who was pulling the dog back by its collar. "Well, I see you've met my dog, then. What do you think of her?" Clarence wasn't sure what Demario was asking, so he tried to answer the way he thought he should, by saying something Johnnyprice or Y would want to hear about one of their fight dogs.

"Well, she's big as shit, so I guess she kicks ass in the pen." Clarence felt sick after he said this. He didn't want to think about any dog in a fighting pen ever again.

Above him, Demario let go of the dog's collar and raised his hands in the air. "Oh no, brah . . . this is no fight dog. This here is my baby girl—it's her name, and it's exactly what she is. I don't fight dogs. That's all my brother." Clarence understood but found himself baffled. There were so many different pieces of Demario. How did they all fit together?

"So I'm going to put Babygirl in my bedroom for a minute, let her calm down. She just loves people so much, and she doesn't know her own strength. You and me—we need to talk." Clarence watched as Demario and his dog walked away down the hall. He could see that Babygirl was Demario's Mona, and he wondered if she helped Demario stay balanced on his personal wire, like Mona did him.

Demario showed back up in the living room, carrying toast and two glasses of orange juice. "How about some eggs?" he asked as he handed Clarence a napkin. Clarence nodded. After his days and nights alone with bags of Chuckie's in the shed, the offer of a homemade breakfast sounded like heaven.

They ate the eggs at the kitchen table, proper style. Clarence couldn't stop looking around at all of the details of Demario's life, a life he'd made for himself, all by himself. He'd obviously been living in this apartment, without Y or anyone else, for quite a while. How could he manage a life like this plus the grades that would get him into college? Demario seemed to be reading Clarence's mind. "Well, we've been together almost three months, brah. You trust me yet?" Demario crossed his thick arms over his chest, like he always did. "Nah, that's not a fair question. You don't have to trust me. You probably shouldn't." Demario gulped his orange juice, and Clarence waited. He was here because he'd asked to be. All he could do was wait.

"But you and me, Clarence"—he started back in while

chomping his toast down to its crusts—"we've got a lot in common. We started in this biz at about the same age. I was ten, you were eleven, but we were both just little men. Kids." Demario paused. His eyes met Clarence's and he nodded, just slightly. Clarence nodded back. "Then, after middle school, you know, I just couldn't see a point in more schooling. I was making money with Y, and at that time, I thought that was all life was: money or no money. And I couldn't see any harm in what Y was doing, I mean, it's what everyone seemed to be doing, right? Whether they were buying or selling or were hooked up with or related to someone who was buying or selling, there was hardly anyone I knew, other than old folks, who wasn't involved in drugs in some way. So it just seemed natural to do what I'd been doing for years. Why not make a buck from someone who wants nothing more than to give their money to you?"

Clarence drank down the rest of his orange juice and nodded again. He understood. He'd been doing the same kind of thinking lately. Why not make a buck from a grown-up who didn't want it anymore?

"See my ma, brah—she had a taste for the crack. That's how Y got started, you know, running for her dealer, her boyfriend. And then her boyfriend just ditched her, like dealers do. Kicked us out, changed the locks. I mean, the crack had aged her something awful, and she weighed next to nothing.

She looked like shit, and she was bat-shit nuts most of the time. A typical crackhead, and to her boyfriend she was a liability. So she and Y and me ended up in a little efficiency over on the east side of the boulevard, and Y started dealing and I—I started running for my brother. Y paid the rent, kept the lights on, made sure we got fed. And Y kept my ma in line by keeping her high."

Demario got up and walked over to the fridge. He pulled out the carton of orange juice, brought it back to the table, plunked it down in front of Clarence, and then just stood there, facing the kitchen. "But then one night, when Y and I were both out, she OD'd. It was bound to happen. And just like that, she was gone, and what was left of my big brother went with her. So on one hand, Y has taken care of me for most of my whole life. On the other hand, he used me—his kid brother—and he killed our mother, and then he completely shut down, just froze right over. He started in with the dogs, and then the girls, and let me tell you—that shit isn't just for the money. He enjoys their pain. He enjoys watching them suffer." Demario walked back over to his chair and sat down in front of Clarence. "So you know, brah? Maybe he did what he had to do at the time, and maybe I did too. But that time will be over, come graduation. I went back to school. I'm on my way out. And he knows it." Clarence sat quietly for a moment, trying to process what he'd heard.

"So why did you take me on, then, if you knew you were on your way out?" Demario's graduation was months away, but Clarence didn't like the idea of dealing with Y on his own. He hadn't let himself be burned for Y. He'd let himself be burned for Demario.

"Well, I did what I needed to do at the time, I guess. And I'm doing what I need to do now." Demario's pale-brown eyes softened for a moment. "Truth is: I didn't expect you, Clarence. I didn't expect you to be so much like me."

Clarence nodded. He hadn't expected it either. "So will he hurt you or something, after you graduate and leave the business?"

Demario shrugged. "Shit, brah. He's already plenty pissed. Nothing to do now but watch my back and wait."

— — —

Clarence left Demario's apartment and followed Tompkins, then Womack, then Carlton back to Bedford Street. When he finally hit the Kwik-Bi parking lot, he cut across it at an angle, moving toward Mr. K, who was outside, holding a big garbage bag and cleaning up Halloween night's mess. "Hey," Clarence said as he walked up behind Mr. K and placed a hand on his shoulder. "Let me help you with that."

Mr. K lifted his hands toward the sky, glancing around the parking lot and shaking his head. "These people . . .

where is the respect?" he asked out loud, though Clarence knew he didn't expect an answer. Clarence was glad Mr. K didn't know that he'd been one of those people last night, if only for a few minutes. He was glad that, so far, there was a lot Mr. K didn't know about him.

A box of trash bags sat over on the sidewalk, and Clarence pulled out a bag and started working. "Sorry I couldn't get by last night," he offered, as side by side he and Mr. K moved across the parking lot, chatting here and there to pass the time. There was no way his dad and Johnnyprice would be stirring at this hour, not on the morning after Halloween, so they wouldn't be heading up to the Kwik-Bi anytime soon for their coffee. For the moment he was free to be here, out in the open, helping his friend.

He and Mr. K worked quietly for a while, and then Mr. K stopped. "You are truly still at your grandmother's then, Clarence?" he asked. Clarence had known this question was coming. It was just a matter of time. With a man like Mr. K, a lie could only last so long.

"Sort of," he answered. "It's a long story."

Mr. K stopped and turned his face up to the unbroken blue sky. "The stories with you, sir . . . they are always the long stories that are somehow, finally, left untold. Is this not true?"

Clarence dropped a beer can into his trash bag. He

shrugged. "Yeah. It's true, I guess. But I don't think there's much I can do about it. Not yet." Mr. K seemed to accept this, and together they moved slowly around the parking lot: a little cleaning up and a little conversation. Clarence's mind kept traveling back to Billie, the boy who he'd thought wanted to be rescued but who didn't, in the end. What was he supposed to do about someone like Billie? How could he help if Billie wouldn't let him?

Soon the parking lot was clean, and it was time to carry the trash bags around to the dumpster on the side of the building. On their last trip over, Clarence just started talking. It wasn't like he'd planned on it, but it wasn't like he hadn't, either. It was just happening, and he was letting it happen. "Okay, so there's this kid I know, Mr. K, and he's kind of a friend. I mean, I guess he's a friend. I care about him, you know; I'm actually his high school mentor. He's in middle school at Stonewall Jackson, where I used to go. So I guess you could say he's a friend." Mr. K tossed his two bags into the dumpster, and Clarence did the same, all the while wondering why, with Mr. K, he always said way too much but, in the end, never seemed to say a thing.

Mr. K gently placed his hand just under Clarence's elbow, and guided him to the metal bench in front of the store. "I locked the store's door in order to properly clean the parking lot, and if the people should come, I will certainly let them in. But for now let us sit outside in the sunlight awhile. It is so warm for the first of November! We should enjoy it together before it passes, no?" Clarence sat down on the bench, squinting into the sun, and Mr. K followed.

"This friend, Clarence. You were saying?" Mr. K turned his tinted glasses up toward the sky.

"Well, this kid, you know—things aren't so good for him at home. He gets hurt, is what I mean. He gets hurt a lot, and really bad, actually. So I decided I would rescue him, you know, just plan it all out and then suddenly show up late at night and just save him, like in the movies. Only, he didn't want to be rescued. He wouldn't come with me, which is probably for the best because I didn't have much of a plan after that. But I can't stop thinking about him, about what might happen next."

Mr. K's glasses glittered gold in the sunlight. "And where would you have taken him, then, had he come with you, Clarence? Would you have taken him back to your grandmother's, wherever that may be?"

Clarence sat, silent, letting the moment be what the moment was. He'd stepped over a line, given away too much, but it was what he'd wanted, somehow. He'd wanted to open that door, and now he'd have to walk right through it. He paused. Inhaled. Exhaled. Spoke. "Well, I'm not actually staying at my grandmother's, Mr. K." That was it. There it was. Mr. K gathered his hands in his lap and sighed.

"Well . . . your father finally told me as much," he said quietly. "He has come here and we have spoken several times, without his friend. Early last night, when he stopped in and I mentioned your grandmother again, he said that you have no grandparents here in Jackson City. And so here we are, the three of us, free of that lie. He is missing you, Clarence, and he is worrying about you very much. As am I, if I must be honest."

Clarence appreciated Mr. K's words, but he had no words to offer in return. Soon he would, maybe, but not now. "Well, I've got to go now, take care of that dog I keep telling you about. But we'll talk again soon, Mr. K. I promise. I heard what you said. I just don't know what to say back yet." With this, he got up and started walking away from Mr. K, back toward Bedford.

"Clarence!" Mr. K called out from behind him, and Clarence turned around and faced him. "As for your friend, that boy, you must wait. You cannot make him be ready for change. He must be ready himself, and if that day should come, you will let me know, and we will see, together, what is possible."

— — —

He took the walk to the park slowly, not wanting to face Y, not even wanting the money he'd take home later, after the run. He knew he'd started running for Y to get even with his dad and Johnnyprice, but today that desire seemed distant. Today, there was no life behind it. How much would it take for the three of them to ever be even? Was there even such a thing as "even"? He nodded as the porch-hangers called and cooed, but his mind was elsewhere. Then, as always, he briefly knocked on the park's bathroom door—one, two, three, four times—but when it opened, revealing Y's smug little face, Clarence felt nothing. He walked slowly away from the park, making his first drop, and then his second, and then on the way to his third, he really, seriously considered just not showing up. But he knew he didn't have the energy or the balls to deal with Y afterward, so he knocked on the door and waited, hoping that for once, no one would answer.

Instead, for the first time in the almost three years he'd been running, a kid opened the door. This wasn't a kid like him; this was a tiny kid in a sagging diaper and nothing else. The lower half of her face was covered in something dried up and brown, making her look like she had a beard. Behind her, an older girl, maybe eight or nine, walked toward the door with some balled-up money in her fist. "Here," she said, glancing back over her shoulder. "Just take it before she wakes up, okay?" The left side of the girl's face was the yellowish green of a week-old bruise, and Clarence felt the fire catch in his belly, like it had with Billie. He took the money and gave the girl the baggie, but he found it impossible to step away.

"Listen—can I help you or something? Do you maybe need some help?" The older girl cocked her head to the side, like a bird, and then she spat out a quiet bitter little laugh. Clarence recognized this laugh. It sounded just like Billie's had that afternoon, when they'd first met in the cafeteria. "*You're* going to help me?" the girl mocked, putting her hand on her hip. "Like how? By teaching me how to run crack?"

Clarence backed away from the door and could feel himself spinning, though his feet were still flat on the porch beneath him. This was the moment. This was what it felt like. The wire had finally snapped, and he was falling.

The last of the daylight leaked through the curtains, and Clarence lay on his back, on Demario's sofa, studying the ceiling. Babygirl stretched out beside him on the floor, licking his fingers. He knew that the Wirewalker had fallen, but if the Wirewalker was gone, who was left? It had been hard to walk the wire, but it felt important, like it mattered. He didn't want to go back to just being Clarence Feather. Clarence Feather didn't feel like anything.

He sat up on the sofa and wrapped his arms around his pillow, playing back what Mr. K had told him, that morning, about his father. His dad missed him. His dad was worried. As he stared at the dimly lit wall above the TV, he felt himself tumbling back in time, and before long, he was watching his father scoop him up in his arms, sunlight glinting in his fiery hair. Clarence didn't know where they were, or when, but again and again he watched himself be lifted and held, and then Clarence smelled him. Cigarettes plus a mellow tang like a just-mowed lawn. And then right there, in the small of his back, he could feel his father's hand, warm and sure, like Mr. K's, and he could hear, flittering in like wind, the music of his mama's laughter.

Clarence pulled the middle cushion up off the sofa and pulled out the black cape. He stared at it for a minute or two and then stood, slipped it on, checked his jeans pocket for the key Demario had left him, and was gone.

— — —

The lights were on in the kitchen window, and he crouched behind a clump of bushes so as not to be seen. It was a cool but comfortable night, and the kitchen window sat half open as his dad and Johnnyprice carried on at the kitchen table, drinking and bullshitting and listening to music instead of sports radio. His dad had pointed a gun at Johnnyprice, and they were already fast friends again. So typical. And to make it worse, the two of them only listened to music when things were good, and there had been little music since his mama's murder. From his spot in the bushes, Clarence could see the dark square of what used to be his bedroom window, and he couldn't help but wonder if life was easier for them now that he was gone.

Inside, the radio deejay announced a song by Teddy Pendergrass, something he'd heard his dad call "fuck me" music when he was deep in the drink. The bottom of a chair scraped the floor as one of the men got up, thunked over to the refrigerator, pulled something out, and then thunked back to the table. Next came the metal-on-glass clank of a bottle opener, the silence of each man drinking, the music shimmying like a porch-hanging girl, Teddy whispering about what he planned to do aaaalll night long, and Johnnyprice's voice agreeing with him in low groans, saying, "Yeah, yeah . . . you know that's right."

Yes. They were happier without him. Nothing could be clearer. But then the music stopped.

"Why'd you turn down Teddy P?" he heard Johnnyprice ask. "I was feeling it, Rowley. For the first time in forever, I was feeling a little bit good." Without the whine and moan of the music to fill it up, the night seemed as silent as a graveyard. Clarence was certain they could hear his sniffling, or the creaking of branches as he shifted positions behind the bush.

"I just miss them," he heard his father suddenly admit. "I miss them both. And I swear to Jesus, I can't even get drunk anymore. I drink and I drink, and there's just nothing." His father paused. "There's no relief from it, Johnnyprice. I didn't know how to love either of them, and now they're both gone."

"I know," Johnnyprice grumbled. "I've been around awhile, by the way." Clarence heard a chair squeak against linoleum again, like it was being pushed or pulled. One of them was moving closer to—or farther away from—the other one. Then nothing. Silence. The deafening sound of his own breathing.

By and by Johnnyprice started the conversation back up. "So, how about my new dogs, right?"

"Didn't know about any new dogs." Clarence could hear the agitation in his dad's voice. Once more Johnnyprice had cut him off, told him how things were going to be without ever saying a word. Both men quieted. And then came

Johnnyprice's voice, as carefree as the Fourth of July.

"Well, that punk Y and me—and believe me, I know this is going to sound crazy, Rowley—but we had a little meeting, and we've come to an agreement." A chair scraping hard against the floor, feet thudding, the refrigerator door opening again. Someone opening the back door, probably going out on the porch to take a piss. To Clarence, it was clear that his dad had left the room right when Johnnyprice was about to break some kind of news about Y, and this meant something. His dad was saying something to Johnnyprice without saying it, using Johnnyprice's own style against him. He was telling Johnnyprice that he didn't give a shit about his news, without even opening his mouth.

Johnnyprice just waited, or so it seemed. Time passed silently. When Clarence's dad finally got back to the table, Johnnyprice picked right up, like his dad had never walked away. "Well, you're not going to believe this, man, but Y and I are going to team up, see if working together might be better than fighting each other for business all the time. Two heads better than one and all that. Partner up for a while and see if both of us might get something out of the whole thing."

He heard his dad huff like he was exhaling a mouthful of smoke. "Yeah, I know what a partnership is, asshole. Thanks for saying it fifteen different ways. But maybe you didn't hear me before, when I was talking about my family, you know, the *ones who are gone.*" Meanwhile, Clarence was trying to get his head around what had just been said. Y and Johnnyprice. Together. A shiver ran through his body that had nothing to do with the autumn wind. "But enough about me. Who gives a shit about me? What I can tell you, though, is that that Y's a straight-up prick. I hate him, even hate the looks of him. But you won't listen to me anyway. This is your game, not mine." A pause. Lips smacking. A loud wet belch. Someone turning the radio back on and changing the channel. "So, are you two going in on everything, then? The crack and the dogs? Sharing resources?"

And with those words, the mood in the room shifted just a bit. By showing just a little bit of interest, Clarence's dad had admitted who was in control, like he knew he had to. "Well, may as well," Johnnyprice answered casually. "Kid has a hell of a lot of resources, and a hell of a lot of gumption." Clarence pictured Johnnyprice leaning back in his chair, maybe putting his feet up on the table. "The way I see it is, I follow the money, or I start looking for another line of work. It's as simple as that."

"Well. Speaking of work." Clarence's dad's voice went hushed and low. Clarence inched up closer to the window, so as to hear him over the radio. "Ran into Benny Jefferson the other day. He's got some daywork coming up. Don't know what the job is, but I figure I'll look into it. I've got to do something. It's no good sitting around, doing a shitload of nothing. When the drinking stops helping, you know you've got problems."

The music stopped, and a man's husky voice came through the radio, saying that the next caller would win a free shrimp dinner at Sharla's Ocean Feast Restaurant, which was open until eleven on weekends. Next came Johnnyprice's voice, cocky and sure as it ever was. "You do what you have to, Rowley, and so do I. Right now I'm thinking about the new dogs I bought from those Mexicans. They kicked some ass at the fight this weekend, am I right?" Clarence imagined that his dad had nodded, because Johnnyprice went right on running his mouth. The usual. "Well, turns out Y has this training compound on the other side of those woods behind the school, you know, way back where those old warehouses are."

"Way the hell back there? Yeah, I know where you're talking about."

"Maybe you remember, there used be some kind of manufacturing operation making I-don't-know-what there, way back in the day. Nothing there anymore, been vacant forever and going to shit. But Y has some kind of connections, don't know with who, and this could mean some serious business, all in all."

Clarence's dad fake-coughed, which meant he didn't really believe what he was hearing, or that he didn't like it. Clarence pictured Johnnyprice nodding and picking at his teeth with his thumbnail, like he did when he was coming up with the next thing to say.

From his spot behind the bush, Clarence felt himself leaving the men's conversation, though his body hadn't moved. Johnnyprice and Y. Together. All he could hear now, over and over, was "a training compound beyond the woods." He closed his eyes and found himself back at the fight, watching Black open Nasty's throat with his grinding jaws, and then he saw Mona, then Babygirl, and then he saw the two of them tangled up in a fighting pen, soaked in blood. A fire sparked in his belly, and for an instant, as he crept back out of the bushes, he stopped and considered what to do about that fire. Then he started walking.

THE EDGE OF THE WOODS

•••

ONCE BACK ON THE street, Clarence tried to focus
on a single piece of what he'd heard under his dad's window.
He kept his mind away from the news about Johnnyprice
teaming up with Y, and he tried not to think about how sad
his dad was, how lost. How lonely. He'd already made his
mind up about where he was headed, and he stuck to the
alleys as always, dodging the occasional streetlight, disappearing into unlit corners, sinking into a groove. In the
dark cave of the cape, his senses bucked and kicked like
they'd just been born and had never been used. He could
smell—almost taste—old meat rotting in a trash can, sour
milk, leaves piled up against the fence in someone's backyard, spilled gasoline. He could hear the padded feet of a cat
crossing the alley behind him, then the flutter of wings as
a bird rose to safety. Over to his left, a can clattered, tossed
by the wind into the side of a garage. And in front of him,
the world unfolded through the small opening in his hood,
a world reduced to shapes and shadows. Cubes, circles, cyl-

inders, spirals all blurred into silvers, golds, and grays as the alley wound in and out of streetlight. The fire in him flickered and danced along the edges of his senses, making them brighter and sharper, making him more alive.

Before long, he found himself behind Stonewall Jackson, traveling right along the edge of the woods. If he followed that line far enough, he'd hit the dead end of Billie's street, and for a moment he was drawn to the unfinished business in that perfect little house. But that moment was fleeting. Mr. K was right. There was but so much he could do for Billie right now. But on the other side of those woods there were warehouses and dogs, dogs not so different from Mona or Babygirl. What was happening to those dogs out there, where no one could even hear them howl? What if there was something he could do to help?

He traveled a long way through unknown territory: yard to yard, over fences and alleys, using the line of the woods as a guide on his left. He sped forward in the moonlight, his cape a dark billowing cloud around his body. Finally the trees started to thin, and as they did, the neighborhood began to change. Streets lined with houses and cars became emptier and darker, just a few boarded-up buildings here and there and hardly any streetlights. Eventually a cluster of brick buildings emerged in the distance on the left, looking like it had been lost to the world for a long, long time.

As Clarence got closer, he could see that waist-high weeds brushed the sills of many of the broken windows. The buildings themselves were covered with words and symbols, most of which he'd seen before around Mayfair Heights, but a series of huge red *Y*s covering the other graffiti meant Y had claimed the whole place for himself.

He was in the right place.

An eerie quiet hung over the complex, nothing moving but Clarence's feet, heartbeat, and the heaving lungs in his rib cage. The wind had died down to nothing, and each of his steps echoed between buildings as he moved past one dark shell after another toward the back of the complex, near the woods. As he got closer to the last building, he heard voices, the clanking of metal on metal, and the occasional high-pitched whine of a dog. This warehouse seemed abandoned like all the others he'd passed, but in the window on the right, shards of light cut through tattered drapes. He slid down along the building's right side, so as not to be seen by anyone coming or going, and this angle gave him a clear view of the tall wooden fence built out from the back wall, extending all the way to the woods' edge.

The fence was even taller than the chain-link one around Gina's house, and he knew that there were dogs in that yard, and maybe people. He took a deep breath, then sank to the ground and slunk like an animal around the fence, looking for a gap that might give him a view of the yard. And then he heard Y's slithery voice, telling someone what to do next. Clarence felt along the back of the fence until he found a spot over on the far corner where the boards were slightly bowed, providing a narrow gap with a decent view of the yard. Inside the yard, spotlights tossed white light onto a concrete square that stretched all the way from the warehouse's back door to each of the wooden fences. On one side of the concrete, there was a row of six small crates, three of which held dogs, three of which were empty. The crated dogs had just enough room to stand or lie down, but not enough room to turn. Two of them stood, hunched over, chains as thick as Clarence's thighs pushing down on their shoulders so that their chins nearly grazed the ground.

Clarence could see the pink of their tongues as they panted, and he thought of Mona's sloppy, gaping smile. And then he saw the dogs' ribs. He could as much as count each one, they stood out so clearly against the thin layer of skin that covered them. *The dogs are starving*, he thought, and then he realized that if they were starving, they'd be desperate for food, and if they were desperate for food, they'd be more inclined to kill a dog they might be able to eat. He suddenly felt dizzy, and he put his hand out against the fence to steady himself while keeping one eye on the yard.

Another dog, mainly white, lay on its side in the third

pen. Its eyes were closed, and its mouth hung open, sucking at air like the others. Beneath its mouth, its neck and chest were raw meat, and Clarence thought of the plastic-wrapped packages of hamburger his mama used to bring home, and the watery blood that pooled up in the corners of the Styrofoam tray. He pulled his right eye back from the gap and struggled for breath. He couldn't get sick now, though his body wanted to, so he focused on his breathing, telling his stomach to calm itself down. In front of him, in the yard, he heard Y say, "Remember, the trick is to really piss them off," and Clarence moved his right eye back to the gap, looking over at the other side of the yard, where two pits were bound by their necks to a thick metal post. Like the pits in the cages, their shoulders were thickly muscled, but their ribs made curved bony shapes against their bodies, like injured wings trying to unfold.

Y stood behind his white dog, Black, the one that had killed Johnnyprice's Nasty just a few months back. A chubby hunched-over Y-boy stood behind one of the dogs, and both he and Y lit cigarettes and started smoking, pulling hard so that the red-hot cherries glowed bright between their fingers. They smoked silently while the dogs fought against the chains, pulling so hard on the pole that Clarence thought they might lift it right out of the cement. And then Y nodded, and he and the chubby kid leaned over and pressed the glowing cherries of their cigarettes hard into the dogs' haunches, applying more and more pressure as the animals flailed. Each dog was fully muzzled, but frantic muffled cries escaped from their mouths, rising into the dead air of the compound, where no one would hear them. The chubby Y-boy took a couple of quick steps back, like he was having second thoughts.

"Lean into it, man," Y instructed, and the boy did as he was told, but he turned his head away from the dog's suffering. "I know this is hard," Y said gently, suddenly using the voice of a parent with a child. "But the madder they get, the better they fight. Trust me. You know I'm right." With this, Y glanced back at a younger boy, about Clarence's age, huddled over by the cages. "Go on inside and get Gina," he told him. "She's got the bait. It's time to have some fun." In front of Y, the back half of Black's body thrashed, but Y didn't look down and he didn't lift the cigarette. It was like he'd forgotten there was a dog there at all and was just chatting now, shooting the shit. "Hey, and tell Gina to bring me a beer, why don't you."

On the other side of the fence, Clarence's whole body went up in flames. This was the same heat that had led him to Billie's house and begged him to ram the gun up against Billie's mom's head. He knew the fire was rage, but he had no gun tonight; he had nothing but his own tiny body covered in thin black fabric. There was nothing he could do as he watched Gina follow the boy back down the stairs, holding a beer in one hand and Babygirl, on a lead, in the other. He could only swallow and swallow, trying to force the rage back down into his belly. He couldn't let it out: he couldn't scream; he couldn't pummel the fence with his fists. He couldn't do anything but bear witness. He'd brought himself to this awful place, and there'd be no way to make a difference if he lost his shit.

Gina was in the middle of the yard now, opening up an empty square pen. She locked Babygirl inside, and Clarence noticed how much larger Babygirl was than the other pits in the yard. "Your beer," Gina said to Y as she stumbled over and placed the can in his hand. He lifted his cigarette, took a drag, and then licked her lips.

"Thanks, baby. But this isn't the bait I want. Not tonight." He pulled away from Gina and took the lead out of her hand. "This one is special. We'll give her a little time." He leaned over and rubbed the fur between Babygirl's ears and then walked over to the row of cages. Clarence remembered the way Demario had looked at Babygirl; it was the way Clarence's mama used to look at him and the way he looked at Mona. Babygirl was Demario's heart, and Y knew it.

Y hiked up his ass-dragging jeans and shuffled back over to Gina, leaning into her and kissing the end of her

nose. "Go back in and get that shepherd you found out behind the Chicken Hut. It'll get the job done for tonight."
Gina shrugged and gave Y a pouty look, like a kid begging for
candy. She held out her hand. Y reached into the pocket of
his jacket and pulled out a little plastic bag, and then he just
held it there in front of her while she squirmed. Finally he
dropped it into the palm of her hand. "Enjoy, lady. You done
good. We make a good team, you and me."

Clarence looked at the dogs, then at Y, then at Gina, and
he stumbled back, spun around, and ran as fast as he could
into the woods. The Gina he'd once known was gone, and
the Gina behind him was dangerous. It was only a matter
of time before Mona would end up as bait in one of Y's practice fights; he could now see how all the pieces fit together.
He ran and ran, and he surrendered to the fire, surrendered to the savage desire to do bad things to bad people, to
do to them what they did to those dogs and to those boys,
and as he ran, the branches that tore at his skin through the
cape felt both like punishment and comfort, like what he
deserved and what Y and Gina and Johnnyprice deserved;
it was what all the shitty, selfish people in the whole shitty,
selfish world deserved, and he was grateful for the pain,
grateful that finally, after months of justifying, wirewalking, and holding back, he could finally just let himself

burn out. Collapse. Hit the ground hard. Weep.

His mama came to him as a huge silver bird with gold wings and delicate gold rings adorning each of her talons. Her own head—the straight black hair, the hot-chocolate-colored eyes—sat atop her own graceful human neck, but feathers fanned out below her shoulders, stretching into broad wings that carried her to where her boy lay sleeping fitfully in the woods, completely spent. "Clarence," she called down to him through the trees, her voice soft and sure. "I'm here. I'm here above you. Look up and listen."

From the edge of sleep, Clarence could hear her, and she flew into his dreams as a woman bird lighting in the top of a pine. The tree bent and swayed with her weight, and as he looked up, he could make out her glittering talons and shimmering feathers, but her face was covered in darkness. "Is that you, Mama?" He could barely find the energy to call out to her. He thought he might be dead—he felt dead—and he supposed his mama might have flown down from heaven to rescue him from all he'd just seen. "Is that you up there?"

She lifted one wing high above her head so that it caught the light from the city beyond the woods. He could see streetlights and headlights in that wing, and neon signs and billboards, and the bright-as-day parking lot of the twenty-four-hour Walmart, and then the sparkling glass high-rises of downtown. There were the glowing windows of sleepless TV watchers, slivers of lamplight floating in a blonde woman's cocktail glass, red cigarette cherries burning down to their filters, flecks of starlight caught in plastic bags of crack. Then he suddenly saw spotlights bouncing off concrete, glinting in the wet whites of dogs' eyes, and right there in the center of this light, his mother's face shone, her wing raised like a torch as she spoke.

"Stand up now, sweetheart. I'm coming for you." With this, she held each wing straight out to her side and stepped away from the tree, drifting into the clearing between him and the pine. "I want to show you something. Get on my back." She bowed as Clarence climbed onto her, pressing himself into the coolness of her feathers. He slid his arms around her warm human shoulders and laid his left cheek there, and with one swift pump of her wings, they rose above the treetops, into the night. Off in the distance, the lights of the training compound were a sickly glow on the edge of the woods, and he turned his face away from them, refusing to remember. His mama was flying in the opposite direction, toward Stonewall Jackson and Mayfair Heights. There was no reason to look back now.

As she swooped down over the baseball field, Clarence told her that he still made As, and that he was mentoring a boy named Billie. He told her that he'd been asked to read at an assembly but had chickened out at the last minute. "I know," she said, nodding. "I saw it all." She flew low now, following the line of the woods behind the school, right past the Kwik-Bi, and he told her about Mr. Khabir, how he was a good man but that he didn't believe he knew any other truly good men, or at least none he could remember. "Your father used to be a good man," his mama said, and she turned gently into the alley behind the box-of-gray and then flew quick and low over to the living room window where she hovered just above the bushes.

Her wings vibrated in tiny, buzzing strokes, keeping them aloft. Clarence looked in and saw his dad pacing in the darkness, lit up blue by the television. His cigarette was a single long ash in between his fingers. "He's suffering," his mama said. "And so are you, and you need each other. So this thing—whatever it is between you, Clarence—it has to end." Clarence looked away from the window as he and his mama rose up toward the rooftop, where she gently landed. "And that one down there"—her right wing stretched out toward a car moving slowly down Barton Street, and Clarence could see it was Johnnyprice's Cutlass Supreme—"that one's got to go. He's no good for the two of you anymore. He hasn't been good for a very long time."

Now his mother used both wings to take him higher, and he could see the Kwik-Bi and its parking lot, Stonewall Jackson just beyond, and Robert E. Lee a few blocks beyond that. Beyond the woods, his eyes could make out the dim lights of Y's compound, and out toward the horizon, the city's center gleamed like Gotham, and he remembered Halloween night, and the young people making room for him on the street, and the towering college building, and all Demario had told him. "The world is bigger than Mayfair Heights," his mama said, and Clarence looked out over the piece of world he could see, and knew it connected to another piece and then another, and that it must go on like this forever, too vast to measure or even imagine. "Wish for more," she whispered as he snuggled down into her feathers. "Wish for more, Clarence, and I promise you'll find it."

"I will, Mama," he whispered back, but as soon as the words left his mouth, his mama was gone, and he found himself waking in the woods, in a little clearing next to a stand of pines. He was still in his cape, his cape smelled like vomit, and he realized he'd gotten sick inside it while he was running or while he was crying in the leaves or while he was tossing and turning in a fitful sleep. The wound in the palm of his hand throbbed, and when he held it next to the light of his watch, he could see he'd opened it back up along the way. He didn't remember it happening, though; he couldn't remember much of anything after the compound except the visit from his mama. Slowly and carefully, he pushed himself up with his good hand, inching the cape up over his head, then letting it drop to the ground. He wouldn't need it again. "Thanks, Mama," he said, and then he started moving in the only direction he could: toward the faint lights of Mayfair Heights glinting far beyond him, through the trees.

It seemed like hours passed as he dragged himself out of the woods to the Kwik-Bi, and when he checked his watch as he shuffled into the parking lot, it read 10:49. The store would be technically open for eleven more minutes. "Gaaaaah," he heard himself mutter as he shoved the door open with his shoulder, and he wished he hadn't moaned: he could feel Mr. K's eyes on him before he even made it into the store. "Good evening to you, Clarence," Mr. K said politely, but his voice was lower than usual, and less singsongy. "Is everything all right?" Clarence nodded but kept his eyes down. He shuffled over to the counter and stared down through the plastic windows at the selection of scratcher lottery tickets. "You are here for a lottery ticket tonight? This is very unusual, no?"

Clarence shook his head but kept his eyes on the tickets. "I'm just looking, just buying some time. Just happened to be in the neighborhood." As soon as he spoke the words, he could hear their falseness. He knew Mr. K could too, but Clarence stood there anyway, just because. He had no choice. He'd come here for a reason, and while he couldn't exactly name what it was, it had brought him here. Now.

"Your hand, Clarence—you are holding it like something is wrong." Mr. K walked around the counter and stood in front of Clarence. "What has happened? Stretch out your arm, please, and let me see." Clarence kept his eyes on the scratchers. This, he knew, was one of those moments—a quiet yet enormous moment—when one decision would change everything. He stood now on one side of that moment, knowing if he pulled in his arm more closely and just walked out the door, his life would unfold in one way. If he extended his arm and showed Mr. K the palm of his left hand, his life would unfold in another way. It was like that day of the assembly, when he'd run out on Ms. Moffett, or the moment he'd decided to run for Y, after Johnnyprice had forced him out into the storm to make his deliveries. It was like that moment—right here in the Kwik-Bi—when he'd seen the black cape on the Halloween shelf and known what he needed to do. One moment + one decision = a life altered forever. Sometimes for the better, sometimes not.

"Clarence." Mr. K extended his right hand and turned its palm toward the ceiling, like Gina had with Y back at the compound, when she'd wanted the bag of crack. "May I see your hand, please?" Clarence hunched down over the scratchers and gnawed at the inside of his lip. He was suddenly terrified. If he showed Mr. K his hand, he would be telling Mr. K the truth, even if he said nothing. He would be

walking out of hiding, out of the lie. From that moment forward, everything would be exposed and everything would
have to change.

"Ah. There now . . ." Mr. K quietly said as Clarence slowly
moved his left arm away from his body and showed Mr. K
his palm. "That is quite a burn indeed. Has no one treated it
yet?" Mr. K gently cupped his hand under Clarence's hand,
supporting it.

"I did. I bandaged it after it happened. But I fell tonight,
and it busted open again." Clarence's eyes closed. He didn't
know why; they just did, and then the whole store gradually
faded until it was just he and Mr. K and his burned hand
resting there in the soft cup of Mr. K's hand. He could hear
himself breathing.

"Wait here for a moment," he heard Mr. K say, and then
he felt his left hand being laid down gently—palm up—on
the cool glass counter. He heard the lock on the store door
click into place, heard the *click-click-click* of Mr. K's loafers, heard Mr. K stop there right in front of him. Clarence
opened his eyes. "You will come upstairs with me, and I will
tend to your hand, yes? The wound, it will get infected oth-
erwise." Clarence nodded and waited for Mr. K to round the
counter's corner, and then he followed him down the aisle,
then back behind the broom closet, where a narrow flight
of stairs led up to Mr. K's apartment. Clarence had always

wondered about those stairs and the apartment at the top, but he'd never expected he'd see it in person. He and Mr. K were friends, but they both were private, separate people. Until now.

When they reached the top of the stairs, he followed Mr. K through his apartment door and into a bright kitchen that smelled of bleach and funny cigarette smoke, just like the Kwik-Bi. Mr. K pulled out a chair at the table and led Clarence to it, placing a hand lightly on Clarence's shoulder as he eased him down into the seat. For what seemed like a long time, Mr. K just stood there, looking down at Clarence, and then he went to the sink and filled up a kettle with water. He set it on a burner and turned the flame on high. "Will we wake up your family?" Clarence suddenly asked, remembering the photo he'd found behind the counter, next to the gun, the one of the beautiful woman and the smiling girls. He'd never seen them around and had always thought they probably lived far away, back wherever Mr. K came from. But he wanted to be polite, just in case. Mr. K was being so kind.

"My family, they are dead, Clarence," Mr. K answered from over by the stove, and then he stood very still. He just fiddled with the lid on the kettle, lifting it up and down, up and down. "They were killed in our home country. It's just me who is living here. No one else." Once this was said, the room went silent until, in time, the sound of bubbling water turned to a whistle, and Mr. K lifted the kettle off the flame and pulled down two lady-cups from the cabinet. He poured the steaming water and then dropped a tea bag into each cup. Clarence just sat there, staring at the tabletop, baffled by how different Mr. K's life was from the life he'd imagined for him. Turned out that for the entire time Clarence had been alone and hurting, Mr. K had been alone and hurting too. It just didn't seem possible.

In time Mr. K walked back over to the table, leaving the tea on the counter to steep. He pulled up a chair but didn't sit down. Clarence glanced up once and then returned his eyes to the tabletop. He didn't know how to say what he needed to say to this man. He didn't have enough words, or the right words. "I have not told this to anyone else except in Bangladesh, where it happened, Clarence. After that, I vowed never to speak of it again, and yet here I am, speaking of it to you."

"Thank you," Clarence whispered. He hadn't planned on saying anything, and he certainly hadn't planned on whispering, but the words had drifted out of his mouth, and he meant them. Mr. K nodded, then stood there for a few seconds more, and then he walked past Clarence into the little living room and then down the hallway.

"I am retrieving the rubbing alcohol and the Neosporin!" he shouted back toward the kitchen. "And I am also bringing a bandage: a bandage is most important. You must keep that wound clean, Clarence, or you will find yourself with all manner of problems!" Clarence just sat there, listening and waiting. As far as he was concerned, he had all the time in the world. There was nowhere he needed or even wanted to be. He wanted to be here. He'd *chosen* to be here.

Soon Mr. K returned with a little white basket of medical supplies. Each item in the basket was carefully lined up against the next one, and Clarence realized how much he relied on the way that everything about Mr. K fit together and made sense. The world outside the Kwik-Bi kicked and snarled, but when he walked through the store's front door, he walked into peace. "Now," said Mr. K. "Please give me your hand again. This will hurt, but the pain will not last. This I promise you." Mr. K's words reminded Clarence of Demario's coaching in the locker room, before he'd burned Clarence's hand.

Slowly he laid his arm out in front of Mr. K and opened his left hand. He looked down at the bloody, yellow-edged circle in its middle, closed his eyes, and started counting, like he had in the locker room. "Now, that was not so very bad, was it, my friend?" Clarence opened his eyes to find Mr. K's thick eyebrows drifting up above his tinted glasses like they always did when he asked a question. "Next, I will wash my hands, and then we will sit and have the tea. This is all right with you, then, Clarence? All is well?"

Clarence didn't think about how to answer. It was too late for that. He was too far in. "I don't know, Mr. K. I mean, no. No, it isn't. Nothing is all right." He said this and then realized there was nothing more to say. This was the whole of it. This was finally the truth.

Across from him, Mr. K gently shook his head, as was his way. "We will save the tea for another time, my friend. Now you go home. Now is the time. All of this—this has to end."

THE WAY BACK

••

CLARENCE AWOKE AND LOOKED around. He didn't know where he was. He wasn't at Demario's. He wasn't in the shed. He remembered his time with Mr. K and thought he might still be in Mr. K's apartment, but then he glanced down at the Batman bedspread draped across his body and he remembered. He was home. He was back in his own bed.

Suddenly he was flooded with memories from the night before, but he only let his mind linger in certain places. He forced his thoughts away from Y's compound but let them settle on the feel of his mama's feathers as she'd lifted him out of the woods. In his mind, he let himself walk through the doors of the Kwik-Bi, into Mr. K's kindness, and he let himself feel sad, for a moment, for Mr. K's terrible loss. There was so much. So. Damn. Much. He finally rolled over and out of bed, and then walked quietly into the kitchen and stopped. He stood very still, just taking in the room once again.

It seemed like years since he'd been here, gathering up

his belongings in a plastic trash bag. In front of him now, his father sat alone at the table, staring out the double windows, onto the front porch, and Clarence's eyes returned to the bullet hole in the glass, like they had so many times before. "You know, Johnnyprice and me, we had a gun that night," his father said, but he didn't turn around. He didn't move at all. "We were drunk and carrying on out on the porch, like we do sometimes. Your mama: she was sitting inside at the table, peeling potatoes, and I knew she wasn't going to take much more of it. She was getting pretty tired of us in general, at that point."

His father paused. Clarence remembered his mama sitting at the table, but he didn't remember much about the carrying-on outside. Like his dad said: carrying-on wasn't anything new. "You know, this was right around the time Johnnyprice started up in the game—a little dealing, a little gambling at fights. Your mama didn't know about it, but she *knew* about it, if you know what I mean. You know how your mama was. She saw everything." Clarence nodded. His mama had seen it all. She still did. Just like Mr. K.

"So all the sudden, Johnnyprice pulls out his gun, just like that, out of nowhere. It wasn't like he was pointing it at me—he wasn't pointing it at anything—he was just waving it around in the air like a drunk jackass, trying to make a point about something, but you and your mama were right there on the other side of that window, just a few feet away. So I just dove for him. It was just instinct, no thinking—I mean, my family was in danger. I dove for him, and then we got to wrestling, and before I knew it, I was grabbing at the gun, and then I heard the shots. And you remember the rest."

Clarence suddenly found himself frozen in his body, and in time. He hoped his dad wouldn't turn around, not yet. There were no words. No thoughts, even. Everything in him had stopped. "I'm not saying I killed her, Clarence, and I'm not saying I didn't. But one way or another, it's time this got said. Because you—you know, with those eyes just like hers, the only person she loved more than me—well, I just couldn't stand to be around you after she died. You were my punishment, and I punished *you* on account of that. And then you got older and smart enough that you could punish me back. Your leaving . . . well, I deserved that. I went as low as I could go, letting Johnnyprice go after your money. Truth is that I've never once done right by you since your mama died. Not really."

The room sat silent until a car flew down the street, honking its horn. Another honking car followed. "Well, are you going to do right by me now, Pops?" Clarence hadn't planned on speaking, but there it was, out there in the air between them. His dad rocked back and forth in his chair.

"I'd like to try. I'd like to think I could. I mean, Johnnyprice is going his way with Y, and I'm going mine. I've found a job, you know, and I'll be pulling in enough to get by. Other than that, though, I can't say as I really don't know how to do right by you. I hardly even know you anymore. Hell, I look in the mirror, and I hardly know myself." Clarence gave his dad's shoulders a little squeeze, and then he turned and walked toward the back door.

"Well, go on and try, Pops. Really do it for once. And then we'll see."

— — —

On the walk to Demario's apartment, Clarence tried not to think about the news he carried. He knew Demario had probably been out for hours now, looking for Babygirl and maybe, most probably, for him. It would only make sense that Demario would think the dude sleeping on his couch was somehow linked to his dog's disappearance. Both he and Babygirl were there when Demario left, and by the time he got home, they both were gone.

Clarence was making his way down Mayfair Heights Boulevard when he heard Demario's voice behind him, calling his name. He turned around, and Demario pulled his black car up to the curb. "Get in, brah," he said. His lips were pulled in a hard straight line. "And make it quick."

"I was just headed to your place," Clarence said as he slid

into the car's passenger seat. "I know what happened. I know what happened to Babygirl." Demario worked the steering wheel with his hands. A thick vein throbbed on his temple.

"What the hell, Clarence? Tell me. And you'd better hope whatever it is doesn't track back to you."

Clarence shook his head. For once, the problem wasn't his fault.

"Nah, man—it's all Y, and it's just so . . ." Clarence didn't know if he could say more. He didn't want to remember. He didn't want to speak the words, but he didn't have a choice. "So Y's got this compound way out past the woods behind Stonewall Jackson—you know there's a bunch of warehouses back there—and I was out walking last night—it's what I do sometimes—and I found his place. And Babygirl: she was there. I definitely saw her, man. She wasn't hurt, but Y said he had special plans for her, and I mean, those dogs out there, well, they're . . . they're . . ." Clarence closed his eyes and felt himself tumbling through the woods. Falling. Weeping. Sleeping in his own vomit. "It's really bad, Demario. It's just really, really bad."

Demario nodded. The vein on his temple throbbed harder. "I know about the place. Hoped I'd never have to see it, but you're going to take me there now. Like, right now." His hands were now two huge fists resting on the steering wheel, and every second or two he'd raise a fist and then drop it back onto the wheel, making a thudding sound like someone being punched.

"Listen," Clarence offered. He didn't think his Big Boy was going to hurt him at this point; it would have already happened. Demario's anger was directed at Y. "You don't want to go blowing into that compound on your own, I mean any manner of shit could go down, and then what would happen to Babygirl? You've got a life, man. You're on your way out. Don't blow it all on your piece-of-shit brother." Demario turned to face Clarence, and Clarence met Demario's eyes with his own. "I mean, don't you want all this to be over already?" He wasn't exactly sure if he was asking the question of Demario, or himself. "I know you know there's got to be a better way. So let's just talk about it, right? Let's just talk it out, and after that, it's up to you."

— — —

Clarence didn't know how to get to Y's compound by car, so he led Demario along the edge of the woods, the way he'd traveled just the night before. They moved silently in the darkness, Clarence out in front, and Clarence knew the hero in him had finally found the right mission. Soon, the houses and yards thinned, giving way to empty streets and abandoned buildings, and he found himself thinking about all that had brought him here. His dream mama, Mona, Mr. K,

Ms. Moffett, and maybe even Demario: they were all people who somehow still believed in him. His dad, Johnnyprice, Y, and now Gina: these were people who had given up on believing in anything. And then there, teetering on the edge of his cracked-open heart, stood Billie Wade, the one he couldn't save, that he might not ever to be able to save. *But I might,* Clarence told himself as he saw the deserted brick complex coming into view. *One day, I might. One day, there might be a way.*

Clarence slowed down and pointed at the buildings up on the left, and as they got closer, Demario slid in next to him, keeping rhythm with his stride. It felt good to be walking with someone else in the night, instead of wandering the streets alone, but he also had a sickness in his belly that he recognized as fear. He and Demario had a plan, but there were so many ways for that plan to go lopsided. And if it did, well, somebody—or a lot of somebodies—were going to end up hurt, or worse. He'd tossed his own gun into the hedge at Billie's, but he knew Demario was packing, and Y sure as hell would be packing, and Y's boys might even have guns. He swallowed, swallowed once more, and then motioned over to the first building where a huge *Y* was splashed in red over the other graffiti.

"It's in the back there," he said in a hushed voice, and though he knew there was no way Y could hear him, it felt like someone had turned up the volume on his hearing, and it was making him jumpy. Even his own breathing sounded like a rushing wind in his ears. "So, the dogs are in the back, like I told you. See that light shining on the woods, right behind the building? That means the yard out back is lit up. Y's got to be there."

Demario stopped and crossed his arms across his chest, taking a long look around. "I don't see any cars, but then again, Y isn't stupid. Cars would draw attention. They must have parked somewhere else and walked in, and that's a good thing. It'll make it harder for them to get away."

Clarence and Demario made their way forward together, keeping to the right of the complex, staying close to the buildings that led back to Y's warehouse, and then they crouched down and ran along the side of Y's building, slipping around to the back, where the fence met the woods. Clarence heard the low moan of a dog, then Y barking orders, then Gina's tiny begging-for-crack voice, and then suddenly Johnnyprice's voice chimed in, and Clarence's stomach went wild. He leaned over, laying both hands on his knees, and he tried to inhale but found it hard to get any air. What if Johnnyprice or Y or both of them could hear him? What if the whole plan fell apart because he couldn't handle his nerves?

Demario reached out and laid a strong meaty hand on

Clarence's shoulder. He nodded, leaned in, and whispered in Clarence's ear. "Keep it cool, brah. I got this." Clarence understood. He was a mess. He was a liability. Demario tightened his hand on Clarence's shoulder, and Clarence let himself be moved away from the fence into the woods. As he looked around, he could feel the night before taking shape all around him. The running, the falling, the crying, the feel of the feathers on his mama's back, the stairs to Mr. K's apartment and then, finally, the familiar comfort of his own bed— it all felt real and like a dream at the same time, just like his memory movies did, in those hours and days afterward.

Demario finally stopped next to a little clearing, deep in the woods, and Clarence glanced up into the treetops. He could almost see his mama lighting there, a beautiful bird in the pines. "The plan's still on," he heard Demario say from behind him. "I'll call the cops on my way back to the compound, then I'll make a run for it, just jump the fence, grab Babygirl, and before you know it, I'll be back here. You just wait for me. I'll be back, brah."

Clarence nodded, then turned around to face Demario, trying to make out his expression, trying to get a read. But the night was too black, and he knew that even in broad daylight, Demario would never let the truth of what lay between them show on his face. Still, Clarence knew this was goodbye, plain and simple. Even if everything went as planned,

Demario couldn't come back for him. Demario was Y's right-hand man, after all, and soon the cops would be looking for him. He'd have to make a run for it, gather up his things, go somewhere else, and do something else, at least for a while, and that was if everything went as planned at the compound. This was the truth of what was about to happen. "Thanks, man," Clarence finally offered, and he held out his hand. "For everything. I would have been in a world of shit without you."

Demario accepted Clarence's hand and shook it, and the moment lingered. One huge hand held a smaller hand until finally, Demario spoke, "The grades, eventually college, that crazy big heart—that's all you, brah. That's who you are. You didn't really need me. I needed you. This whole plan, saving my girl? That was you. All you." He gave Clarence's hand a squeeze, and then released it. "So just wait. I'll be seeing you soon," he said, and then turned, took a few steps out into the darkness, and was gone.

Without even thinking about it, Clarence felt himself lying down in the pine needles, just like he'd done the night before, and in time he heard a gunshot and then, by and by, sirens started up in the distance, and he made himself remember his mama's great silvery wings and all she'd shown him. His eyes closed as the sound of sirens drifted into the woods and then got louder, and he imagined himself lifted now, beyond those woods, beyond Mayfair Heights, high enough to catch a glimpse of how the pieces of his world were sewn together, and how he fit into the pattern. Johnnyprice, Y, Demario, and the Wirewalker were gone now. Mr. K, Mona, Billie, Ms. Moffett, maybe even his dad—they were all still here, and he was still here too. Clarence Rowley Feather. Evangeline Feather's son.

And his mama, well, she seemed to be everywhere and gone all at once, and maybe that was what happened when people died, or when they died slowly while still walking around breathing, like his dad had for so long. Maybe death— and life—were full of comings and goings, like when Mr. K would drift off into thoughts about his family then snap back into the moment, or when Billie would slip silently into his body and mind then show back up, swearing like a Y-boy. So many times he himself had abandoned scared, aching Clarence for a wirewalking superhero, only to find himself back where he'd started. Maybe by leaving for a while, people eventually found some reason to stay.

He waited for a few minutes more, listening for the sound of Demario's footsteps, just in case. "Guess I'm back, Mama," he finally whispered, and then he pushed himself up, walking out toward the edge of the woods, toward the streets that would lead him home.

ҳ — ҳ — ҳ —

THANKS TO MY EARLY READERS, who supported. Thanks to Leigh Feldman, who believed. Thanks to Ken Wright, who took a chance. Thanks to Regina Hayes and Alex Ulyett, my shepherds. And thanks to Clarence Feather, who showed up just when I needed him.